For Dara

If I am not for myself, who will be for me?
If I am only for myself, what am I?

—Rabbi Hillel

What if we chose the wrong religion?
Each week we just make God madder and
madder.

—Matt Groening

AGGADAH TRY IT

The End of Daze

Andrew Fox

A Madness Heart Press Publication

PART ONE

Chapter One

A dear, dead friend had led Jacob Zvi to this place.

Not just any dead friend. Saul Tannenburg, who had died of a heart attack during the final moments of Yom Kippur after Jacob had told him the news that the Old City of Jerusalem had suffered an atomic bombing. Saul Tannenburg, whose spirit had somehow become infused within a cybernetic shopping cart created by Jacob's friend Wyonna Rhinegold in her lab at Tulane University's Williamson Science Building.

The cybernetic shopping cart, speaking in Saul's voice, had led Jacob into a flood-ravaged section of Uptown New Orleans, to the block where a decrepit, long-ago abandoned synagogue, Beth Judah, sat precariously on the edge of an expanding sinkhole.

Only a couple of weeks ago, the world had been a different place.

A normal place.

✡ ✡ ✡

Jacob hurried up the worn front steps to Saul Tannenburg's home. He'd spent much of his twenty-six years running late. This morning was no exception. But he had committed to making the morning and evening *shiva minyanim*, for without Jacob to complete the *minyan*, Saul could not recite his mourner's *kaddish*.

This section of Uptown New Orleans was composed entirely of comically narrow shotgun houses and slightly less comical double-shotguns. They were all shoved so close together an average man could stand between two neighboring houses and touch the walls of each without straining too hard. The neighborhood had been spared the ravages of the last great storm's flooding. These blocks retained their antediluvian patina, the grime and funk and weathered charm they'd accrued over more than a century of hard use.

"Ahh! The crown of our *minyan*. Thank *Hashem!* Come in, come in, Mr. Zvi!" Rabbi Pincus Karnofsky enthusiastically ushered him inside. Jacob accepted with abashed pleasure; it always felt good to be the tenth man, even if he was mainly showing up for a free breakfast. The burly Chabadnik, built like a Russian circus bear, grabbed his shoulders and propelled him to the front row of dining room chairs assembled in the Tannenburg family room. The rabbi thrust a *kippa*, a *tallis*, and a *siddur* into Jacob's hands, then scooped up his thick black prayer book and returned to his rhythmic speed-mumbling.

Jacob had never met the sad, hunched little man who sat two chairs from him, the left side of his button-down plaid shirt torn in a place above his heart, a ritual of grief. Saul had just lost his wife of forty-seven years. He looked as bewildered and lost as a little boy who'd gotten separated from his parents in the women's lingerie department at Dillard's.

Jacob was happy to do him the favor of making his *shiva minyan* a reality. He was even more happy about the bagels, lox, orange juice, coffee, and kosher pastries he could look forward to for the next six mornings, and the kugels and dairy casseroles which would be set out in the late afternoons. *Shiva minyanim* were great for stretching his food budget. The obituary column was about the only section of the *New Times-Picayune* he bothered looking at regularly anymore. Between the newspaper and synagogue or Chabad notices online, he generally managed to line himself up with two or three *shiva minyanim* a month.

Saul wasn't a regular synagogue-goer, Jacob figured; certainly not a Chabadnik. In all likelihood, he and his wife had made their annual appearances at one of the big Reform temples, Touro or Temple Sinai, during the High Holy Days, then dutifully paid their membership dues for the privilege of never attending services for the remainder of the year. In all likelihood, Saul had let his membership lapse, which meant that he was unclaimed territory, spiritually speaking. When Saul's wife passed on, Rabbi Karnofsky would have leapt into the breach, offering his support, his guidance, and his *minyan*, which was a pretty decent thing to do for a stranger, no matter what else one might think about the Chabad movement.

Rabbi Helvetica Rhinegold, director of the Tulane University Hillel Center, had obviously tried to do the same, but she had arrived on Saul's doorstep a half-step after Rabbi Karnofsky, to her obvious consternation. She sat in the back of the room, glowering on the men's side of the curtain, claiming her spiritual pound of flesh by defying Pincus Karnofsky's old-fashioned prohibitions. As he'd done many times during her occasionally interminable sermons on Friday nights at the Hillel Center, Jacob tried to imagine what Rabbi Helvetica would look like with a little makeup. She rejected the entire cosmetics industry for its imposition of tyrannical beauty standards and its reliance on animal testing. She was just as pale as he was, only her paleness was further accentuated by her dark brown hair, pulled back in a bun, which conformed to the slope of her impressive skull like a bow wave clinging to the prow of a Navy destroyer. She wasn't unattractive, he thought; but of course his male, heterosexual standards of attractiveness were irrelevant in this case. The robotics expert Wyonna Shaver, with her John Lennon glasses and shaved head, hovered at her elbow. She was Rabbi Helvetica's trusty sidekick; her fiancée, actually.

Jacob forced himself to concentrate on his prayer book. The service seemed to drag on like a marathon of Ingmar Bergman films, even though he knew there were just *Aleinu*, the Mourners' *Kaddish*, and *Yigdal* left to go. He listened to Saul Tannenburg painfully stumble through the Hebrew words of the Mourners' *Kaddish*, frequently pausing while Rabbi Karnofsky gently corrected his pronunciation.

The service concluded. Jacob folded his *tallit* as fast as he could, then headed for the breakfast table. An undeniable bonus of the ongoing competition between Rabbis Karnofsky and Helvetica was that they competed in the realm of nosh, too; this made for a bountiful breakfast, exceeding those offered by most French Quarter luxury hotels.

Rabbi Karnofsky had brought fresh bagels, mandelbrot cookies, and blueberry blintzes from Dorignac's Kosher Bakery. Rabbi Helvetica had relied upon Wyonna's culinary skills; they'd brought a broccoli and cheese soufflé, home-baked banana bread, and a dried fruit assortment. Helvetica, bless her stormy little heart, had also thought to bring a bag of Community Dark Roast with Chicory; the coffee suffused the Tannenburg dining room with its life-giving aroma.

Rabbi Karnofsky met Jacob next to the coffee pot. "Mr. Zvi," he said, clapping Jacob on the shoulder, "I truly appreciate your being here. By being the tenth man, you have performed a double *mitzvah*. Who knows? Maybe you've given *Moshiach* just the little extra nudge he needs so that he will tarry no longer."

Rabbi Karnofsky sometimes gave him the creeps. Although Jacob's parents had raised him Modern Orthodox, the law of the Exaggeration of Small Differences applied quite strongly between the Modern Orthodox and the Chabadniks within the small New Orleans Jewish community. Still, Jacob appreciated being appreciated.

"Thanks, Rabbi," Jacob said, stirring a large portion of Half-N-Half into his coffee. "Yeah, I seem to have a talent for coming in tenth."

"Actually, Rabbi Karnofsky," Rabbi Helvetica said from behind Jacob, "Mr. Tannenburg already had his *minyan* before Jacob arrived. With Wyonna and me, eleven adult Jews were present, one more than necessary."

Jacob didn't have to see Rabbi Karnofsky's eyes roll toward the ceiling to know they had. "Ms. Rhinegold—" Rabbi Karnofsky started to say.

"That's *Rabbi* Rhinegold, Pincus." She held her prayer book to her bosom like a shining shield. It was the latest edition of the Reconstructionist-Renewalist *siddur, Will-to-Believe: A Daily Guide to Spiritual Practice,* to which she'd contributed a preface, ten watercolor illustrations, and a section on Womynist observance of the harvest festivals. "I must ask, Rabbi Karnofsky, that you address me by my proper and *earned* title, especially at communal events like this one."

"*Ms.* Rhinegold, perhaps you would earn more professional courtesy if you would stop trying to force your dubious standards onto life-cycle events where you have no jurisdiction. Mr. Tannenburg invited *me* to lead his *shiva* services, not *you*. *Halacha* is not a piece of wire which you can twist into pretzel shapes anytime you wish. It is a strong scaffolding, an unmovable bridge upon which we walk our whole lives, leading us from birth to death to the World to Come—"

"Any tradition which refuses to adjust itself to the evolving morality of humankind is a *dead* tradition. We are thinking beings, *Pincus. Creative* beings. Religion is simply one of the modes we utilize to interpret and live in our world. By stating that the Jewish people's religious creativity *stopped* eight hundred years ago, you are denying us one of the central faculties of our Humynity. Have you not read even one of my articles in *Tikkun* or *Moment*?"

Rabbi Karnofsky crossed his thick arms. "I restrict my reading materials to Torah, Talmud, Mishnah, and Gemera. I deny myself the dubious pleasures of fantasy fiction and self-hate manuals."

Hot coffee, knives, Rabbi Karnofsky, and Rabbi Helvetica—not a good combination. "Uh, guys," Jacob said, "can't we cool it here?" He gestured toward Saul Tannenburg, sitting alone on one of the chairs in the family room, an untouched plate of food on his lap. "I don't think this is the place or the time to decide who gets voted off Jew Island."

Rabbi Karnofsky tugged sheepishly on his beard. "Of course, Mr. Zvi. You are right. Again, I must thank you." He lumbered into the next room and sat next to the bereaved.

Jacob glanced at Wyonna. He felt sorry for her; it couldn't be easy, being in love with someone as stiff-necked as Rabbi Helvetica. Wyonna appeared even more breakable and forlorn than usual. Throughout the altercation, she stood back and looked as though she'd wanted to sink into the floor. Her eyes met Jacob's. She saw his understanding; her eyes clearly told him, *"Thank you."*

Rabbi Helvetica stared at Rabbi Karnofsky's back and compressed her thin, pale lips. "He didn't apologize."

Jacob dumped two heaped tablespoons of sugar into his coffee. "Did you really expect him to?"

"He should."

"He called a truce. I'd say that's good enough for now, considering we're visiting a house of mourning."

"*You* called a truce. *He* owes me an apology. This isn't over. His pointed lack of collegiality —I plan to take it up with the Council of Tulane University Chaplains. If he wants Chabad House to continue to have a place on campus, he'll need to behave himself like a professional, not some *Haredi* hooligan from the streets of Meah Shearim."

"How about this lox, huh?" Jacob asked, piling strip after strip of the expensive smoked salmon onto his poppy seed bagel. "This stuff is pink gold. Have you tried some?"

Helvetica's eyes darted toward Rabbi Karnofsky. "I won't eat his lox."

Out of the corner of his eye, Jacob caught Wyonna spitting something pink into a napkin, then quickly tossing it into the trash.

"There's a program coming up in a couple of nights that you might be interested in," Rabbi Helvetica told Jacob. "In conjunction with Federation, Hillel is sponsoring a talk by the Israeli assistant consul from Dallas at McAlister Auditorium."

"Oh?" Jacob replied through a mouthful of bagel and lox. "Must be a new assistant consul—the poor schmuck doesn't realize the buzz-saw he's walking into. If I wanted to watch a crucifixion, I'd go to a Passion Play."

Wyonna dabbed the last traces of cream cheese from her lips and warily approached him. "Helvetica and I just thought—with your parents still living in Haifa— maybe you would want to hear the latest news about the situation over there?"

"Thanks, but I heard all the news about Israel's situation I'll *ever* want to hear during the four years I lived there. I came back to New Orleans to get *away* from all that shit."

Saul Tannenburg stared across the room at him. As though his words had been recorded and immediately played back to him at ten times their original volume, Jacob realized how rude and inappropriate he had just been. Was there something in this house, some invisible *dybbuk* that had turned him, Rabbi Karnofsky, and Rabbi Helvetica into oblivious assholes?

Oddly enough, Wyonna looked far more affronted by his outburst than her fiancée did. Rabbi Helvetica seemed equivocal; her small smile might almost pass for approval. Whereas her wife-to-be, the recent convert and onetime Seventh Day Adventist, glared at him as though he'd kicked a stray kitten.

"I'm sorry," Jacob muttered to Wyonna. "That was dickish of me. Wyonna, I appreciate your thinking about me, I really do." He turned to Helvetica. "Rabbi, what night is that talk again?"

"Tuesday at eight. Come forty-five minutes early so you can get through security."

"You guys are going?"

"Hillel is co-sponsoring, so we plan to attend."

"How about some folks from Federation and the synagogues? Are they going to invite this guy here and then abandon him to the wolves? Or are they going to actually show up and give the man some moral support?"

"I've been assured of a good turnout from the local Jewish community. You won't be stranded in a sea of protesters."

"Yeah? That's good. Maybe I'll bring my *keffiyeh* anyway, in case I need to blend in with the crowd."

"Jacob?" Wyonna's irate expression had faded as quickly as it had manifested. Her large eyes, made to seem even larger by her glasses and lack of hair, peered up at him hopefully. In her bald, elfin way, she really was quite beautiful, he thought. "There's something, well, I've been meaning to ask you. Do you think you might be interested in visiting me at my lab on campus sometime? I'm in the Williamson Science Building, with the Consortium for Advanced Automation and Artificial Intelligence Concepts."

"I'd get to check out the robots?"

"That's why I want you to come. Well, one reason, anyway."

"Heck, yes! I *love* robots—I practically grew up with them. But don't I need a security clearance or something?"

"Oh, that's all right. I can get you in. I'd like to talk about—well, maybe we could discuss an opportunity for, uh, academic collaboration."

Academic collaboration? "That sounds really interesting," Jacob said. Far-fetched or not, academic collaboration might open up the door to his sharing in a grant. Grant money meant grocery money. "Although I'm having a hard time figuring out how I'd be able to contribute anything. My academic work doesn't have anything to do with robotics. As for my outside activities, when I'm not attending *shivas*, I'm kind of a repo man for grocery carts; I collect them after they're stolen and return them to stores for a fee. I've been doing it about three years now, watching people sneak carts away from stores, tailing them to their homes, and retrieving the carts once they unload their groceries."

Wyonna blushed from her excitement. He found watching a bald woman blush to be utterly transfixing; her head transmogrified into a shapely tomato. "I, uh, already knew that, Jacob. That's—well, that's actually a *plus*, not a minus."

"Really?"

"Oh, with all the restrictions, I'm afraid I'm not at liberty to discuss those matters off-site." She tapped her nose. "Homeland Security. Come see me at the lab, and I'll be able to explain."

"Do you have a date in mind?"

"I'll email you. Or, you know, we'll see each other back here for another *minyan*."

"I need to get back to the Hillel for Sunday morning bagel brunch," Rabbi Helvetica said. "Wyonna, why don't you help Mr. Tannenburg put away the food? It looks like we're the last guests still here."

"I'll help, too, Wyonna," Jacob said. "I'm not in a hurry." He glanced over at Saul, who still hadn't eaten a bite. "Give me just a minute, okay?"

✡ ✡ ✡

Jacob wandered over to the widower and sat down next to him. What would he say to him? He silently berated himself; after so many months of attending the *shiva minyanim* of strangers, he had scripts worked out in his head — *Sorry for your loss; nice home; thanks for the delicious meal; is there anything I can do for you (that doesn't involve spending money)?* — but none of those felt right, so he just went with, "Uh, hi, Mr. Tannenburg."

The old man, who hadn't noticed Jacob sit beside him, turned. He regarded his companion with surprise. "Oh! Hello! I'm sorry — my memory's not working so good nowadays. Do I know you?"

"Your memory's fine; we've never met, Mr. Tannenburg. My name's Jacob Zvi."

Saul set his plate of food down on an empty chair and shook Jacob's hand. "Zvi, huh? Can't say I've ever met any Zvis. Do you have family here in New Orleans?"

14

"I used to. I was raised in New Orleans, in Lakeview. But my parents emigrated to Israel when I was in high school."

"What? They left you behind?"

"Huh? Oh—uh, no, they didn't leave me behind. I went with them. But I came back."

"What for? What type of work do you do?"

"I'm a graduate student at Tulane."

"Law? Medicine?"

"Cultural Studies."

"Oh? That must be a new one. Where did you go to synagogue when you were growing up? Maybe we know some of the same people."

"My old synagogue's not around anymore. It was in Lakeview. It got flooded out in the big storm."

"Oh." Saul shook his head sadly. "I'm very sorry. I remember when that happened. Hannah and me, we evacuated to Birmingham for four months. Stayed with cousins of hers. Oy, that's an experience I never want to repeat. By the way, my brother lives in Israel. He used to live in Jerusalem, in one of the ring neighborhoods on the outskirts. But the government made him move when they gave away that part of the city to the Arabs. Now he lives in a new development in the Negev Desert. He'd come to see me, you know, what with Hannah being gone, but flights out of Israel are so expensive nowadays, with the terrorism and whatnot, it would cost him half his annual pension. Do your parents live anywhere near the Negev?"

"They're in Haifa. They both work at the Technion, the Israel Institute of Technology."

"They're professors?"

"In the Computer Science Department, yeah. The Technion's known for that."

"How come you didn't go into their field? Sounds like it's a family thing, like running a dry goods store used to be."

"I wasn't interested." This was false enough to be a hair's breadth away from an out-and-out lie, but Jacob didn't feel like dredging up his family history.

"Eh, too bad—everything today, it's computers, computers. Me, I wouldn't know how to send an email, much less do a Google or a Twitter or whatever. Maybe if I had someone to help me, I might try it, but I don't have any kids, and you say you're not interested in computers, which seems very strange for such a young man, but to each his own, who am I to judge?" He glanced at his dining room table, which was now almost entirely cleared of food. "Oy! While we've been sitting here *kibitzing*, that little bald girl has put everything away, all by herself! Do you know her? You were talking with her."

"Yeah. Wyonna and I are friends. I know her from the Hillel Center."

"She has cancer, right? I should be ashamed, letting a girl in chemotherapy do all my cleaning up for me—"

"Don't worry, Mr. Tannenburg. Wyonna's fine. She doesn't have cancer."

"It's in remission, thank God?"

"She never had cancer."

Saul looked confused. "So why is she—what's with the bald head, then?"

"It's, uh, a fashion thing."

"*Fashion?* What kind of a 'fashion' is it to cut off all your hair? They did that to me in the Army, before I shipped off to Korea, but it had nothing to do with fashion."

Jacob glanced at his watch. "Uh, I've got to be going, Mr. Tannenburg. There's stuff I need to do over at school."

"So soon? It's Sunday! Why don't you and little Miss Helpful stay for another cup of coffee? There's still half a pot left. We could talk some more about Israel, or something?"

"I'll tell you what," Jacob said. "I'll come back tonight, for your evening *shiva minyan*."

Saul grasped Jacob's right hand between both of his. "You will? Really?"

"Definitely. I'm a single guy, you know? Footloose and fancy-free. I could use the company myself."

Saul didn't let go of his hand. He squeezed it more tightly. "Let me tell you something, Jacob." His eyes looked suddenly moist. "Hannah and I, we used to wonder about something. How the Jews managed to stay a people after so many centuries without a country of our own. So many pogroms, so many massacres—why didn't we fade away into history, like the Phoenicians or the Canaanites did? Do you know why we didn't?"

"I, uh, I don't know. God, maybe?"

"Yes, yes, God, maybe. But after today, after so many strangers came to my house to help me—to help me mourn my wife, I think I know another reason. You all came not because I'm a *macher*, a big shot—but just because I'm a fellow Jew. That's all. And Jews have been willing to do that sort of thing for fellow Jews all throughout our history. I didn't really realize that, not until today. We've kept each other alive, as Jews, from generation to generation."

He lifted Jacob's hand to his lips and kissed it. "So …" He smiled, and his eyes were brighter than before. "I'll see you tonight, then?"

"Tonight, for sure," Jacob said softly. "And at every one of your other *minyanim*. Count on me." The words tasted strange, coming out of his mouth. He realized he hadn't asked anyone to count on him, with real sincerity, in a very, very long time.

Chapter Two

Jacob was due to meet Wyonna in a little over an hour at her lab on Tulane's campus. Necessity and a hearty appetite had taught him not to let spare hours go to waste. With sixty minutes to play with, he could retrieve a wayward shopping cart for a bounty, maybe even two carts.

He scuttled, crab-like, along the narrow alleyway that led to the midget-sized gate to Smilin' Jack's postage stamp of a back yard. He side-stepped a broken-down lawnmower and a grill with a large hole rusted through its bottom, then made certain his city-issued commercial ID badge was clearly visible, in case any of Jack's neighbors happened to be awake at this early hour, drinking *café au lait* or more potent beverages on their back stoops. The official badge might not keep them from pulling a gun on him, but he sure hoped it would make them hesitate before they jerked the trigger.

He no idea if the man's real name was Jack; he'd nicknamed him Smilin' Jack after the comic strip character, because every time Jacob had tailed the dude from the store, Jack had semi-strode, semi-bounced behind his shopping cart, *smiling*, bobbing his head from side to side as though he were listening to some really great music. Except he never wore headphones and never carried a radio.

Jacob peered into the yard. Sure enough, there was the cart from Labouef's Market. And sure enough, resting beside it, there was Smilin' Jack's pit bull. The dog raised its massive head and growled. Jacob retrieved a small plastic sack of organ meats from his backpack. At least, he *assumed* the red and gray entrails in the sack were organ meats; managers at the Vietnamese market in Gretna had unhelpfully labeled the bag "Parts." Whatever it was, dogs of all sizes and breeds lapped it up as though it were ambrosia. Moving as nonthreateningly as he could, Jacob lifted his sack o' meat over the gate, letting the bag's lip droop open so the meat's odor could waft out.

The pit bull's demeanor changed immediately. He stood and scuttled over to the gate, his tail wagging furiously. Jacob dumped the sack's slimy contents next to the dog's slathering jaws and opened the gate. "Come to papa," he said to the grocery cart.

Two minutes later, he had the Labouef's Market cart shackled to the bed of his Dodge Ram truck. He calculated his prize's worth: *Ten bucks redemption fee, minus the cost of sack o' meat, minus a quarter gallon of gas, minus administrative overhead, minus State and federal income taxes... comes to about $6.75.* Such was the economy of New Orleans.

Almost not worth doing, considering the degree of physical peril he sometimes subjected himself to. But, on the other hand, he got to be his own boss. Jacob mentally waved goodbye to Smilin' Jack's house, knowing he'd return for another cart in three or four days.

✡ ✡ ✡

Jacob worked up a good sweat running from his parking spot eight blocks off campus to the Williamson Science Building, one of Tulane's more modern structures. The rough-textured concrete Brutalist edifice, the height of architectural fashion when it had been built in the late 1970s, looked distinctly out of place among the Colonial Revival academic buildings, like a hydraulic steel press dropped into a rose garden.

Embarrassed that his greed for shopping cart bounty had made him ten minutes late, Jacob fumed when he saw he'd need to go through a security checkpoint to gain entrance. But then he remembered what Wyonna had said about the work being done here for the Department of Homeland Security, so the precautions made sense. He asked a woman security guard for directions to Wyonna's lab. Luckily for him, her lab was easy to find, on the ground floor in the central research complex. Before he was allowed to enter, Jacob was instructed to cover his clothes with a disposable, sterile paper uniform and his face with a surgical mask. Only then did the doors open. Wyonna awaited him.

"So this is where the magic happens," Jacob said. He glanced around Wyonna's lab, his eyes meeting an array of sophisticated 3-D printers and computers that individually cost more than he could expect to earn from collecting a decade's worth of stolen shopping carts. Various work stations housed components of roughly human-shaped robots. In this particular section of the lab, the work stations focused on the fabrication either hands or feet. Everything was as clean and dust-free as the most up-to-date filtration processes could manage. "I'm impressed you were able to get me in here. Isn't the Department of Homeland Security kind of squirrely about who gets to see their latest toys?"

"Well, you've got a good pedigree," Wyonna said.

"That helps. Did you, uh, know that your parents are among my colleagues?"

"No—I didn't." This cast a whole new light on his invitation here. A clarifying light, but not a welcome one.

"The Technion in Haifa is one of the members of my consortium, along with M.I.T., Cal Tech, and the École Polytechnique Fédérale de Lausanne in Switzerland."

"Given the way things are, I'm surprised those other universities are willing to have anything to do with the Technion," Jacob said. "Aren't academic boycotts of Israel the hip thing?"

Wyonna dropped her gaze to the floor. "Oh, there have been rumblings. The Williamson Building gets picketed fairly regularly. But we'd be cutting off our noses if we denied the Israelis participation, and the Department of Homeland Security recognizes that. Just as the Israelis were pioneers in the field of automated drones, they're also on the cutting edge of robotics and applied artificial intelligence. Your parents are both highly respected researchers. Much of what I do here wouldn't have been possible without their pioneering monographs on the analogy between nanobots and human-symbiote microbes, as it applies to robotics." She smiled weakly. "But I'm sure I'm not telling you anything you don't already know."

"Actually, that stuff is news to me," Jacob said. "I mean, I've got a rough idea of what my folks do at the Technion. But we haven't talked a whole lot in the last three years or so."

"I, uh, sort of picked up on that…"

"Right." He bristled under the unspoken pressure for him to talk more about the rupture in his family relationships. Time to change the subject. "So, do you work on hands or on feet?"

"Neither. My work station is through these doors."

The End of Daze

✡ ✡ ✡

She led him into another, smaller room. Sitting in the room's center was the spiffiest shopping cart Jacob had ever laid eyes upon. Its metal armature, composed of alloys far more exotic and expensive than the cheap steel comprising the sort of shopping carts Jacob redeemed, gleamed beneath the lab's bright lights, and its plastic bits, the handle grips and protective bumpers and information screen and wheel housings, weren't plastic at all but made of some sort of carbon fiber material appropriate for a Lamborghini supercar. "Wow!" was his involuntary exclamation, although it could just have easily been *Zounds!* or *Holy moley!* or *Great Scott!* "I've never seen one anything like it—it's the Starship Enterprise of shopping carts."

Wyonna blushed, but she also smiled. "I call it P.R.E.T.E.C.T., or Proactive Response Eliminating Terror Events Cart Technology. It looks as inert as a typical grocery cart in a high-end food store—lots of those already have built-in video screens and touch pads for relaying advertising and entertainment to customers— but P.R.E.T.E.C.T. is every bit as autonomous and potent as any of the humanoid robots you saw in the other lab. It's also got the advantage of being less intimidating to the customers it protects. I designed it to be as unobtrusive as possible in the kind of 'soft target' settings that appeal to terrorists plotting mass casualty events … places like grocery stores, shopping malls, big box stores, anywhere you might imagine a shopping cart could be. It can also be reconfigured to resemble the sort of pull-carts people bring to outdoor festivals or parades. P.R.E.T.E.C.T.'s meant to be a guardian that won't make the people being protected feel like they're living in a police state."

"May I take a closer look?"

"Oh, please, please do."

Jacob let his eyes play upon the cart's sleek interactive console, mounted on its handle bar. Parallel rows of red, green, and yellow light emitting diodes ran along the rubberized gray molding on the rim of its basket. He knelt by the cart's four pairs of wheels, which to a casual glance appeared little different from the wheels on the carts chained in the bed of his truck; but he spotted the electric motors tucked within the wheels' inner bearing housings. "What's the fastest it can go?" he asked.

"Its top speed is classified, but it can accelerate to thirty miles per hour as quickly as a Ford Mustang GT. In any case, its speed capabilities, just like its capabilities in all areas, are improving constantly."

"You mean you're constantly inventing better motors?"

"No, *it's* constantly inventing better motors," Wyonna explained. "It steadily reinvents itself. I come in each morning, pull up its schematics on my computer, and find that they've been changed. As though the machine were providing me hints with how to make it better."

"That sounds like something out of a 1950s sci-fi movie," Jacob said. "You sure it's not some other engineer pulling a gag on you?"

"No one will own up to it. And it's not just P.R.E.T.E.C.T. Every robot in the lab is experiencing something similar. If we could isolate the phenomenon, study it as it occurs, this could be a tremendous breakthrough—the first instance of an emerging machine intelligence initiating communication with human beings."

Jacob took another look at the shopping cart, realizing how much processing power must be disguised within its common-looking haptic screen mounted atop its handle grips. "What else can it do, aside from drag race Camaros?"

Wyonna took in a deep breath. "It can recognize, identify, and appropriately respond to up to ten thousand different voices. It can interface with worldwide databases of fingerprints and retinal scans, limited only by permissions granted, and then perform its own fingerprint and retinal scans to obtain matches. It is capable of carrying out continuous scans across the full electromagnetic spectrum of a room up to a thousand square feet in size, and it can monitor the behavior, body language, facial expressions, and other physical 'tells' of up to two hundred persons simultaneously for signs of incipient aggression. It can extinguish medium-sized fires. In terms of active anti-terror protection, it's equipped with a variable-response taser and can fire micro-darts loaded with fast-acting tranquilizers—"

Jacob shook his head with boundless admiration. "Okay, okay, enough! Tell me anymore and the government will have to kill me. Jesus, I'm in *love* with this thing. I want to take it to bed with me."

Wyonna blushed at Jacob's choice of hyperbole. "I'm, uh, glad to hear that, I guess," she said. "I hope P.R.E.T.E.C.T. feels as warmly toward you."

"Why do you say *that?*"

"Because... well, Jacob, I'd like you to become one of P.R.E.T.E.C.T.'s tutors."

"*Me?*"

"P.R.E.T.E.C.T. continuously learns," Wyonna said. "And like I said, so far as we can determine, it's steadily evolving itself, encouraging the team and me to improve it. Our first prototype, which we developed only ten months ago, had barely one-twentieth of the current model's capabilities. It's advancing so quickly that we don't even have time to designate different version numbers anymore. I mentioned before how nanobots can be made to act much as microbes do in the human body. Without allied microbes, millions of them, in tens of thousands of distinct varieties, infesting all parts of our bodies, we would be unable to survive our environments. Did you know the human gene only contains about twenty thousand chromosomes? That's not nearly enough processing power to handle the onslaught of foreign micro-invaders we need to fend off every minute of our lives, not to mention resource-intensive internal-external processes like digesting highly complex foods. Our allied microbes do that for us, increasing our bodies' defensive intelligence and organic manipulation capabilities by several magnitudes. They adapt continuously to changes in the environment—they *learn*, and we don't even realize they're doing so. P.R.E.T.E.C.T.'s entire structure, just like those of the robots in the other lab, is coated in a dense but invisible layer of nanobots. Those nanobots are P.R.E.T.E.C.T.'s microbes—they help it learn, they help it to adjust, and they even help it to evolve its own capabilities."

"Well, P.R.E.T.E.C.T. sounds several magnitudes smarter than I am. What could I possibly teach it?"

"You can teach it about how human beings interact with shopping carts. You can provide it with insights it will need to have before we test-deploy it in the field. Your parents mentioned to me that you're an expert on the sociology of human-shopping cart interactions. You're working on a monograph, aren't you?"

"Uh yeah, but it's been on the back-burner for the last year or so. The working title is, 'Rolling Gold: The Underground Economy of Grocery Store Carts Among the Underclass and Working Poor of New Orleans.' I mean, I guess it's more of a cultural-economic study than a sociological or psychological one—it might not be what you're looking for—"

"No, it sounds *perfect*. Your parents didn't exaggerate. There will be a lot a paperwork for you to fill out, of course, since the Department of Homeland Security is involved, and you'll have to undergo a formal background check, but my people can accelerate that. The Consortium will compensate you for your time, and you'll be eligible to have your name listed as a consulting researcher and author on several monographs currently planned or in development—"

Jacob waved his arms in a sign of distress. "Whoa, whoa, *whoa!* I haven't said 'yes' yet."

"You—you *haven't?* But I thought—"

"You thought I'd be thrilled? Well, I am, *sort of*. This is pretty much a dream job. But I need to get one thing straight before I sign on the dotted line. Is this charity?"

"Charity? What—what do you mean?"

"What I mean is, did my parents put you up to this? Being a semi-impoverished graduate student, it's not that I have anything against charity. I just want to know where I stand."

Wyonna blushed more deeply than she had before. She stared at her feet. "Well—I, I wouldn't call it *charity*—I mean, you'd be providing valuable data to the project, but ..."

"But what?"

"Well, your parents—to be perfectly honest, Jacob— they *did* ask me a favor."

Jacob's anger flared more than he'd imagined it would. "So it *is* Mommy and Daddy looking out for little Jakey, after all! Is doing this also supposed to accrue me some credit toward my compulsory Israeli Army service? Are they trying to fix things so I can go back to Israel without spending a year in the slammer for having skipped out on the IDF?"

"Jacob, please, *please* don't make it sound like I'm

doing something underhanded! Your parents are some of the best people I've ever worked with—and some of the sweetest. Do you realize how much they *miss* you? Not ever hearing from you after you left Israel—it tears them up inside. They'll forgive you everything, if you'll just take even a baby step in their direction—"

Jacob turned his back on Wyonna and paced to the far side of the room. "Just mind your own business, okay?"

"But Jacob, cutting off important relationships, it's not *healthy*—"

"So Rabbi Helvetica's been coaching you, too? I've got a whole *conspiracy* of do-gooders working my sorry little case?"

Wyonna shook her head vigorously. "Helvetica hasn't coached me on anything. Jacob, please listen— our family lives are more similar than you know. The difference is, my parents broke with *me*. Once I— when I wasn't able to lie to myself or them anymore about the type of person I am. There's not a day that goes by when I don't wish, when I don't *yearn* for that to be different. When I don't crave the ability to go home for the holidays and have things feel as normal and *good* as they're supposed to in a loving family. I don't know if I'll ever get that, Jacob, because I can't control what's in my parents' hearts. But you—you're the lucky one. *You're* the one who's in control. Change your heart just a little, and they'll welcome you. I *know* they will!"

"I wish I was as confident of that as you are," he said quietly. "You don't know how much I wanted to get away from all that—that pressure cooker society they dunked me into. I just wanted to live a *normal* life. The kind of life I remembered from New Orleans."

"Nobody can blame you for that. So why don't you give your parents a call? Just a short one, to wish them happy holidays?"

"I just—" A security gate slammed shut in his mind, closing down his indecision. "No. Uh-uh. I'll do it when I'm ready. I won't be manipulated."

"I'm not trying to—to *manipulate* you! I only want to be *helpful*—"

"I get that, Wyonna. And I suppose I appreciate it. But I have to ask you to *please* butt out. If I'm going to fix things up with my parents, it's got to be on *my* terms, when *I'm* good and ready. Okay? Can you understand?"

She stared at the ground near his feet. "I—I'll try to." She walked silently to the cybernetic shopping cart. "What about P.R.E.T.E.C.T.? Will you still think about tutoring it?"

"Give me a couple of days to think about it, all right?"

"I suppose there's no big hurry." She walked over to him and hesitantly smiled. "Still friends?"

"For sure," he said. "Always."

"Will I see you tonight at the talk at McAlister Auditorium?"

He'd almost forgotten about the Israeli assistant consul's scheduled talk. "The Israeli Love Fest? Sure, I guess I'll make an appearance. Can't let the home team down. But I need to go to Saul Tannenburg's afternoon *shiva minyan* and then meet another friend of mine, so I might run a little late."

"I'm glad you're going. We'll see you there," Wyonna said.

He stared one last time at P.R.E.T.E.C.T. before turning to go. "Maybe you should bring it along. With the kinds of folks expected to turn up at McAlister, a state-of-the-art terror prevention gadget might come in handy."

Chapter Three

Like a medieval alchemist, Jacob had taken the most-base materials—a drunken session of bullshitting at the Boot Bar; the family fortune of an acquaintance who wasn't really a friend; contacts with old high school buddies who could use some extra cash; and a willingness to take advantage of others' prejudices, even if it meant somewhat degrading himself—then mixed them into pure gold.

His gold? A dissertation topic wildly popular with the Cultural Studies Department. A long line of research assistants from the Experimental Psychology, Religious Studies, and Sexology Departments begging to work with him. An almost assured tenure track position following graduation, either here at Tulane or at another university of at least mid-level rank. And, as a bonus, a possible best-seller along the lines of Camille Paglia's *Sexual Personae*—he already had an agent dropping hints to editors at the big New York houses about a popularized version of his dissertation, *Jonesing for Submission: Psycho-Sexual Responses of Diaspora Jewish Intellectuals to Dhimmitude Pornography*.

Yes, he was fixing things so he would be recognized as the world's premier authority on dhimmitude porn.

A unique genre of pornography that produced sexual excitement in its very niche audience by portraying erotic abasement of submissive non-Muslims (particularly Jews) at the hands, tongues, penises, whips, and sadistic torture devices of dominant Muslim men. Sure to be the hottest thing in the academic field of sexology since Baron von Krafft-Ebing invented the field with his tome *Psychopathia Sexualis*. Jacob couldn't take credit for initially coming up with dhimmitude porn; nor would he want to, since he would then be accused of inventing a self-licking ice cream cone. However, he could take credit for the genre's recent effusion of content (although it would be unwise for him to do so); in order to ensure himself adequate feed stock for his dissertation, Jacob had reached out to his circle of Jewish New Orleans high school friends, several of whom were still seeking ways to afford their escape from their childhood bedrooms in their parents' homes, and explained he could offer a good-paying gig they could work in their spare time on their laptops. He'd assembled half a dozen dhimmitude porn writers, male and female who could crank out an entire book in a week. Jacob acted as middleman, collecting their manuscripts and paying them in cash once their submissions (*double entendre intended*) met with approval. He never answered his friends' queries about where the money was coming from. He suspected the majority of them would back out if they knew the books and their distribution were being paid for by Yishmael Hashmed, a Saudi princeling with a less than benign outlook on Jews.

The only downside for Jacob of this convoluted arrangement was his twice-monthly humbling before Yishmael, a fellow Tulane grad student. He had a strong sense that his mother in Haifa would slit her own throat if she ever learned the actual details of the books he was midwifing and the research he was overseeing in the Sexology lab.

And now he had a new concern. The near certainty that his new friend, Saul Tannenburg, would drop him like a sizzling-hot donkey turd if he were to learn the true nature of Jacob's academic career.

Jacob walked into the Boot, his latest harvest of dhimmitude porn manuscripts under his arm. Yishmael Hashmed waited for him at a table near the middle of the mostly empty bar.

"Greetings, son of apes and pigs," Yishmael said.

"Howdy, towel-headed goat fucker," Jacob replied. "I thought we'd agreed to shorten my honorific to S.O.A.P.?"

"Indeed, we did. My apologies. Buy you a beer?"

Jacob glanced around the Boot. At this hour of a Tuesday late afternoon, the campus bar, located just off-Broadway Avenue's fraternity row, was nearly deserted, housing only a few graduate students grabbing some cheer between classes. He sat across from Yishmael. "Sure," he said. "My usual. I'll spring for the cheese fries."

Yishmael called over a waitress. "Two Rolling Rocks, please. And two orders of cheese fries. I'll have mine with extra jalapenos." After taking a few seconds to admire the blonde waitress's undulating posterior as she returned to the bar, he turned back to Jacob. "You have the manuscripts for me?"

Jacob placed a stack of thick manila envelopes on the table. "Here. All my authors included DVD copies, too, in case your publisher ever wants to join the twenty-first century."

"Cordoba likes to do things the old-fashioned way," Yishmael said. "The editor there wants to see everything on paper. What did your friends offer up this time?"

"Some of the same old, same old—lesbian bondage,

gay S&M, and goat sequences. But there's some fresh material, too. I got a great idea for a new sequence from my latest experimental volunteer. Passed it along to my writers. Get this—CIA agents captured in Afghanistan by the Taliban, forced to wear *burkas* and take it up the ass like women. And there're goats involved, too."

"Sounds very promising. My family compliments me on my wise choice of partners in this endeavor." Yishmael smiled. At twenty-four, the Saudi MBA student was a couple of years younger than Jacob, and not a bad-looking guy. With his family's money propping up a notably extravagant lifestyle, Yishmael never seemed to lack for American girlfriends, although he burned through them faster than the Flash punched out Gorilla Grodd. The waitress brought the two green bottles of Rolling Rock. Yishmael popped the cap off one and slid the other across the table and asked, "How is your study going?"

"My research is coming along really well," Jacob said. "I should be done with the dissertation within four or five months."

"Good. The quicker you get your book published, the quicker I start earning a return on my investment in you."

"Your family isn't making a profit on the dhimmitude porn I've arranged to be written?"

Yishmael frowned. "*Erotica*, please. Well, yes, of course, there is money to be made on that. But it is a niche market, very small. That is not to say that distributing the erotica does not have ancillary benefits, which my family appreciates far more than the inconsequential cash flow."

Jacob debated whether to tell Yishmael about that morning's study volunteer. He wouldn't be violating Alvin Schwartz's privacy, not in a legalistic sense. But in a broader sense, he would be shaming the man and, to an extent, himself. Still, the unwritten agreement between him and Yishmael insisted that he surrender whatever morsels of salacious gossip his study turned up. The cheese fries arrived. Jacob pulled a pair of potato wedges from the molten mass of bright yellow processed cheese food to allow them to cool. "You wouldn't believe who walked into the Sexology Center this morning and let a plethysmograph be strapped to his dick."

"Oh? Who?"

"A policy research analyst from the American-Israeli Political Action Committee."

"*AIPAC?* Surely you cannot be serious."

"As serious as a suicide bomber."

Yishmael smiled and gravely shook his head. "You are all doomed."

"Israelis? American Jews? Or Jews in general?"

"The whole lot of you. At the Last Hour, the stones and trees will not need to scream to *jihadis*, 'Here, oh Muslim, servant of Allah! There is a Jew behind me! Come and kill him!' You will reveal yourselves from your hiding places and offer us your necks."

Yishmael reached across the table and clinked the neck of his beer against Jacob's bottle. "*L'chiam*, my doomed friend." Before Jacob could think of a suitable riposte, Yishmael reached into his wallet, pulled out a fifty, and set in on the table. "I need to go. Pay the bill. Do leave the waitress a generous tip. You may keep the rest yourself."

He took the manuscripts and the bottle of Rolling Rock but left the cheese fries, loaded with soggy jalapenos, behind.

Jacob took a long swallow from his beer. He stared at his hands. They were large, pale hands, with tufts of almost white blond hair covering their knuckles and tops; when he wore a jacket, which was seldom, the hair on his wrists protruded like the frayed sleeves of an alpaca sweater. His friends at Hebrew school had always teased him, repeating, ad infinitum, that old Borscht Belt punchline, *"Well, you don't* look *Jewish."* Maybe that's why Yishmael had taken to him as a companion and business partner; Norwegians were among the most anti-Zionist and pro-Arab Europeans, and Jacob easily passed. The fact that he'd skipped out on Israeli Army service and reneged on his *aliyah* to return to New Orleans had helped lessen his pariah status with the Saudi, too.

Maybe his oppositional-defiant relationship with his Israeli heritage had made him less of a pariah with Yishmael. But Jacob couldn't help but feel that every time he handed over a stack of manuscripts to the Saudi, he became a bit more of a pariah to himself.

Chapter Four

Jacob, contrary to habit, did not arrive late for the Israeli assistant consul's talk at McAlister Auditorium. He arrived to take his place in the security line forty minutes before the talk was scheduled to begin. The line stretched two and a half blocks, past the Student Activities Center, almost all the way to Freret Street and the edge of the neighboring Loyola University campus.

While walking to the back of the line, Jacob had searched in vain for any recognizably Jewish faces. Members of the Islamic Student Union were out in force with their banners and placards. There were also noticeable contingents from the International Students Union, the Black Students Union, National Council of La Raza, CACTUS-the Community Action Committee of Tulane University Students, the Arab American Anti-Discrimination League, J Street Campus Outreach for Peace in the Middle East, International A.N.S.W.E.R. Coalition to Act Now to Stop the War and End Racism, Mothers and Others Against War, the Service Employees International Union, Methodists for Social Justice, and the Gay-Lesbian-Transgendered Student Progressive Alliance. He saw a swaying sea of *keffiyehs* on the heads ahead of him, about half in the traditional Palestinian black-and-white checked pattern, the rest in a motley assortment of tie-dye, plaid, and, surprisingly, pink. A microcosm of the worldwide Red-Green alliance — with "Green" having a double meaning in this case, since many of the *keffiyehs* were made of biodegradable natural fibers with no artificial dyes.

What he didn't see was any identifiable contingent from Hillel, Jewish Federation, Chabad, or any of the local synagogues. He looked in vain for Rabbi Helvetica or Wyonna, but finding them in a crowd this massive would be like trying to pluck the queen ant from a bustling colony using a pair of chop sticks.

Finally, three minutes before eight o'clock, he reached the front of the line. The campus security guard asked to see his backpack. Jacob handed it over.

"Hey," the guard said, "where're your vegetables? There's nothing in here but a note pad, some pens, and some comic books."

"Uh, did I get in the wrong line? I thought I'd be attending a talk on the Middle East, not a nutrition lecture."

"Vegetables aren't for eating, wise-ass. They're for throwing. You're allowed to have fruits, vegetables, eggs, fake blood as long as it's in a plastic container, no glass containers, no alcohol, no flammable liquids, no weapons, no genuine blood, and no urine or feces, human or animal."

"That's nasty."

"Yeah, you right. You should see some of the stuff I been forced to confiscate tonight. Now empty your pockets, stick your stuff in these trays, and step through that metal detector."

Jacob shuffled into the auditorium. The talk hadn't even started, and already the huge room overflowed with barely controlled pandemonium. At the stage's center sat a large box, about eight feet square, which was covered with a black tarp. A handful of audience members had decided to calibrate their aim and splatter the box and the surrounding stage with overripe tomatoes and rotten berries. Jacob saw that the only seats still available were those closest to the front. The seats where many of the poorly thrown tosses would land. Suddenly, he wished he'd brought his *keffiyeh*, after all. At least it would keep the gunk out of his hair.

He picked a seat off to the side. He'd be craning his neck throughout the talk, but at least he wouldn't be directly in the line of fire. Still, he crouched low in the seat, the back of his scalp tingling with anticipation of the impact of a badly aimed egg.

A shrill siren sounded, the signal, apparently, for all audience noise and boisterous activity to temporarily cease. Once the room had settled into something approximating decorum, Professor Emeritus Khalid Sheik Al-Nassar, the head of the Department of Middle Eastern Studies, poked his head from the wings, assured himself that no objects or edibles were airborne, then strode quickly onto the stage.

"Good evening, members of the Tulane University community," he said into a wireless mic pinned to his lapel. "I greatly appreciate you all coming out this night to hear what promises to be a most interesting presentation. In a moment, you will be introduced to the Israeli assistant consul from the Dallas regional consulate, Mr. Menachem Levine. Given the great passions which have flared, both within our community and worldwide, regarding the controversy over *Al Wadib*, Mr. Levine's consulate was anxious to have him present the Israeli government's side. My department, dedicated to an impartial, scholarly pursuit of knowledge, was interested in allowing him to speak. Please remember that the core mission of our university is the free and open exchange of ideas and opinions, no matter how reprehensible. With this in mind, I ask that you offer a warm Tulane University welcome to Mr. Levine, despite your fully justified outrage at the racist, colonialist, apartheid policies of his government."

Ropes began lifting the tarp from the large box on stage. Professor Al-Nassar scurried off stage as quickly as his stout legs could carry him.

Once the tarp was completely removed, Jacob saw that the box was actually a portable cage, one which could be used to transport livestock or circus animals. Its steel mesh would obstruct large thrown objects, but not pulp, liquid, or egg yolk. Inside, seated on a plain wooden chair, was a man not much older than Jacob was, someone he could have attended high school with in Haifa. He wore a gray suit, a red tie, and safety goggles. His clothes were covered by a transparent plastic rain poncho. The poncho and safety goggles quickly proved their worth, as a hail of tomatoes, zucchinis, eggs, and Ziploc baggies filled with red-dyed kayro syrup exploded against the front of the cage.

"Good evening, Tulane University," Mr. Levine said. He paused for a second to wipe a smear of kayro syrup and tomato seeds from his cheek. "I see I am not speaking with a friendly audience. That's all right. If we Israelis insisted on speaking only to friends, we would have very few people to speak with. All that I ask is that you listen—I may not change many minds here tonight, but I hope that once we leave this auditorium, you will depart with a better understanding of my government's positions on the issues of the day. Perhaps in time, understanding will lead to empathy, and empathy will lead, at last, to peaceful coexistence."

"*Death to the Jooos!*" someone five or six rows behind Jacob shrieked.

"The issue I'm sure most of you are interested in my speaking about is Meah Shearim, the current flashpoint between the Israeli and Arab peoples. Unlike so many other issues which have divided Israelis and Arabs over the past seventy years, this issue is a very simple one. It is an existential issue for Israel. Meah Shearim was founded in 1874 by members of the Old Yishuv, the Jewish community which had remained in the Holy Land following the destruction of the Second Temple in the year 70. Its founders were residents of the walled Old City of Jerusalem, then inhabited by only two thousand people, half of them Arabs, half of them Jews, but plagued by overcrowding and poor sanitation. Meah Shearim, established on empty, barren land, served as a suburb and farming center. As Jewish immigration increased, and Jerusalem grew, Meah Shearim was absorbed into the city proper. At the end of the Israeli War of Independence, it was on the Israeli side of the armistice line, the Green Line. It was never an Arab village. It is, and always has been, an integral part of the Jewish State. For an Israeli government to abrogate its sovereignty over Meah Shearim and surrender that sovereignty to Palestine would be an act of national suicide."

"How can we help?" a woman wearing a Mothers and Others Against War shouted.

"It would be an admission that Jews have no legitimate standing in the land of Israel," Levine continued, "that the Israeli nation has no legitimacy, and thus could only be a prelude to the gradual dismantling of the Jewish State. Let me make it clear—no Israeli government will ever do this. No Israeli government will willingly slit the throat of its own nation."

This seemingly self-evident declaration ignited a chorus of boos and a fresh shower of produce and kayro syrup.

Levine took a towel and wiped pulp from his forehead and hair. "Our friends in Europe and here in America ask us, 'Why make such a big deal out of Meah Shearim? It is just one little neighborhood. You have already given back Gaza, the West Bank, and East Jerusalem—even the Temple Mount—and have handed over sovereignty of the Golan Heights to international control. What is one more tiny neighborhood on top of all that? Will you turn your back on peace for the sake of a few dozen acres? Is not peace worth any price?

"Let me tell you about the peace we have purchased. It is a good we have tried to buy many, many times. The best peace we ever purchased was the peace with Egypt. Its price was the Sinai, territory won by Israeli blood during two Egyptian wars of aggression, oil-rich land three times the size of the current State of Israel, which made up eighty-one percent of all the land Israel captured during the Six Day War. Even that peace, the best of the many 'peaces' we have bought, was never better than a bitter, cold peace. And it was partially renounced by Egypt following the overthrow of President Mubarak."

"Death to the traitor Mubarak!"

"Hail the Muslim Brotherhood! Hail the Salafi! May they pluck out the Mubarak family's eyes!"

"Israel once maintained a security zone in southern Lebanon," Levine continued, "to prevent attacks on the villages and cities of northern Israel. Israel unilaterally withdrew from that security zone in 2000. The result was the ascendancy of Hezbollah, until recently internationally recognized as a terrorist organization—"

"One man's terrorist is another man's *freedom fighter!*"

"— a terrorist organization armed with tens of thousands of short and medium range missiles by Iran. In 2005, Israel unilaterally uprooted its citizens from Gaza and withdrew every soldier. We left them the greenhouses our people had built so that they could develop their own agricultural economy. We did this as a test, to see whether the Palestinians in Gaza were more interested in building their society or in warring with us. We received our answer when they destroyed the greenhouses and elected Hamas—"

"*HAMAS! HAMAS! Jews to the gas!*"

"Upon Hamas's ascendency, the rain of rockets into southern Israel intensified into a daily offensive. Following two years of forbearance, after eight thousand rocket attacks, our government finally responded with an incursion into Gaza. Our efforts at self-defense were condemned by much of the world, as were our subsequent efforts to prevent the rearming of Hamas. Now Iran has succeeded in transforming that territory into a heavily armed forward base of operations."

"Long live Ayatollah Khamenei, champion of the oppressed peoples!" a man wearing a pink *keffiyeh* and a matching dyed pink goatee cried in a nasal voice.

Jacob thought Levine might go off-script to say something about the fate of homosexuals in Iran, but he avoided the detour. "These unilateral concessions by Israel," the diplomat continued, "unmatched by any concessions or even flexibility on the Palestinian side, were but a prelude to the events of the past four years. The Peace Now Coalition replaced the previous Knesset coalition headed by Likud. The new government responded to economic and cultural embargoes on Israel from China, Russia, and the European Union and similar measures threatened by the U.S., Japanese, and Australian governments with unprecedented unilateral concessions. The Peace Now Coalition did what the world demanded—we withdrew from every inch of territory beyond the Green Line. Although the territories were legally disputed, Israel, at enormous sacrifice to its social fabric, withdrew each and every one of its citizens, oftentimes by force. We turned over billions and billions of dollars' worth of housing, commercial real estate, and farms. We reconstructed the Security Fence to precisely match the dictates of the Green Line. Most painfully, we re-divided Jerusalem. We surrendered our sovereignty over Judaism's holiest site, the Temple Mount. We willed ourselves to believe in the world's promises that international supervision would preserve the rights of all faiths to worship at their holy places.

"And what have we received in return? Has it been peace? Has it been Israel's attaining the status of a normal nation among the nations, not subjected to barrages of boycotts, delegitimization, and demonization?"

"*This* is what you'll receive, you *child-murdering fascist SCUM!*" A dreadlock-wearing woman from the International A.N.S.W.E.R. Coalition hurled a gallon-sized Ziploc bag filled with cloudy yellow liquid. As soon as it burst against the cage, Jacob knew by its odor what it was. Given that he'd seen the security guards insist that attendees take a sip from any questionable liquids they refused to have confiscated, Jacob had to at least respect the strength of the woman's convictions.

Levine's nostrils flared. "Not that it will make any difference, but I would like the security guards and administrators to know that *wasn't* lemonade. At least the young lady had the decency to say 'fascist' rather than 'Nazi'—"

"Nazi! Nazi!"

Levine rolled his eyes. "Please tell your parents that the thousands of dollars they have spent on history and political science instruction at this school have been utterly wasted. As I was saying—what sort of peace have we received in return? The apartment towers which we gave to the Palestinians have been turned into snipers' nests and rocket launching pads. Our commercial aircraft cannot land at or take off from Ben-Gurion International Airport without expensive anti-missile defenses installed, and no other nation's airliners will land there because of the dangers. International supervision of the Holy Basin in Jerusalem has become a farce. Half a dozen terrorist groups have taken de facto control of chunks of the former East Jerusalem while U.N. soldiers have looked the other way. Eighty-five percent of the population of the State of Israel is now exposed to rocket and missile attack. Most egregious of all, UNRWA, a U.N. body, pays for New Fatah's erection of a waste treatment plant on the site of the *Kotel*, the Western Wall of the Temple Mount—"

A Middle Eastern man in his early twenties sprang from his chair a few seats over from Jacob. "Sons of apes and pigs! You made the Palestinian people eat your shit for seventy years! Now it is your turn to eat *our* shit!"

The crowd cheered.

"Are you willing to listen?" Levine shouted back. "Are you students at university, or a pack of savages? We have tried 'land for peace,' over and over and over again. The land is gone forever, and the peace never comes. So, no, the Israeli government will *never* surrender Meah Shearim—"

"I will give my life for *Al Wadib*! A thousand million *Shahids* will march on occupied Jerusalem until *Al Wadib* is *ours!*"

"Oh, listen to yourselves!" Levine shouted. "This '*Al Wadib*' of yours is a malicious, childish fairy tale! Nowhere in any hadith of the Koran is there any mention of Muhammed stopping on his Night Journey to water his flying horse outside the walls of Jerusalem. *Al Wadib* is a fabrication, a pretext for aggression, a lie—"

The Arab a few seats down from Jacob sprang up again. Now Jacob recognized him—Yakub bin Saladi, a Yemenite member of Yishmael Hashmed's loose circle of drinking buddies and hangers-on. "Your filthy lips profane the name of the Prophet (blessings and peace be upon him)!" Yakub shrieked. "For that you will *die!*"

Levine shielded his face from the splatter of a fresh barrage. "Should we be so foolish as to give away Meah Shearim, next we will be called upon to give away Rehavia, and then Kfar Saba, and then Jaffa. There will be no end to it, until there is an end to *us*, the Jews—"

Jacob heard a wail of electronic feedback. Levine's voice suddenly vanished, although his lips continued moving. *Someone's screwed with the sound board*, Jacob thought. The audience erupted into a frenzy of cheers and ululations. Like the climax of a Fourth of July fireworks display, all of the saved-up ammunition seemed to take flight at once, exploding against the steel mesh of Levine's cage in a pulpy, gooey tsunami.

Menachem Levine now looked like a three-dimensional Jackson Pollack painting. After another moment of trying to speak and having to spit out raw egg and who knew what else, he clamped his mouth shut and held up his left hand, its middle finger projecting toward the auditorium in mute defiance.

As an example of hasbara, *public diplomacy, that presentation pretty much sucked*, Jacob thought. *Epic fail. But who could've done a better job than he did?*

Ruminating on his critique, Jacob realized how much of a detached observer he'd been. As though none of this really touched him, as though he were just a tourist on this planet. He glanced back at the hundreds of people behind him and stared at their faces. Brown faces, white faces, black faces; straights, gays, lesbians, and men who loathed the very air homosexuals breathed; Muslims, Christians, atheists, and probably a few Jews mixed in, too. All screaming, all glaring with varying degrees of the same passionate, self-righteous hatred.

If it weren't for that cage, Menachem Levine would be a dead man.

Because he was an Israeli. Because he was a Jew.

Like a bucket of ice water dumped on his thick head, the thought occurred to Jacob that the same applied to him. Despite his having fled Israel for New Orleans, despite his facilitating the writing of dhimmitude pornography and sharing beers with Yishmael Hashmed.

He smelled something burning. He looked to his left and saw Yakub bin Saladi using a match to light a rag inserted into a plastic bottle. The man stood and raised his arm to hurl the bottle at the stage.

"Yakub! *Don't!*" Jacob tried to reach him over the laps of three other audience members. He stumbled and tripped, but his outstretched hand bumped against Yakub's arm just as the Yemenite completed his throwing motion.

The blazing bottle flew wide of the cage. It split open and spewed what smelled like cleaning fluid over a good portion of the stage's wooden floor. The fluid, possibly smuggled in before the event or lifted from janitorial supplies kept in some backstage closet, ignited into puddles of shimmering blue flames. The auditorium's sprinkler system sputtered into life. Klaxons began their ear-splitting wailing.

The audience, united in their passion and outrage into a single righteous fist only seconds before, fled for the exits.

Chapter Five

After he returned to his apartment and showered to clean his hair and neck of *schumtz*, Jacob caught broadcasts or reruns of all four local nightly news shows. Two of them featured brief segments showing the protesters outside McAlister Auditorium and snippets of interviews with representatives from the Islamic Student Union, International A.N.S.W.E.R. Coalition, or Mothers and Others Against War. None of the broadcasts mentioned anything about the arson attack.

The next morning, after he'd gulped down a few swallows of leftover coffee, he threw on a pair of shorts and a tee shirt and went downstairs to the vending machine on the corner of State Street and Tchoupitoulas, in front of the corner bar which stood below his second-story apartment, and bought a copy of the *New Times-Picayune*. The front section lacked any story about the assistant consul's talk. The story was also AWOL from the Metro Section. Finally, midway down the page of the Living Section set aside for coverage of local religious issues, he spotted a small story, half a column long, about the event. But all it ended up being was an abbreviated regurgitation of the press releases the Tulane University Department of Middle Eastern Studies and the Hillel Foundation had sent out.

Every crummy one-alarm fire in this tinderbox town gets on page one of the lead section or Metro, Jacob thought. *But an arson attack witnessed by five or six hundred people gets ignored? What the hell's going on?*

He wasn't in any mood to go looking for grocery carts, so he left the Ram in front of his apartment and rode his bicycle to campus. He locked up in front of the Student Center, grabbed a free copy of the *Tulane Daily Hullabaloo,* and plopped down on one of the center's couches. Unlike the *New Times-Picayune,* the *Hullabaloo* hadn't ignored the story. It was front page. The headline read:

ISRAELI CONSUL "SHOOTS THE BIRD" AT T.U. COMMUNITY

Right below the prominent headline was a close-up photo of Menachem Levine raising his middle finger to the audience after his mic had been cut off. Jacob saw that the picture had been photoshopped so that the egg, tomato, and urine splatter did not appear on the consul's defiant face. He began reading the story.

It's not easy, putting lipstick on a pig. Yet that is precisely what Israeli Assistant Consul Menachem Levine attempted to do last night in McAlister Auditorium. Speaking to a crowd of approximately six hundred Tulane students and community activists, Levine offered up an unappetizing banquet of stale platitudes, half-truths, and twisted history, shunting aside the ongoing tragedy of the Palestinian Nakba in a vain effort to paint Israeli intransigence on the issue of Al Wadib as a principled stand on a matter of existential import …

He began skimming, running his eyes over adjective-choked column inches crammed full of *"Zionist imperialism"* blah blah *"apartheid wall"* blah blah *"fascist brutality"* blah blah *"victims turned victimizers"* blah blah, looking for a description of how the evening had ended. Finally, in the second to last paragraph, he found it:

… When his propagandistic remarks failed to elicit the applause he had been expecting, the Zionist "diplomat" cut his talk short and directed an obscene gesture (see photograph above) at students and activists alike, displaying a profound disdain for the civilized norms of democratic discourse. Fortuitously, a small electrical fire caused by worn wiring backstage necessitated an orderly emergency evacuation of the building, bringing the evening's misbegotten presentation to a premature but welcome end …

An *"electrical fire?"* Jacob read the paragraph again to reassure himself that he'd just read what he thought he'd read. The *Tulane Daily Hullabaloo* had certainly lived down to its nickname—the *Hezbollahbaloo*.

Who had written this tripe? He looked to the top of the article for the byline. *Norm Zucker*. Well, that explained a lot. Zucker, self-proclaimed Trotskyite and darling of the Political Science Department, was editor of the *Hullabaloo*, campus president of the International A.N.S.W.E.R. Coalition's local chapter, and the organizing force behind the Muslim-Jewish Progressive Alliance for Peace and Understanding.

And a prick.

Well, Zucker wasn't going to get away with this. Not this time. Not when Jacob had been sitting four seats away from the man who'd thrown the Molotov cocktail; not when he knew the arsonist's name. If nobody else among the six hundred attendees had come forward to tell the truth, he would have to do it himself. Even if it meant upsetting his partnership with Yishmael Hashmed.

He marched himself over to the Campus Security building and said to the woman officer sitting behind the reception desk, "I'd like to report an arson."

"A fire? Is it on-going? You need to call 911—"

"No, it's out now. The arson took place last night. In McAlister Auditorium."

She raised an eyebrow. "Oh, you mean that demonstration about Israel and the Palestinians?"

"Yeah. The *Hullabaloo* said the fire was caused by an electrical short. That wasn't how it happened at all—"

"Stop!" She held up a hand to quiet him. "Don't tell me another thing about it. Let me get one of the sergeants to take your statement. In private."

She disappeared into one of the back offices. A moment later, she emerged with a male sergeant in tow. The man gestured for Jacob to join him in his office.

"Close the door behind you," the sergeant told Jacob. He pointed to a chair in front of his desk. "Sit down. This is about last night?"

"Yes. I'd like to report an arson and an attempted murder. I was sitting in the third row from the front, just four seats away from the guy who threw the Molotov cocktail—"

"Whoa, slow down," the sergeant said. He looked tired and vaguely queasy. "Are you *sure* you want to make this statement?"

Jacob didn't understand the man's meaning. "Of *course* I want to make a statement. Why else would I have come in here? The *Hullabaloo* said an electrical fire caused the sprinkler system to go off. That's *bullshit*. I was right there. I saw everything that happened. I even know the name of the man who threw the bomb."

The officer sighed. "You know, of course, that officially, the cause of the fire was an electrical short. That's the report I gave to the New Orleans Police Department."

"Well, you gave an inaccurate report, then. Good thing I'm here to correct it. Didn't any of your security people see what I saw?"

"None of them were inside until the alarms went off. We were told to stay outside the auditorium unless things got out of hand."

"And the stuff you were hearing—'Death to the Joooos!' 'Hamas, Hamas, Jews to the gas!'—that didn't sound like 'things getting out of hand' to you?"

"This is a university. We deal with that stuff all the time."

"Do you deal with *arson* all the time? Come on—didn't any of your people even take a *look* at that stage after the fire? There must've still been traces of chemicals all over the place. That was no electrical fire, and you know it."

"Look, what's your name?"

"Jacob Zvi."

"Mr. Zvi," He spoke slowly, as though Jacob had a hearing impairment or a severe learning disability. "I happen to like this job. It's a whole lot safer than working for the NOPD, and the pay is comparable. But did you know that all my officers and I are contract workers? Our contract can be terminated for nonperformance, or convenience, or for any of several dozen other reasons, at any time. All the university has to do is give my boss thirty days' notice, and we're all out on our asses, with no recourse. All that aside, I am legally required to take a statement from you, if you insist on giving one. Maybe you aren't too good at reading between the lines. In case you aren't, let me fill you in on a little secret—there are certain people you do not want to piss off, and I'm not referring to *me*. Are you *sure* you want to give me a statement?"

This only served to make Jacob more ferociously certain he was doing the right thing. "Hell, *yes*," he said.

The sergeant's shoulders slumped. He turned to a filing cabinet and pulled out a form. "Okay, grad student," he said, "it's your ass."

✡ ✡ ✡

Jacob didn't like feeling angry. Or aggrieved. Or vengeful. He didn't like feeling under siege by shadowy forces that might drop a bomb in his pants at any moment. That's what he had left Israel to get away from.

He decided to head over to the Hillel House. It was just a couple of blocks off campus, tucked between a couple of fraternity houses on Broadway Avenue. Rabbi Helvetica would be a good person to talk with. Maybe she could offer some sensible suggestions about what he should do now, after giving his seemingly radioactive statement at the campus security office. He wanted to get her take on it all. Had she been there? How had witnessing all that made *her* feel?

He walked up the brown building's front steps to the porch and entered the center's den/library/dining room/prayer space. The only people inside were a pair of undergraduates he sort of knew, a skinny guy with a curly beard and a slightly zoftig but very attractive brunette he'd tried to ask out once and had been rebuffed by. He couldn't remember either of their names.

"Uh, hi," he said. "Is the rabbi in her office?"

"Nope," Curly Beard said. "I think she might be back in a couple of hours."

"Oh," Jacob said. "That's a bummer."

Ms. Zoftig-but-Attractive pretended he wasn't there.

Jacob stared at old, faded travel posters of Israel that had been cheaply framed and stuck up on the walls years ago, long before either he or Rabbi Helvetica had come here. A *kibbutz* in the Galilee. An ancient Crusader fort somewhere on the West Bank. The Temple Mount with the Dome of the Rock and Al Aqsa Mosque, the Mount of Olives in the background with its centuries of Jewish graves.

He wanted to talk with his parents.

The suddenness of the idea surprised him. But then he realized the desire had been sneaking up on him for days, ever since he'd attended Saul Tannenburg's first *shiva minyan*.

He headed back to his apartment to make an Internet call to his parents' home in Haifa. He checked his watch. With the time difference, his parents should've left work at the Technion at least an hour ago.

E.T. phone home …

He put on a USB hands-free head-set and logged in. As he typed his parents' number, his stomach felt like he was riding a roller coaster after he'd scarfed down four Hebrew National dogs. And a couple of those giant pretzels. And a wad of cotton candy bigger than a Volkswagen.

A moment later, he heard his parents' phone ringing.

"*Shalom?*"

It was his mother.

"Uh, hi, Mom," he said. "It's Jacob."

"Jacob?" A long pause. Had she forgotten who he was? "Hold on—don't go anywhere—let me get your father on the other phone."

He waited.

"Hello? Is this Jacob?"

"Yeah, Dad. None other."

"Tovah? Are you back on the other line yet?"

"Yes, I'm here," she said.

Another long pause.

So we're all here. Now what? Jacob rubbed the back of his neck. "Uh, how are you guys doing?"

"Forget how *we're* doing," his mother said. "How are *you* doing?"

"Okay, I guess."

"That doesn't sound so 'okay' to me. Is anything the matter? Are you *sick?*"

"No, no, I'm fine, it's nothing like that. I don't have colon cancer. I know two of your great uncles died from it, and Cousin Mortie on Dad's side has had to wear a colostomy bag since he was twenty-eight. But my bowels are just fine. It's just I wanted to talk."

"That's good," his father said. "Did—did Wyonna Shaver speak with you?"

"Yeah, she did," Jacob admitted. "She showed me around her lab, too. But that's not why I decided to call."

"So why *did* you?" his mother asked.

"Well, you know, the High Holy Days are coming up. I just wanted to wish you a happy new year."

"Several Rosh Hashanahs have come and gone since the last time you called," his mother reminded him. "So why is this year different from all other years?"

"It just *is,*" Jacob said. "Would you rather I *didn't* call?" He listened to the silence on the other end of the line, realizing that, in less than ninety seconds, he'd fallen back into the emotional defensiveness that for years had made it impossible for him to talk seriously with his parents. He was getting too old for this adolescent role playing; he needed to extricate his foot from that bear trap, if only for his own sanity. "I'm—I'm sorry," he said. "I called because—because I miss you. And because I'm worried about you."

"Worried about *us?*" his father said. "That's a turn-around."

"I went to a talk last night," Jacob said. "Given by the assistant Israeli consul from Dallas. Things sound pretty rotten over by you. It looks like that 'Al Wadib' thing is coming to a boil, with the whole world piling on again. It's never going to end, is it? No matter what the Israelis do, no matter what they give up. It's not going to end until one side chokes on sand. How do you two *live* with that?"

"It's nothing new," his mother said, making it sound as though she were talking about a recurrent plumbing problem.

"We knew what we were in for when we decided to make *aliyah*," his father said. "The politicians have been making themselves blind and crazy trying to 'process peace' ever since Oslo. But we decided the best way we could show that Israel would never go away was to come here and make a life for ourselves. A *good* life."

"But haven't you sacrificed more than enough just to make a point?" Jacob asked. "How safe do you feel in Haifa? You're not that far away from Hezbollah."

"We're probably safer here than we were living in New Orleans, to be honest," his mother said. "We're not as bad off as the border towns are. Haifa is far enough away from Lebanon that the Iron Dome and David's Sling anti-missile systems have time to target whatever missiles the Hezzies fire off. The defenses take down eighty-five percent of them."

"And the other fifteen percent?" Jacob asked.

"That's why every building in the city has a bomb shelter," his mother said. "We generally have about a minute and a half of warning time."

"You know what's worse, actually?" his father asked. "It's that we have to counter cheap Hezbollah missiles with expensive Israeli anti-missiles. Between paying for the anti-missiles, paying for water desalination thanks to the Syrians and Chinese diverting every drop of the Jordan River, and all the boycotts targeting our economy, we're living like we're back in the 1960s. Everything's rationed. My taxes were raised four times this past year. Your mother and I are renting out your old bedroom to make ends meet—"

"Herman," Tovah said warningly, "enough, already. Jacob didn't call to hear you *kvetch*."

"Actually," Jacob said, "that's exactly what I called to hear. Is there any way—I mean, could you *possibly* consider joining me back here in New Orleans? With Wyonna's help, you could probably continue doing the same work you're doing now, at Tulane instead of the Technion. And we'd be together again."

"Jacob, really," his father said heatedly, "*these* old battles again? You know how your mother and I feel—"

"Wait just a minute!" Tovah interjected. "What Jacob just said—not that I'd do it, but those are the first *sweet* words I've heard from my son in over three years. Let me savor them, just a little bit, before you two start back in on the fighting."

Everyone stayed quiet for a moment.

"So," Tovah said at last, "Jacob, darling, are you seeing someone?"

"Do you mean 'seeing someone' romantically or therapeutically?"

"The *former*, of course! That latter, that's none of my business. Not that there's anything wrong with seeking professional help; your cousin Mortie, the one with a colostomy bag, he's a certified family therapist and he does very well for himself."

"I'm not seeing anybody special," Jacob said.

"Anybody not-so-special?"

"Not even someone not-so-special," Jacob admitted.

"Well, there are *plenty* of girls here," his mother said. "Just three offices over from mine, there's a lovely girl, Sephardi family, parents originally from Iraq. She's twenty-four, never been married, finishing a doctorate in applied artificial intelligence. Very sweet. I hear she cooks, too. May I email you a photo?"

"Email her over here," Jacob said, "and I'll try out her cooking."

He heard his mother sigh. "Your loss, Jacob."

"Jacob," his father said, "you know, if you ever want to come back to Haifa, maybe once you finish your degree, I could fix things for you with the IDF. I'm very close with the commander of my Reserve Division. I could probably work things so that you wouldn't face any penalties, just have to put in your normal service time—"

Jacob rolled his eyes. "Dad, that's *way* premature. I mean, thanks for offering to go to bat for me, but what I decided three years ago still stands. Oh, heck, maybe once I've got the doctorate under my belt, I'll be willing to reconsider. *Maybe*. Assuming the Knesset hasn't given away the rest of the state by then, and you all are living on big pontoon boats in the Mediterranean."

"Jacob!" his mother scolded him. "Spit between your fingers!"

"It was a joke, Mom."

"How about the other part?" his father asked. "Was that a joke, too?"

Was it? He didn't know himself. "Check back with me in a couple of years, Dad."

"Well, at least that's something. Something's better than nothing."

What else was there to talk about? He couldn't very well give them details about his dissertation research. He couldn't tell them about his friends at Hillel, either—if he were honest about attending the services Rabbi Helvetica led, they'd be more offended than if he told them he'd joined Jews for Jesus.

"Well, I guess I need to be going," he said.

"So *soon?*" his mother asked. "You call us for the first time in over three years, and we get less than ten minutes from you?"

"Tovah," his father said, "it's the middle of the work day over there, I'm sure he has classes."

"I won't let another three years go by," Jacob said. "I *promise*. I'll call again during the High Holy Days."

"Do you need us to send you money for the call?" his mother asked.

"No, please, don't bother."

"Well, have you been attending services?"

"Uh, yeah. At the Hillel Center."

"Oh, the *Hillel* Center? Why aren't you meeting any women there? What sort of a rabbi do they have?"

"The non-Orthodox kind. Hey, gotta catch my next class. We'll talk again soon. I—I love you. Both of you."

"We love you, too, Jacob. Goodbye, son. *Shalom.*"

"*Shalom*, Mom. Be safe, all right?"

"Will do."

PART TWO

Chapter Six

Sayyid al-Wahhab hurried past a load of blue steel aqueduct pipe sections piled at the southwestern edge of the Al-Buraq plaza, soon to be the site of Palestine's newest waste treatment facility. He had a meeting to make with the Chechen. A very important meeting.

Already, three quarters of the waste treatment plant's structural skeleton rose above the ancient stones of the plaza's floor, almost to the height of the base of the Noble Sanctuary. The project was coming along splendidly, he noted with pleasure. Of all the infrastructure projects which the European Union and the U.N. had funded following the Zionists' unilateral surrender of all of the West Bank and East Jerusalem, this one had proceeded by far the quickest, approaching completion an unheard-of six months ahead of schedule. He, Sayyid al-Wahhab, chief supervising construction engineer, could claim much of the credit for this astounding efficiency. But in truth, the credit for this accomplishment belonged to the workers themselves, who viewed this task as a sacred national duty. They had applied themselves with the same vigor they had once devoted to resistance activities. Perhaps even greater vigor, for who did not delight in the utter humiliation of his enemies and desecration of that enemy's so-called holy places? Upon its completion, the Chairman Yassar Arafat Memorial Solid Waste Treatment Facility would perform both functions, around the clock, every day of every year.

Still, glorious as this public project was, his secret project, the one for which the Chechen was key, promised a far vaster payoff. Sayyid al-Wahhab would one day soon be spoken of in the same hushed, awed tones as Saladin. For he, acting on his own initiative, would have broken the national spirit of the thrice-accursed Zionists and perhaps induced them to leave their illegitimate Crusader colonialist outpost of a statelet *en masse*.

Officially, Sayyid expressed adherence to the public charter of New Fatah, which called for a single, bi-national state between the Jordan River and the Mediterranean Sea. Less openly, he pledged loyalty to the code of the Al Wadib Martyrs Brigade, New Fatah's armed resistance wing, which mandated expulsion of all the Jews, or, should individual Zionists prove resistant, their extermination. Other factions' codes and charters were less merciful. The Black Septemberists declared they would drive all the Jews into the sea. The fighters of Hezbollah South would drive all the Jews *and* all the Christians into the sea. The militants of the Palestinian Revolutionary Guard Corps would behead all of the Jews and all of the Christians, ship their heads to Iran, and then dump their lifeless, headless bodies into the sea. The *shahids* of Islamic Maoist Jihad were the most hard-assed of all; they would imprison all of the Jews and all of the Christians in rural reeducation camps and force them to study both Mao's *Little Red Book* and the Holy Koran until they had been convinced of their true identities as part of the Sharia-compliant worldwide proletariat. Then they would employ the newly enlightened ones' joyous labor on collectivist farms until they starved to death, and finally grind their bodies into nutritious paste for export to the Democratic Republic of North Korea.

But once Sayyid's plans came to fruition, all the loyalists of those *poseur* resistance factions could beat their own heads with their own worn-down shoes. For his bold, heroic act would have made the Al Wadib Martyrs Brigade supreme above all.

He hurried down the steps to the sub-basement of the Chairman Yassar Arafat Memorial Solid Waste Treatment Facility. The Chechen awaited him, accompanied by Nassari and Hassan, two of Sayyid's most trusted subordinates. Sayyid had never met the Chechen face-to-face until now; he almost laughed when he saw man's beard. The elongated inverted triangle of hair looked like a fake beard that one might order from a novelties firm advertising its wares on the back of a comic book. But the Chechen's fierce, icy blue eyes made Sayyid's half-formed laugh wither in his throat.

"Greetings," Sayyid said. "I trust you have my package with you?"

"I do," the Chechen said. He pulled a bulky, wheeled footlocker from a corner and deposited it at Sayyid's feet.

Sayyid eyed it with a reverence he generally reserved for the Al Aqsa Mosque or memories of his mother. "This is the little package?"

The Chechen nodded. "The confederates who helped me bring it across the Jordanian border believed it to be a smuggled shipment of medical isotopes. Your men here have already confirmed the box's contents. I assume you have the second of three portions of my money?"

This was a part of the transaction Sayyid particularly

looked forward to. Having seen it done in dozens of American espionage thriller movies, he felt himself virtually a peer of Tom Cruise and Leonardo de Caprio. With a flourish, he undid the stainless-steel clasps of the black leather briefcase he had been carrying, then laid it upon a table and opened it. "Five hundred thousand in unmarked American dollars," he said proudly. "Procured for New Fatah by the American Congress for schools and hospitals. You will receive your final payment of five hundred thousand dollars when you deliver the big package. When is that to be expected?"

The Chechen frowned. "Perhaps somewhat later than I had originally indicated. I have been required to initiate negotiations with my Syrian contacts."

"What about the Iranians?"

"My contacts in the Iranian Revolutionary Guard Corps have been liquidated ..."

Sayyid stifled an impulse to grab back the briefcase of American currency. "What does this mean? Has our operation been compromised?"

The Chechen formed a somber minaret of his fingers and stared down at them. "Possibly," he admitted. "In my final communication with my primary Iranian contact, he mentioned that his top leadership was leaning towards providing the missile to their clients in the Palestinian Revolutionary Guard Corps, rather than to your Al Wadib Martyrs Brigade. If indeed they made that decision, it would logically follow that they have informed the PRGC of my delivery of the special munition to you. You understand, of course, that without the munition, the missile is of little consequence. The men of the PRGC understand this, too."

It did not take long for Sayyid to put two and two together. However, he found himself more relieved than worried. Of all the rival factions which the Iranians could have chosen to set against him, the PRGC was perhaps the least formidable. He allowed himself a confident laugh. "The Palestinian Revolutionary Guard Corps? Those boot-licking, Shiite-worshipping lackeys of the Persians? *Hah!* They are *poseurs*—there is not a true *shahid* among them. They are little girly men who dream of their seventy-two virgins in Paradise teaching them to sew and to cook, and how to wet-nurse real men's babies. If they dare to cross swords with the fighters of the Al Wadib Martyrs Brigade, they will slice off their own toes before they spill even a drop of my men's blood."

"For your sake, I hope your confidence is well-founded," the Chechen said, running his fingers through the oddly artificial-looking fur of his long beard. "In any case, the most difficult part of the procurement is behind us. The contents of the little package are far rarer and more valuable than any short-range ballistic missile. And it is now in your hands—a choice bit of Soviet Army surplus, a ZBV3 152-millimeter artillery shell, its forty-year-old plutonium core refreshed by Pakistani Intelligence."

"Having the shell, perhaps we could make do with a locally manufactured rocket?"

"No. Your Kassams do not have the necessary carrying capacity. Although it is a tactical device, not a strategic one, still the ZBV3 shell weighs in excess of sixty kilograms. Also, Kassams have been known to be not always very reliable. A misfiring Kassam with conventional explosives? At worst, it causes ten or fifteen deaths of your own people, and if you are lucky, you can blame it on the Zionists and have BBC newsmen interview the grieving relatives. A misfiring Kassam with a one kiloton nuclear shell attached, however? Ahh, a different tale entirely. I do not think your masters in New Fatah would look upon such a misfortune with nonchalance."

"What, then? Where shall the missile come from?"

"The Syrians will likely be forthcoming. If they will not, I will speak with my contacts in Turkey or Pakistan. Do not worry, you will have your missile."

"When?"

"In less than a month, surely."

Sayyid wasn't so sure he liked that answer. The longer he had to safeguard the nuclear shell, the greater likelihood there was of other factions learning of its existence. Still, the Chechen had come through with the more difficult of the two procurements, as he had said. "Please sit. Make yourself at home. Nassari, Hassan, have you prepared refreshments for our guest?"

"I have taken it upon myself to prepare servings of coffee," Hassan said. A dapper little man with a trim mustache, Hassan could easily pass for a waiter at one of Ramallah's most exclusive coffee houses.

"I would prefer vodka," the Chechen said, sitting at the table, "but I understand that New Fatah has religious prohibitions to uphold."

"Alas," Sayyid said, "that is true."

"Alas. Coffee will do, then. By the way, has the change of names been very expensive?" the Chechen asked.

"Hmmm?"

"You belong to the Armed Resistance Faction Formerly Known as the Al Aqsa Martyrs Brigade, do you not? Has the change in your faction's name caused you much expense?"

"Oh—you mean switching over the letterhead, updating the web sites, swapping out thousands of tee shirts, having to dispose of all those old banners and paint over the outdated wall murals?"

"Yes."

"Well, it has been an inconvenience, that is for certain. But an expense? Not so much. UNRWA, the United Nations Relief and Welfare Agency, has picked up the bulk of it."

"Ahh, yes—'infrastructure updates.'"

"Yes, quite fungible and handy. I cannot deny, however, that actually achieving *de facto* territorial sovereignty over East Jerusalem significantly set our cause back. I mean, how could we still be the Al Aqsa Martyrs Brigade when the Zionist Crusaders no longer surrounded the Noble Sanctuary with their infidel presence?"

"I see the problem," the Chechen said, tugging at his beard.

"Fortunately, Allah provided a solution. Foolish Zionist archaeologists, funded by the international Jew-Rockefeller conspiracy, began a dig in the heart of the Meah Shearim district, within the currently Zionist-occupied portion of Jerusalem. They discovered traces of an ancient *wadib*, a desert stream, and the remains of a basin from which sojourners to the Old City would have drawn water for themselves and their animals. Thank merciful Allah, one of the workers employed on the dig was an Israeli Palestinian. That was the man who discovered the preserved footprints of the Prophet Muhammad, peace and blessings be upon him, and hoof marks and the imprint of a feather from his winged horse, Buraq, who carried him on his Night Journey to the farthest mosque in Jerusalem. Undeniable physical proof that the Prophet stopped there to water his horse at the midpoint of his journey."

The Chechen smiled. "Which, quite conveniently, provided you with a religious claim to the Meah Shearim neighborhood, even though it is entirely populated by black-robed Jews and lies on the Israeli side of the Green Line." He leaned forward. "Tell me—is there any truth to the rumor that this amazing happenstance was actually the work of Jordanian Intelligence, working through Islamic Maoist Jihad?"

Sayyid shot him a sour look. "*Psshaw!* Would you scoff at the validity of our holy relics? I, myself, have personally gazed upon the holy imprints, after they were liberated from the foul *kafir* hands of the Zionist archaeologists and spirited away to Palestine. I can vouch for their authenticity. True, the Hashemite scum in Jordan have every reason to keep the attention of their Palestinian citizens focused to the west, rather than upon their teetering monarchy. But once you have gazed upon the footprint, the hoof print, and the feather print, you will have no doubt. We shall reclaim the Holy *Wadib* and all the land which adjoins its ancient shores, you will see. No true Muslim can rest until the Holy *Wadib* is restored to the Ummah! We shall spill the blood of a million martyrs, a *million-million* martyrs, to recover that which by the dictate of Allah is rightfully ours! *Shahid! Shahid!*"

"The coffee is ready," Hassan said.

"Would you like two sugar cubes in yours, or three?" Sayyid asked, smiling.

"I'll take mine black, thank you," the Chechen said.

Hassan carried the coffees to the table. "I'll let you in on a secret," Sayyid said. "You spoke of names and renaming before. Well, the name 'New Fatah' is about to become passé. Oh, we changed it a few years back so the European Union could tell itself our political processes were progressing, we were building up our civil society, promoting openness and transparency, preparing to move forward on our nine-times delayed elections, blah-blah-blah. Well, it has had a good run and all, but everyone is becoming tired of the name and the logo. 'New' can only remain *new* for so long, yes? So, the Central Committee has decided that, after the nuclear shell explodes above Zionist-Occupied Jerusalem, we are changing our name again."

"To what, may I ask?"

Sayyid beamed proudly. "'Fatah Classic,'" he said. "Do you like it? It will honor the martyred Chairman Arafat."

The Chechen returned a measured smile. "It has a certain poetry to it." He lifted his tiny cup of coffee. "To Fatah Classic," he said.

Sayyid raised his cup. "To Fatah Classic. Long may it reign over the Arab Quarter of the Old City, the governmental district of Ramallah, and the southeastern corner of Jericho."

"Indeed."

"Well, I presume you are tired from your long and arduous journey. Have you a need to relieve yourself?"

"I'm fine, thank you."

"Is your bladder at least partially full? Do you need to pee?"

The Chechen looked nonplused. "Eh, not especially, no. I used a bathroom about an hour ago."

"Could you *make* yourself go, if you really, *really* wanted to?"

Now the visitor looked perturbed. "Why this sudden obsession with my bodily functions?"

Sayyid clapped his hands together and grinned most broadly. "For your services to the Palestinian people and to the Al Wadib Martyrs Brigade, I desire to offer you a boon. However, in order to partake of this hospitality, you must have an at least partially full bladder."

"This is a most irregular offer—"

"Oh, but I *insist!* Truly, this is an experience not to be missed. Nassari, prepare another, larger cup of coffee for our guest."

"That will not be necessary," the Chechen said a bit huffily. "I suppose I could manage to relieve myself, if it is as imperative as you make it sound."

"Splendid!" Sayyid said. "Please follow me." He

brought his visitor outside. They walked across the Al-Buraq plaza, avoiding piles of construction materials dimly illuminated by a quarter moon, until they came to the western wall of the ancient stone platform which held the Noble Sanctuary. Weathered granite blocks, quarried more than two thousand years earlier, formed the last remnant of what the Jews claimed had once been their Temple. At its base, the stone block wall, stained with Arabic graffiti and other defacements, now held a long, stainless steel basin, stocked with ice chips and disinfectant-deodorizing cakes.

"Is this what I think it is?" the Chechen asked.

Sayyid unzipped his trousers. "Indeed, it is. During the day, worshippers atop the Noble Sanctuary rain rose pedals down upon my workers as they relieve themselves. Try to aim for the little notes stuck within the seams between the stones. We considered disposing of them, but this is better, actually."

"I understand now why you insisted," the Chechen said, unzipping his own trousers.

"Enjoy, my friend," Sayyid said. "The experience never grows old."

He relaxed his prostate muscle and thought of the glorious day to come, when the little package would be united with the big package and the Knesset Building, recently relocated underground, would be buried in radioactive rubble. The foolish rabble of the Palestinian Revolutionary Guard Corps would pose no obstacle, surely.

But then he remembered something else about the PRGC. Hadn't that bumbling organization been thoroughly infiltrated by spies from—dare he think it?—Islamic Maoist Jihad? The *shahids* of the Al Wadib Martyrs Brigade were hard men, greatly to be feared. Fanatics, most of them. But the *shahids* of Islamic Maoist Jihad, *they* were bat-shit *crazy*.

Sayyid felt his right sock grow wet. Looking down, he saw that he had missed the trough and peed on his own shoe.

Chapter Seven

Generally, it was not a good thing to be summoned to a meeting with the Dean of the Graduate School of Arts and Sciences, one's department head, the university's legal counsel, and the Associate Dean for Intercultural Relations. The sole exception to this normally applicable rule would be the bestowal of an especially prestigious academic award.

Jacob knew he wasn't up for an award.

The Dean of the Graduate School of Arts and Sciences, Dr. Gilbert Lonahan, cleared his throat. "Mr. Zvi," he said, "we have a situation."

"A *serious* situation," Jacob's department head, Dr. Hershel Bromide, who had elected to wear a solemn (for him) dark red, pleated *campesino* shirt, said.

"A situation," said Dr. Naomi Smith-Alwaari, Associate Dean for Intercultural Relations, "which threatens the fragile fabric of inter-ethnic and inter-religious comity within our university community."

"A situation which could lose us millions of dollars in promised endowment funds," Bruce Quentin Williams, Esq., head legal counsel, said.

"Would this situation have anything to do with studies of the effects of dhimmitude pornography?"

Jacob asked.

"No," said his department head. "Although it might have something to do with your ability to *continue* those studies."

"Would it have anything to do with an act of arson at McAlister Auditorium?" Jacob asked.

"The *alleged* attempted arson, yes," Bruce Quentin Williams, Esq. said.

The door to the conference room opened. Rabbi Helvetica Rhinegold entered. "I'm sorry I'm late, Dean Lonahan," she said. "A student required spiritual counseling." She took a seat next to the Associate Dean for Intercultural Relations, after giving her a light peck on the cheek.

"Jacob," Dr. Bromide said, "I want you to know, this counseling session is in no way a reflection on the quality of your academic work. We in the Cultural Studies Department have been very pleased with your scholarship."

"This is a *counseling* session?" Jacob asked. "Am I being officially reprimanded?"

"Not at all," Williams the lawyer said. "In fact, we very much don't want things to reach that stage. We greatly value you as a member of the Tulane University community—and I'm sure that you value your university equally as much. But we need to clear up several sensitive matters. On the morning of September fifth, following Israeli Assistant Consul Menachem Levine's talk at McAlister Auditorium, did you dictate, then sign, this statement alleging that the fire on stage was caused by a, I quote, 'Molotov cocktail' thrown by fellow student Yakub bin Saladi?" He pushed a piece of paper across the table.

Jacob looked down at his statement. "Yes, I did."

"That is your signature at the bottom?"

"Yup."

"You gave this signed statement after Sergeant Lemuel, chief of Tulane Security, told you that his official investigation of the fire incident had determined its cause to have been an electrical short?"

"Yes. He asked me if I still wanted to offer my statement, and I said I did."

Williams frowned, turning his high forehead into a mass of creases. "Are you aware of the legal penalties for libel and for giving a false statement?"

Christ, why don't they just get out the rubber clubs already? "Mr. Williams," Jacob said, "official investigation or no official investigation, I know what I saw. And what I saw is described in full detail in that statement. I'm not 'libeling' Yakub. I'm telling the truth."

"Jacob," Rabbi Helvetica said, "the truth can be a very elusive thing. Are you *certain* you saw Yakub bin Saladi throw a fire bomb? Many, many attendees in that packed auditorium were throwing all manner of innocuous things. I imagine your surroundings were very chaotic at the time you saw what you believe you saw. How far away were you sitting from Yakub?"

"Three or four seats down," Jacob said. "But I'm telling you, I *know* what I saw. I saw him light a lighter—"

"Your statement says you saw him light a *match*," the lawyer said.

"All right, a *match*—I'm kinda under a lot of stress right now, okay? I saw him light a match and set fire to a rag stuffed in a plastic bottle. I saw him throw the bottle at the cage where Mr. Levine was sitting. My hand bumped his arm as he was throwing, and I saw the bottle miss the cage and land on the stage. Then I saw part of the stage catch fire—"

"The electrical short," the lawyer said.

"Oh, come *on*," Jacob said to him. "What are the chances that the McAlister electrical system should happen to suffer a catastrophic mishap just at the very *instant* a lit Molotov cocktail lands on the stage? I may be a little thick at times, but I'm not *stupid*."

"Jacob," Rabbi Helvetica said, "you're among friends. There's no need to get hostile—"

"I'm *not* getting hostile. I'm just getting a little freaked out, okay?"

"Mr. Zvi," the lawyer said, "are you aware of Yakub's political situation in his home country?"

"Uh, not really. We're just acquaintances."

"Should Yakub lose his student visa and be forced to return to Yemen, his life could be in danger, due to his father's political activities. Were you aware of that?"

"Maybe he should've thought of that before he threw that Molotov cocktail," Jacob said.

"Jacob," Rabbi Helvetica said, "that remark shows a *shocking* lack of empathy on your part. Yakub, your near-namesake, wasn't raised with all the advantages you were. He was brought up within tribal, rabidly patriarchal society, but he has struggled mightily to overcome that burden."

Jacob sighed. "All I know is this," he said. "If Yakub's aim had been better, Mr. Levine could've been killed. What Yakub did wasn't a prank. It wasn't a protected act of political protest, either. It was a *crime*. I *saw* that crime being committed. You want to talk about culture? Here's mine. I was raised that if you see a crime being committed, you don't ignore it—you *report* it."

Dr. Bromide, Jacob's department head, cleared his throat. "Jacob, I admire your ideals. However, there comes a time when dedication to one's ideals goes over the line and devolves into blind fanaticism. What do you wish to accomplish here? The Israeli consul wasn't injured. Yakub bin Saladi will be discretely spoken to and informed that any further violent actions on his part committed on university property may result in his expulsion. The matter will then be over. Isn't *that* what you wish to see accomplished? Or do you seek *vengeance* of some sort? Do you want to see young Yakub's academic career destroyed, his life possibly endangered, because of some *ethnic animus* you bear?"

The only ugly thing Jacob harbored right now was a burning sense of resentment. And it had little to do with Yakub bin Saladi.

"Jacob," Rabbi Helvetica said, "the moral and ethical thing for you to do, given the entirety of the situation, is for you to withdraw your statement. You owe Yakub that mercy because of your privileged status. And what can you *expect* of him? The West has degraded him and his people, and you want him to abide by Robert's Rules of Order at an inflammatory speech delivered by a representative of his nation's mortal enemy? In this season of our atonement, as your rabbi, I strongly advise you to be the bigger man and help seal yourself in the Book of Life through an act of loving-kindness and civilizational penance."

But by making him a sanctified victim, Jacob thought, *wouldn't I be doing him the greatest favor of all, at least by your lights?*

He remained silent.

"Mr. Zvi," Williams the lawyer said, "it appears we've reached an impasse. Dean Lonagan has kindly authorized me to put a little something extra on the scales. The University likes to be helpful to its friends. You would be a friend, indeed, Mr. Zvi, if you would let this matter drop. You may not be aware of it, but there are numerous scholarships and student stipends funded by our alumni which go unclaimed every year. Be helpful, and I'm fairly certain Dean Lonagan could prevail upon some of those alumni to be most helpful to you."

A little something extra on the scales. Jacob sensed scales falling from his eyes. "This is all about *money*, isn't it? Forget Yakub bin Saladi and his precarious position back in Yemen—this is about Gulf Arab donations to Tulane, isn't it?"

Williams grew red in the face. "No one said a *thing* about donations—"

Jacob rolled his eyes. "*You* did, when I first walked in here. You mentioned 'millions of dollars in endowment funds' which could be at stake. Yakub's family may not have any money to speak of, but he's got *connections*, doesn't he? He's good buddies with lots of little Saudi and Qatari princelings here on campus, students whose extended families pump *lots* of money into this school."

The five men and women facing him remained stony silent, some as red as the rocky buttes of the Southwest.

Rabbi Helvetica shook her head. "Jacob, Jacob," she said sadly. "As intelligent as you are, have you never heard of *projection*? You're projecting your own obsessions with money and status onto us, we who are *pleading* with you to recognize your own interests and the needs and interests of the fellow members of your academic community."

"Uh, Jacob," Dean Lonahan said, "it may not be especially tactful of me to mention this, but it *is* pertinent—you happen to be the beneficiary of a considerable annual gift of Saudi money yourself. I would imagine that should you persist in your stubbornness, your benefactor would be among the first to shut off that 'golden spigot' you referred to. Are you prepared to replace that funding?"

The thought had briefly occurred to him. But he hadn't let himself dwell upon it—why borrow tomorrow's troubles today? "No," he admitted. "I'm not."

"Well, I'm sure the Cultural Studies Department would hate to lose you."

So this is what it came down to. The Jacob Zvi of

a few weeks ago would have happily lapped up the hinted-at bribes and let the whole sordid mess drop. He might have even laughed it all off over beers shared with Saudi princeling Yishmael Hashmed. The Jacob Zvi of this morning, however? He was "stubborn." He was "idealistic," maybe to the point of being "blindly fanatical" and "vengeful."

Could he have changed so greatly in just a few weeks? It didn't seem plausible. But maybe what events had scraped away from him had been a veneer — a protective coating of cynicism and willed myopia. Maybe he was like a *mezuzah* on an old house which had been owned for a few decades by *goyim* who had painted over it, but which was then revealed by a new Jewish owner with a thorough application of paint thinner.

Maybe plying orthodontists and foreign policy analysts with dhimmitude pornography and then sticking a plethysmograph onto their dicks wasn't a proper occupation for a nice Jewish boy, after all?

He rose from the table. "Do whatever you have to do," he told them. "I'm not retracting my statement."

And he walked out of the room.

Chapter Eight

Jacob felt his *tuchus* falling asleep. He'd run late, walking to services, and thus been relegated to one of the folding chairs in the far back of the chapel. He squirmed on its cold, unyielding metal. In retrospect, one of the pluses of the Orthodox Rosh Hashanah services of his youth was that they'd forced him to frequently stand, stretch his legs, and give his gluteal muscles and tailbone a break. Rabbi Helvetica's Reconstructionist-Renewalist service avoided all the standing. Maybe her movement considered standing during a service an affront against egalitarianism? An inappropriate mark of subservience from the congregation in the face of a willfully imagined deity?

Finally, the time came for Rabbi Helvetica's sermon.

"Commentators throughout history have remarked upon what they see as a special genius of the Jews," Helvetica said, scanning the congregation of four hundred students and half as many faculty and adult visitors. "Some, taking their cue from the Old Testament, have attributed that genius to the Jews' status as God's Chosen People. Others, aspiring to a more scientific approach, have attributed it to genetics, a fortunate heredity which has been preserved by thousands of years of ostracism from the larger society, self-selection, and inbreeding. Still others attribute it to a cultural endowment handed down from generation to generation, reinforced by a history of ghettoization.

"I wish to postulate a fourth possibility. The genius of the Jews is to be found in their Victimhood. Think about it. How many of our great heroes, even those of the Bible, have been Victims? There's Jacob. He was the Victim of his brother Esau's jealousy and rage. There's poor King Saul, doomed to be killed by the Philistines, his lineage deposed by his younger rival David, all because of the mercy he granted, against his God's instructions, to the monarch and the animals of the conquered Amalekites. And then there was Moses, the greatest leader, teacher, and prophet the Jewish people ever had. For a trivial 'sin' of momentary anger, he was denied entry into the Promised Land, following more than forty years of devoted struggle and sacrifice to lead his people there. Could there be a more tragic Victim of the unyielding dictates of his own God?

"With the destruction of the First and Second Temples and the subsequent scattering of the Jews throughout the known world, the Jewish people became the supreme Victims of their own story. It is no coincidence that, from that point forward, the Jews, a tiny, insignificant sliver of the teeming masses of Humynkind, have excelled in science, medicine, commerce, and all the productive arts. Victimhood ennobles. Adversity calls forth adaptation, versatility, determination, and creativity. Even massacre can serve a worthy purpose, pruning those branches of the communal tree which have grown weak, dull, brittle, infested, or diseased, allowing the remaining branches to flourish in the sunlight."

Jacob noticed a few heads shaking in dissent. *Starting to lose a few of us, Helvetica,* he thought. *But I'm still willing to see where you're going with all this.*

"What I am about to suggest may not sit well with some of you. To some, it may seem perverse. To those of a more rigid mindset, it may even seem treasonous. Yet say it I must. We, the Jewish people, must reclaim our Victimhood. Ever since 1948, we have squandered our communal spiritual strength and towering moral authority, accumulated through two thousand years of suffering, on a misbegotten dream of sovereignty, nationalism, dominion, and domination, thinking a state of our own would save us. We, the spiritual Athens of Humynkind, have transformed ourselves into a cruel, militaristic Sparta. We have dispossessed the Palestinians. In so doing, not only have we earned the opprobrium of the world, but we have performed a perverse trade—we have traded our Victimhood for the Palestinians' land.

"It has been a wretchedly poor trade, akin to Esau trading away his birthright for a bowl of pottage. Sovereignty has been a curse, not a blessing. It was ever so, even in the days of the Bible. Aside from the few happy years of David's and Solomon's kingdoms, Jewish sovereignty in Israel and Judea was a blight on the communal soul of the Jewish people. Don't take my word for it—read the words of our own Prophets. Only one solution will ever bring to an end the wars and conflicts of the Middle East. We, the Jews, must recognize the tragic error of our reclamation of our anachronistic self-sovereignty. We must renounce that cancerous sovereignty. We must *abrogate* that sovereignty. I ask you, my congregants and friends, if you have not already done so, to support the establishment of a *single state* between the Jordan River and the Mediterranean Sea. A state of all its peoples, a state with no set religious or ethnic identity, a state which will open its welcoming arms to displaced

Palestinians now living in squalid camps all over the Middle East. A truly democratic state.

"Some may call this national suicide. I call it national redemption. And if, someday, the Jewish residents of this future Palestine find themselves expelled by the majority—then so be it. Our communal destiny is to be a light unto the nations. Better to be millions of scattered, wavering, brave candles than a single malign conflagration."

Two students, both undergraduates—maybe freshmen, new to the culture and mores of higher education—rose from their chairs and quietly walked out of the chapel. Jacob tried to sort and catalogue his own emotions. He was irritated. Affronted, even. Perhaps almost as indignant as his parents would be if they were here with him.

More than anything else, he was just *pissed*. First that ridiculous, infuriating inquisition in the dean's office, and now this. He hadn't come to a Rosh Hashanah service to be lectured at and harangued. *Fuck* victimhood. It was all well and good for Helvetica Rhinegold to pontificate that the Jews of Israel should put their fates in the hands of their neighbors. She lived in the United States. *Her* neighbors were a bunch of liberal university professors.

"Before we return to our prayer books," Helvetica continued, "I would like to direct your attention to an addendum, a responsive prayer I composed especially for today. It's the folded blue sheet inserted near the backs of your prayer books. Please join me in reciting responsively the Prayer of Thanksgiving to Our Oppressors. I ask that everyone please rise."

Jacob had a sour premonition about this. But feeling a residual sense of loyalty to Helvetica, he rose and unfolded the blue sheet.

"Almighty God," Helvetica began, "we thank you for

Pharaoh and the Egyptians, who enslaved us for four hundred years—"

"For they taught us the bitterness of slavery and that we must identify with enslaved peoples everywhere," Jacob mumbled back.

"We thank you for the Amalekites," Helvetica said, "who harried our flanks during the Exodus from Egypt and who preyed upon our weak, our slow, and our old—"

The congregation responded, "For they hurried our steps to the foot of Sinai, where we received the divine revelation which made us the Jewish People."

"We thank you for the Babylonians," Helvetica intoned, "who destroyed the First Temple, and for the Romans, who destroyed the Second Temple—"

"For they drove us into Exile, so that we might spread the light of our faith throughout the entire world."

And on it went. Torquenada got thanked, along with the whole Spanish Inquisition. Then the tsars and the Cossacks received hosannas for carrying out the pogroms.

Jacob could see where this was progressing. *Know when to call it quits, Helvetica, don't go over the edge— don't jump the shark—Don't go where I think you're going, Helvetica. Just* don't.

"And lastly, Almighty God, we thank you for Chancellor Adolf Hitler, the SS, the *Einsatzgruppen*, and the builders of the extermination camps—"

Jacob flung the blue paper onto his seat, as though it had burned him. He was torn between two warring impulses—the mandate for politeness and decorum, drummed into his head since childhood, and an overwhelming sense of disgust. *A sermon only Yishmael Hashmed could love ...*

He waited mutely until the people around him began sitting down. Then he exited as inconspicuously as he could.

He wasn't the only one who left the chapel. About twenty others also streamed out into the bright sunlight, disoriented and stunned, as though they were theater-goers who'd bought tickets to a Disney musical but who'd instead been shown a snuff film.

There should have been more who walked out, he thought. His one consolation was that Saul had not been in the congregation. His old heart might have given out.

✡ ✡ ✡

Wyonna felt starved. Starved for the attention of her fiancée. She fully understood that the advent of the High Holy Days meant that Helvetica would be especially preoccupied with her professional responsibilities. Yet Wyonna felt like a book that had been placed on a shelf partially read, then hidden from sight by a pile of other, newer books, and then coated with dust.

She poked her head into Helvetica's study. "Uh, hon?" she said timidly. "It's been nearly five hours since you've taken a break."

Hunched over her computer keyboard, wearing noise-cancelling headphones, Helvetica either did not notice Wyonna or refused to acknowledge her. Wyonna entered the room and stood in front of Helvetica's desk, anxiously shifting from foot to foot until her fiancée finally doffed her headphones and looked up from her screen.

"Yes?" Helvetica said, her voice flat. "What is it?"

"I—I'd like to spend some time with you. I took the day off from the lab so we could be together before the holidays, but …"

"But I'm only half-way done with my sermon, one of the two most important sermons I'll deliver this year. Surely you can understand I don't want to be interrupted right now?"

"But don't you need to eat, at least? I could fix you something, something quick?"

Helvetica sighed. "Only if you promise this will be the last interruption tonight. Agreed?"

Grateful for Helvetica's willingness to be pulled away from her work desk, Wyonna hurriedly threw together a mixed greens salad, a bowl of buttered whole wheat noodles, and a plate of cruelty-free gefilte fish. While she was setting the dinner table for the two of them, she rehearsed in her mind all the questions she had planned to ask her fiancée during what she had hoped would be a relaxed shared day at home, but which had now been compressed into a mere half-hour, at most.

"Tell me some about your girlhood again," Wyonna said. "Yours seems so different from mine, growing up on the farm in Nebraska with my five brothers—like it took place on a different planet, almost …"

Helvetica thoughtfully masticated a bite of salad before speaking. "My mother told me she and my father met and fell in love while they were backpacking through Europe. That was the summer of 1968, the summer of revolution. They ended up in France during the strikes and the mass youth protests against capitalism and the Vietnam War, right in the middle of it all, in Paris."

"Do you remember much about your dad?"

"No. He died before I turned two."

"Do you miss him? Or miss having known him?"

Helvetica remained quiet for a few seconds. "My mother became both a mother and a father to me. But she made sure I was very proud of my father, what he had accomplished. In the entire history of the Rainy Day Womyn, he was the only man ever named an honorary Womyn."

Wyonna set the bowl of buttered noodles, Helvetica's

favorite, in front of her fiancée. "Your mom's group, they were an offshoot of the Weather Underground, weren't they?"

"A late-blooming offshoot. My mother always said she had missed the party. By the time the Womyn got organized, the Vietnam War had ended, Watergate had happened, and the peace, justice, and gender equality movement was falling apart. Only the Panthers and the Weather Underground showed a possible way forward—the formation of a revolutionary vanguard in America, a vanguard unafraid to utilize narrowly targeted violence."

Wyonna was thrilled that Helvetica had opted to open up to her. Even though this account of Helvetica's girlhood was so far beyond Wyonna's realm of experience as to seem a story from a distant continent and a different century. "When your father died—was anyone else killed?"

"No. He was setting a bomb in an empty military recruitment office when it exploded prematurely."

"How—how did your mom take it?"

"I was too young to remember," Helvetica said, forking a piece of gefilte fish. "But later, the other Womyn told me she took it like a pillar of stone, barely cried. Went on with her work the next day, organizing underground memorial events for my father. She had her sisters in the movement to support her, of course. They gave great parties, the Womyn. Those were the happiest memories from my childhood, those parties in forests and farms throughout the Pacific Northwest— the bonfires, the drumming sessions— The parties were my version of heaven."

"We didn't have parties when I was growing up," Wyonna said.

"Not even birthday parties? No Christmas parties?"

"Nope. We didn't celebrate birthdays. My dad thought

celebrating birthdays was immodest and promoted narcissism." Wyonna stiffened at the anguished memory of a whole childhood of deliberately ignored birthdays. "On Christmas, we just went to church, like we did every Saturday. Aside from that, we never went anywhere. I could never even get my hair styled—just *trimmed*. It had to be *long*, like my dad liked. I used to dream about running away for my birthday, going somewhere where some group of kind, wonderful strangers would throw me a party. You traveled lots, didn't you? You and your mom were always having to move around, right?"

"Always. We'd go from state to state, moving from one safe house to another. One day my mother would be robbing a bank in some little town in northeast Washington State, and the next day we'd be in Wyoming."

"She robbed *banks?*" This shouldn't have surprised Wyonna as much as it did, but astonishment bloomed like a swollen pimple on her face.

"Banks, liquor stores, gas stations when she had to. Once, during the 1984 presidential election, she set fire to a Reagan campaign headquarters in Tacoma. She became a minor legend in the Pacific Northwest. The feds finally caught up with her in 1985, when I was ten. She was sentenced to fifteen years. Served eight and was paroled for good behavior. I spent my adolescence with my father's parents in Oakland. My mother got out when I was a sophomore in college. She earned her law degree the same month I got my undergrad degree. We shared a graduation party."

"And now she defends unpopular people?"

"Like accused terrorists? Yes. She has tremendous empathy for those who have been persecuted for their beliefs."

Wyonna's heart stuttered. She felt she couldn't avoid

bringing up a subject she feared would inexorably cause a breach between them. "My—my work—it doesn't bother you, does it? That I do work for Homeland Security?"

Helvetica coldly contemplated this for ten very long seconds before replying. "Your robots are designed to be impartial, aren't they? They're not like human security guards; they won't racially profile—not unless they're programmed to?"

"Oh, of *course* they *won't* be!" Wyonna said quickly.

"Are you the one who will make that decision? Or will it be some ex-military man at the reins of the Department of Homeland Security?"

Wyonna couldn't answer that question truthfully— not without antagonizing Helvetica. Honestly, she could no more control the purposes to which P.R.E.T.E.C.T. would be put than she could the weather. In the absence of a fibbed denial, she watched Helvetica's face turn stony. She felt exposed, vulnerable—afraid. Afraid of losing the only woman she loved with her entire being.

An idea had been gestating in her head. Actually, an idea *about* gestation had been gestating in her head. At first, it'd seemed crazy—then audacious—but now, maybe vital to her and Helvetica's shared happiness.

"Helvetica," she said, "I've been thinking. Maybe I should go to a fertility clinic ..."

Helvetica stopped chewing her noodles. "For heaven's sake, why?"

"I think I may want to get myself inseminated."

Helvetica dropped her fork. "You want to have a *baby?*"

"No—not a baby. I want to have an abortion."

"Hold on—you want to have an *abortion?*"

"Yes, yes I do. When I think about poor women in rural Louisiana, the ones who desperately need and want to have an abortion, and what they have to go through—the state-mandated counseling, the emotional assault by protesters outside the clinics—I just want to *cry* for them." The look on Helvetica's face shifted quickly from astonishment to admiration. Wyonna, thus encouraged, found herself talking faster and faster. "I—I want to experience what those poor women do. I really think it'll draw us closer together, help me understand the depths of your compassion for the downtrodden. I—I want so much to give you a special wedding gift, a present you'll adore. I'd like this abortion to be my wedding gift to you, my dearest darling. A gift from my own body, and from my soul."

"Why, darling," Helvetica said, slowly smiling, "I think that's a *wonderful* idea. Very creative, very daring. I agree with you a hundred percent that it will teach you empathy for the downtrodden women of rural Louisiana." She reached across the table and took Wyonna's hand in hers. "I made a good choice when I agreed to marry you, Wyonna Shaver."

Wyonna felt her heart leap. This was precisely what she had yearned to hear.

"I—I *love* you, Helvetica."

"I love you, too."

Chapter Nine

Jacob sat on his threadbare futon and read a stack of Jack Kirby and Steve Ditko monster comics, *Strange Tales* and *Creatures on the Loose* and *Monsters on the Prowl*. He hoped their goofy banality would wash the taste of Helvetica's awful Rosh Hashana service from his mind. But neither "I was Captured by the Creature from Krogarr!" nor "Gigantus, the Monster that Walked like a Man!" proved compelling enough to drag his thoughts away from his Israel-hating rabbi and his vulnerable parents in Haifa.

What would he do about tomorrow's service? He certainly wouldn't go back to the Tulane Interfaith Chapel for a second dose of post-modernist anti-Zionism. Temple Sinai and Touro Synagogue were both within walking distance, but they charged a pretty penny for admission, and their Reform services would seem like watery milk to him.

He wanted the hard stuff. The Old-Time Religion, ninety-five percent in Hebrew, ancient melodies that dated back to the fifteenth century. The type of service he'd grown up attending.

Chabad House wasn't much further from his apartment than the Interfaith Chapel. But the small space would be packed, and he doubted he could get over there early enough to get a seat. Then Jacob remembered Congregation Anshe Sfard, an old Orthodox *shul* in Central City, a neighborhood which had once been heavily Jewish and bustling with Jewish-owned businesses, but which was now almost entirely African American. Decades after all the neighborhood's other synagogues had moved out, first for Uptown New Orleans, and later for Metairie out in the 'burbs, Anshe Sfard had clung to its old location, serving a steadily diminishing and aging congregation.

He had another idea. Saul Tannenburg's house wasn't that far off the route Jacob planned to walk tomorrow. Why not call him and see if he wanted to go, too? Saul might not have anywhere else to go. And Jacob could use the company. It would be a long *schlep* from Tchoupitoulas and State down to Carondelet and Jackson, reversing the exodus of upward mobility the Jews of New Orleans had taken from their original neighborhood. A walk back in time.

✡ ✡ ✡

Jacob waited on Saul's doorstep. He cringed when he saw the heavy wool jacket his companion had pulled on. "Uh, Saul," he said, "are you *sure* you want to wear that? It's ninety-four degrees out."

"But we're going to *shul*. I *have* to wear a jacket to *shul*."

"I'm not wearing one." Actually, Jacob had dressed several notches above his usual standard. He had selected a light blue button-down Oxford, albeit a thrift store Van Heusen short sleeve, and had actually worn a tie. A polyester tie emblazoned with the faces of the original Three Stooges, but a tie, nonetheless.

"Jacob, you're a squirt, if you'll pardon my saying so.

You can get away with no jacket. I'm an old man. I have to dress properly."

"How about you don't put it on until we reach Anshe Sfard?"

"But then I'll have to carry it."

"Look, *I'll* carry it. I'm starting to sweat, just standing here looking at you."

They walked down Baronne Street for a while, then switched over to Carondelet Street to avoid the direct sun.

"Hannah and I used to walk to *shul* on the holidays," Saul said. "When we were much younger. It's been years—*decades*—since I've done this."

"Where did you two used to go?"

"Chevra Thilim, when it was at the corner of South Claiborne and Napoleon Avenue. It was Orthodox, but for some reason, they allowed mixed seating. We thought it was the best of both worlds. But after Marsha, our daughter, went off to college, we sort of drifted away from the *shul*. The old building got turned into a Baptist church, then got flooded during the storm."

After walking a couple more blocks, they came upon a shopping cart left lying on its side next to a bus stop post. "There's money lying on the ground," Jacob said.

"Where?"

"You're looking at it. If it wasn't Rosh Hashanah, and if I had my truck with me, I'd scoop that little beauty right up. Ten bucks, sitting right there."

"That's how much a scrap yard pays for a shopping cart nowadays?"

"Scrap yard wouldn't take it. Too much plastic, not enough metal. No, I'd return that to the store it got lifted from. That's what I do for a living. One of the things, anyway."

"*That's* what you do? A smart Jewish boy like you? I thought you were in graduate school."

"I am. But I still have to eat."

"Isn't it beneath you? What do your parents say?"

"They don't say anything. What *I* say is, work is work. Money is green whether it comes from redeeming stolen grocery carts or from a summer internship at daddy's law firm. And I meet some interesting people. And their pit bulls, guarding those shopping carts."

"How do you still have all of your fingers?"

"A sack o' meat from Vietnamese market in Gretna, on the West Bank of the Mississippi. Mostly red and gray entrails and other assorted parts. I toss it over the wall, grab the cart and I'm outta there."

Saul grinned. "Maybe the new generation of Jewish boys isn't as soft as I thought. When I was coming up, I worked twelve hours a day in my pop's shoe store on Dryades Street. You know what I did when a customer wanted a particular style, *insisted* on that style, and we only had it in a half-size smaller than their size? I took the shoes in the back, spit in them, and *then* they fit. Of course, that was when shoe salesmen were expected to place the shoes on customers' feet. No self-service back then." He laughed.

Once they'd crossed Washington Avenue, now well within the Central City ghetto, the frequency of odd looks they received from fellow passers-by and neighborhood residents sitting on their stoops increased sharply. The looks weren't unfriendly or menacing, just surprised. Jacob smiled at a woman sitting with her baby granddaughter on a double shotgun's porch, then imagined the woman's inner monologue—*What're two white guys in ties doin' walking through* this *neighborhood, when it's hot enough to fry an egg on the sidewalk?*

He felt sweat trickle down his back. He was glad he couldn't see what the rear of his shirt looked like. Good thing he hadn't been counting on meeting any young, available Jewish women at Anshe Sfard; probably the youngest available female would be a sprightly widow of seventy-five.

"Hey, look over there," Saul said. "Wasn't that your old synagogue? I mean, the original location of your old synagogue, before it moved out to Lakeview?"

Jacob looked toward Baronne Street, where Saul was pointing. In the middle of an overgrown, double-sized lot, on a block where the neighboring houses stood as abandoned and forlorn among the chest-high weeds as trees in a petrified forest, he saw a large white building, more than two stories tall, topped with a shallow dome and fronted by six massive stone columns. The western third of the building looked weirdly tilted, ready to split off from the remainder—great cracks ran parallel to the columns, two of which formed a V, and the building's lower western corner had disappeared, as though it were an ice sculpture melting away.

"I think you're right," Jacob said. "I remember hearing that Beth Judah Synagogue's original location had been in Central City, before they moved out to Lakeview in the early 'sixties. But I never knew where, exactly. Let's go take a closer look."

They detoured a block to Baronne Street. Part of the building's sign had remained erect and visible above the weeds. It read Holy Salvation Full Baptist Church, but Jacob could still make out the Hebrew lettering carved into the building's crown above the columns. It was the old Beth Judah, all right. "What a mess," Jacob said. "I wonder how long it'll take the city to clear all this away. You can't fix that building. It's virtually split in half. I've seen plenty of flood damage around town, but nothing quite like that."

"The flood waters would've barely made it to this block," Saul said. "Everything between Baronne and the river in Uptown only got wind damage, mostly."

"I want to see what's making that whole side of

the building tilt away." Jacob handed Saul his jacket, then pushed his way through the weeds. At the abrupt border of the overgrowth, he nearly slid down the slope of a steep canyon. Chunks of earth broke away from beneath his shoes and rolled down into a pit fifteen feet deep, splashing into muddy water at the bottom. "Jesus! I think I found the problem," he called back to Saul. "It's a sinkhole. A *big* one. No wonder everything on this block's completely abandoned. The old Beth Judah's the heaviest building on the street, so it's getting eaten first. I'll bet six months from now, most of the building won't even be there anymore. You ever hear of sinkholes in New Orleans?"

"The storm screwed everything up," Saul said. "In some parts of town, the weight of the flood waters made the streets settle a foot or more. I'm surprised all of Broadmoor and the Claiborne corridor isn't one big sinkhole."

✡ ✡ ✡

Fifteen minutes later, they stood in front of Congregation Anshe Sfard. The narrow, tall synagogue, built in the Byzantine Revival style, tucked between camelback houses and large Victorians in reasonable states of repair, had retained its ninety-year-old dignity, unlike the crumbling Beth Judah.

"We're *here*," Saul said.

"Air conditioning will never have felt so good," Jacob replied. He handed Saul his jacket.

As soon as they walked through the front doors, however, Jacob's happy anticipation melted into sodden disappointment. The air in the *shul*'s foyer was heavy as soup. Ominously, he heard the distant roar of multiple box fans.

A short man, whose bald, white-bearded head

on an ovaloid body made Jacob think of a snow owl perched on an ostrich egg, came into the foyer to greet them. "*L'shana tovah*," he said. "I'm very sorry. Our air conditioning unit died this morning. We're trying to make do with fans, but it's very uncomfortable in the sanctuary, even with some of the windows opened."

Jacob flicked sweat droplets from the tips of his eyelashes. He felt sorry for the man. He looked as bedraggled and sweat-soaked as Jacob felt.

"Have services been cancelled?" Saul asked.

"No, no, we're trying to avoid that," the man said. "We had more than twenty-five people here earlier, at the start of the morning. But lots of them—well, they're on medications and whatnot; they can't take the heat. Many have left. I can't blame them—health comes first. But, well, we're two men short now. We have a wonderful rabbi with a fabulous singing voice—we fly him in from Belgium every year to lead our High Holy Days services—and he's been skipping around the liturgy, doing all the parts he can, absent a *minyan*, while we wait—well, while we wait for a little miracle. Like the two of you showing up. I know it's an awful lot to ask, given how hot it is here—but do you think there's *any way* you might consider staying with us?"

Jacob glanced at Saul. The heat was no big deal for Jacob to deal with; he'd gotten used to stultifying summers without air conditioning from riding around in his old Ram, whose a/c hadn't worked since Lee Iacocca had been hawking Dodges. But Saul had visibly wilted on the walk over here. Whatever they decided, Jacob wanted to get him a glass of water as quickly as possible. "What about it, Saul? Are you up for this?"

"We've come this far," Saul said weakly. Then he seemed to pull strength from an interior reservoir, thinking, perhaps, of the strangers who had shown up at his house twice a day for a week so that he could properly mourn his wife. "We'll stay," he said to the man. "Of *course* we'll stay. You need us, right?"

"You two would complete our *minyan*, yes. Some of the others were talking about walking Uptown to the Chabad House. But that's five miles, maybe more, in this heat …"

"There's no need to go anywhere else," Saul said. "We'll stay as long as we're needed. Isn't that right, Jacob?"

"I've got nowhere else to be," Jacob said. "Sir," he asked the man, "before I go inside, would it be possible for me to get my friend a cup of water, and one for me?"

"Please, let me get it for you. We have cups in the kitchen. I'll be right back."

Saul sank gratefully onto a chair near the doors to the sanctuary. Jacob found the men's room and brought back damp paper towels so they could swab their necks and faces. By the time he returned, their host had brought cups of cool water for them.

"Is there a prayer of thanksgiving for water?" Saul asked.

"There's a prayer for rain, and one for dew," the man said. "There's a prayer of thanks for everything, you know. I'll have to ask the rabbi."

The three of them entered the sanctuary. Its high ceiling, tall stained-glass windows, and monumental ark made the small group of elderly congregants seem even more minuscule. The six men and four women clapped when Saul and Jacob entered, a breach of decorum the rabbi, given his broad grin, didn't seem to especially mind. The rabbi, a barrel-chested young man, not much older than Jacob, with a long, dark, curly beard, approached the two newcomers eagerly.

"Our prayer was answered," he said, clasping Jacob's hand between his. "I'm Rabbi Randy Izzenschimmel. It's *so* good to meet you both."

Odd—the rabbi spoke with an Australian accent. "Aren't you from Belgium?" Jacob asked.

"Actually, initially from Sydney, but by way of Antwerp," the rabbi explained. "I'm the original Wandering Jew."

"I know the feeling," Jacob said.

Rounds of introductions followed. The rabbi, indulging in a Belgian custom, kissed Saul and Jacob on both cheeks. They were ushered to two of the best seats in the house, next to the most powerful fan. The fan's loud whirring made it difficult to hear the rabbi's *davening*, but the breeze blasting Jacob's hair and skin felt like the breath of life.

"Jacob," Saul whispered, "between the heat and the noise of the fan, I'm afraid I'll fall asleep. If I doze off, will I still count as part of the *minyan*?"

"You'll still count," Jacob said. "Let's make a pact. If you fall asleep, I'll elbow you in the ribs. If *I* fall asleep, you elbow *me* in the ribs."

"And if we *both* fall asleep?"

"Then we fall on our faces."

Far from putting him to sleep, the mental and auditory effort Jacob expended to follow the rabbi's *davening* and that of his fellow congregants over the noise of the fan helped concentrate his thoughts. He realized he hadn't focused this intently on a Rosh Hashanah service since the year prior to his *bar mitzvah*, a time when he still took the concept of approaching Jewish manhood and the responsibilities it entailed seriously. They reached an *Al Chait*, one of the frequently repeated group recitations of communal and individual sins and shortcomings. Some of the sins listed were ritual sins, the breaking of commandments which delineated man's duties to God. But the majority of the sins he and the others recited were sins of man against man—envies acted upon; business transactions tainted by cheating; the spreading of gossip and malicious lies. These were sins which, for their atonement to be completed, required not merely confession, but also efforts to make the injured parties whole. It did not take much imagination or too great a stretch of memory for Jacob to recognize his own behaviors.

He found himself looking forward to other parts of the traditional service he remembered, the Torah portion, the reading from the Prophets, the *kiddish* with its ritual consumption of bread and sweet wine. The service drew him back to those months before his *bar mitzvah*, when he stood on the cusp between childhood and adolescence, when all choices were still before him; when he hadn't yet rebelled against decisions his parents were still to make, hadn't yet defined his identity around an amorphous ideal of contrarianism, and hadn't yet taken a blowtorch to many of his most precious relationships.

The final words of the Torah service haunted him:

Turn us to You, oh Lord, and we shall return.
Renew our lives, as in days of old.

Is that what he wanted? Is that what he needed?
He didn't know.
But he did know that he wanted to be here. He loved Saul, and he loved these people, and the intensity of that love shocked him. It amazed him that through the simple act of depositing his grubby self on this bench, he could help sanctify their season—*that* was a blessing.

It wasn't every religion that gave points just for showing up.

Chapter Ten

Wyonna had never felt so at peace.

This warm, calming, reassuring sensation flowing from her embracing the sleeping form of her beloved, this sensation of firmly anchored well-being, this was what she had yearned for all throughout childhood. This was what her parents' manias had denied her with their ceaseless demands and unattainable standards. But the love Helvetica had lavished on her during the past nine days, ever since Wyonna had shared her idea of a wedding gift, had cracked open the door to paradise that Wyonna's parents had nailed shut. Yesterday she had pushed the door further open by getting herself inseminated at the fertility clinic. In a couple of months, right after their honeymoon, she would deliver her gift by having the fetus aborted. This feeling of well-being was worth more than all the currencies and precious treasures of the world. To keep it, Wyonna would gladly suffer a hundred pregnancies and a hundred abortions.

She glanced at the clock. Eight more minutes until Helvetica's alarm would go off and she would rise and shower and dress and go over her Yom Kippur speech one more time before they would walk together to Tulane's Interdenominational Chapel. No breakfast this morning; no coffee, either, the lack of which caused far worse pangs.

Eight more minutes to luxuriate next to Helvetica's languorous warmth. Eight more minutes to softly nuzzle her fiancée's neck and breathe in the scent of her warm skin, not so different from handmade bread fresh from the oven. Eight more minutes to remain still and listen to the sounds of the house and the sounds of the world outside, to the ticking of the clock and the hum of air conditioning and the harmonious songs of robins and jays in the branches of the mango trees outside.

Then the chimes of Helvetica's alarm would temporarily exile Wyonna from this tiny version of paradise, but the realm of exile would not represent much of a step down. For it was Yom Kippur, according to Helvetica the Shabbat of Shabbats, Judaism's most holy day of the year. A day when Wyonna could bask in Helvetica's presence from waking until past sundown, a day when Helvetica's charisma and personal luminescence would be at their zenith as she shared her wisdom and rectitude and ideal of holiness with hundreds of Tulane staff and students. Wyonna would be so proud.

She looked at the clock again. Six more minutes of this intimate paradise …

Her phone began vibrating fiercely on the nightstand next to her pillow. Someone had sent her a text message.

Damn! She had meant to mute her phone for the entirety of Yom Kippur. But caught up in the bliss of last night's passion with Helvetica, she had forgotten.

She could ignore it. Or try to ignore it. It was probably just a trivial "happy holiday" message from one of her non-Jewish friends or colleagues who thought Yom Kippur, the Day of Awe, the Day of Repentance, was an ordinary holiday, akin to Thanksgiving or St. Patrick's

Day. But it might be important. It might be from someone who knew what Yom Kippur was and who knew not to bother Wyonna on such a day but who had been forced to do so anyway because of an emergency.

So if she didn't check to see what it was, it would nag her all throughout the day. She would wear her former aura of anxiety. Helvetica would notice, and it would concern her, and Wyonna's nagging distress would distract the rabbi from what she should be one hundred percent focused on—her conducting the Yom Kippur services and ministering to the spiritual needs of her congregation.

Despite whatever religious prohibitions existed against checking text messages on such a day, Wyonna knew it would be horrendously selfish of her *not* to set her mind at ease. So, taking care to not rustle the bed covers and inadvertently awaken Helvetica, depriving her of her precious remaining four minutes of rest, Wyonna checked the message on her phone.

It was from Tim Oberfeldt, her student assistant. Since he wasn't Jewish, he would be at the lab today. He said she needed to come to lab right away. This was an emergency. He'd explain when she arrived.

Crap! Why today, of all days?

She'd have to go. If she didn't meet Tim at the lab, she would go half-crazy with worry, and that would be even worse for Helvetica than her not having looked at the text in the first place. She'd just have to deal with whatever it was as quickly and efficiently as she could and then rush over to the Interdenominational Chapel, which was just a few blocks away from the Williamson Science Building.

She shook Helvetica awake. "Darling?"

Her fiancée's semi-conscious expression was as formless as congealed pudding left too long in the refrigerator. "Whuu …? What is it? Alarm hasn't gone off yet …"

"Darling, I'm afraid I have to go."

More awake now. "Go? Where? Why?"

"There's some sort of emergency at the lab."

"Wyonna, it's the morning of Yom Kippur—"

"I *know*. I feel terrible. But Tim knows he shouldn't be messaging me on today of all days. So if he says it's an emergency, he must mean it's really *bad*. And if I don't go, I'll be horribly worried about it until the end of the holiday, and I won't be able to concentrate on the service, and I'm afraid I'll end up distracting *you* …"

Helvetica sat up and rubbed sleep out of her eyes. "All right. Go. Take care of whatever it is. But be as quick as you can."

✡ ✡ ✡

Wyonna rushed into the lab. "I'm here, Tim."

"Ms. Shaver," her student assistant said in a panic. "I'm *so* sorry I had to call you into the lab this morning. I know it's Yom Kippur and all—"

"It's all right. *Really*, it *is*. I know you wouldn't have called me if you hadn't run into an emergency. Bring me up to speed as fast as you can."

"Okay. You remember how you told me to keep a close eye on P.R.E.T.E.C.T.'s nanobot replication rate?"

"Yes. The rate's been steadily increasing for the past two weeks," Wyonna said.

"I came in early this morning to take my measurements, because I knew just about all the researchers planned to take the day off for the holiday. The last time I took measurements was two days ago. Since then—it—I mean, the rate of increase, it's gone off the *scale*."

"What do you mean? Doubled? Tripled?"

"No—I mean by a factor of *ten*. And it's *still* increasing.

Not just the nanobot replication rate—processing speeds, electro-neuronic connection webs, battery efficiency, transmission speeds, memory capacity—the works. On every performance metric I could think to measure, P.R.E.T.E.C.T. is evolving at lightning speed. It's—well, it's as though the evolution of amoeba to man, instead of stretching out over a couple billion years, had been compressed into a few *thousand*. When I left here two nights ago, we had a Tinkertoy to play with. What we've got now—I'm not *sure* what we've got now."

"You've compiled reports?"

"Sure. I've emailed you copies. But they'll all be out of date by the time you look at them."

Wyonna felt the hairs on her arms rise, as though she were being charged by whatever supranormal electricity that had jump-started P.R.E.T.E.C.T.'s accelerating evolution. Her desire to run to her computer and jump headlong into the rush of fresh data felt so intense that its frustration by the holiday's prohibition on work struck her like a physical blow. *Damn! Why did this have to happen on Yom Kippur, of all days?*

"I'll have to contact other nations' labs as soon as the holiday's over, to see if they've been seeing any comparable results," she said. "I—I really have to run, Tim, much as I hate to. You'll keep an eye on things until I can come back tonight, after sundown?"

"Of course I will. But there's one other thing I've got to tell you before you go—"

Wyonna, already on her way to the door of the lab, stopped short next to P.R.E.T.E.C.T.'s shopping cart-like chassis. Everything was out of place. "Tim, what are these nano feedstock vats doing next to the diagnostic equipment? And why are all these transfer tubes hooked up between the vats and P.R.E.T.E.C.T.'s intake nodules? I didn't leave any instructions for you to make those adjustments."

"*That's* what I was about to tell you," Tim said. "I didn't do it. None of that stuff was there two nights ago."

"No one else had authorization to touch P.R.E.T.E.C.T. in my absence. So who would've moved all this equipment and these feedstocks?"

"I've got no idea, Wyonna. I'm really freaked out."

"I really, *really* need to get to services. But before I head out, I have to take a look at the humanoid robots in the primary lab."

"Why?"

"Call it mother's intuition."

She'd so hoped she would be wrong, because being right meant her world was rapidly sliding from a rose-scented paradise into an abyss of the uncanny. But her intuition proved as correct as the law of gravitation. Every robot in the primary lab was hooked up to its own vat of nano feedstocks, too.

Chapter Eleven

The night air in Jerusalem was refreshingly cool. *It won't remain that way for long,* Sayyid al-Wahhab thought. *At least not in Zionist Jerusalem. The air there will soon burn at the temperature of the sun's core.*

He thought of the teeming masses of Jews now leaving their synagogues after their Day of Atonement, scurrying like dung beetles towards their homes or to break their fasts in restaurants and cafés. On a mild, pleasant night like tonight, many of those Jews would linger outside to enjoy the refreshing breezes; they would chat with neighbors in their alleyways and sip tea at café tables lined up on the sidewalks. The flash of the weapon would blind them, the shock waves would pulverize them against stone walls, and the fireball would melt the flesh from their bones, just as the American bombs had done to the Japanese.

He took a moment to train his night vision binoculars on the lights of West Jerusalem. From high atop the Noble Sanctuary, at the edge of the broad plaza that lay between the Dome of the Rock and the Al Aqsa Mosque, he could view the Zionist sector quite easily. His workmen had erected a tent beneath which he, Bhudro, Nassari, Hassan, and a missile engineer named

Achmed had assembled the launch device. The tent was meant to hide them from prying Zionist eyes, although the precaution could be considered redundant—no Israeli commander would *dare* fire upon the Noble Sanctuary, both due to fear of hitting their Wailing Wall and aversion to damaging either the Dome or the Al Aqsa, and thus enraging the entire Muslim world into war against them. The Noble Sanctuary provided the perfect launch pad: symbolically perfect, and perfectly safe.

The Chechen had stopped communicating four days ago. An ominous sign. However, Sayyid had planned for the contingency that his arms dealer would prove unable to provide a suitable missile. Ten days earlier, he had arranged for several of New Fatah's weapons engineers to link three of the available Grad missiles into a single launch device, one which could handle the weight of the payload the Chechen had delivered. Achmed had been chief of the fabrication team. Now he led Sayyid's men in assembling the launcher and making final adjustments. Very soon now, the "hot potato" would be out of his hands and, far, far hotter, into the hands of the Israelis.

Before reentering the tent, he nodded to the three New Fatah guards holding their AK-47s at the ready. "Thank you for your vigilance," he said. "You have your protective goggles at hand?"

"We do," the lead guard said.

"Put them on as soon as we launch the missile. Then you will have the honor of watching the destruction of Zionist Jerusalem and the nerve centers of the Zionist conspiracy. It is only one-thirteenth as powerful as the bomb Americans used on Hiroshima, but its impact will be far, far more wide-reaching. This is the beginning of the end of the Zionist malignancy. You will see."

"Praise Allah," the guard said, "and may it be so."

Sayyid entered the tent. "Is all in readiness?" he asked Achmed.

"All preparations are complete," Achmed said. "The three missiles' firing sequences have been synchronized. The munition is snug within its nest, awaiting its arming."

"There is no chance of an Israeli anti-missile battery disabling the device?"

Achmed smiled. "That is the beauty of using an artillery shell. Once armed, it is percussion primed. Even if one of their Iron Dome batteries can be deployed quickly enough and is successful at striking the missile, the munition will still explode. The only difference is that the Israelis will suffer an air burst, rather than a ground burst. For our purposes, there is no difference at all."

"Splendid," Sayyid said. Another advantage of using a small, low-yield device, fired at relatively short range, was the ambiguity of its origins. A ballistic missile would be tracked to its source by Israeli spy satellites, providing the Zionists with a return address for their reprisals. This baby-size munition, however, launched from a place so near? It could come from Pakistan. It could come from Iran. It could come from one of the newer atomic programs built in response to the Iranian project, that of Saudi Arabia or Egypt or Turkey. Or, as this one actually had, it could come from the morass of poorly controlled military depots contained within the states of the old Soviet Union. The Zionists would have no idea where to strike back. Nor would they would have any idea whether the militant group which had fired the missile had another one waiting, or five more, or twenty. That uncertainty, even more than the physical damages the one-kiloton device would inflict, would drain their blood of vigor and reduce them to the paralysis of complete terror.

And if the Israelis were foolhardy enough to level the holy buildings atop the Noble Sanctuary in revenge? So much the better. They would bring a global *jihad* down upon themselves, with every nation in the Islamic Conference lining up to war upon them, and not even America would be willing to come to their aid.

"There is no reason to delay launch any longer," Achmed said. "I leave to you, oh Sayyid, the honor of entering the activation code and pressing the final arming switch."

Achmed shone a flashlight's beam onto the munition, tucked between the three linked rockets. Sayyid reached into the gap between the missiles and punched a thirteen-digit code onto the artillery shell's built-in keypad. "Oh, my arm!" Sayyid said with delighted surprise. "It tingles! As though it has entered Paradise and is being caressed by the loving hands of seventy-two virgins!" Then he flipped open a protective cover and pressed the arming button twice. The diode next to the button glowed green.

Sayyid heard a distant shout from outside, from far above. It almost sounded like the beginning of the call to prayer. But it was not a time for prayer.

He exited the tent and asked one of the guards, "What was that?"

"It came from up there," the guard said, pointing to the top of one of the Al Aqsa Mosque's minarets. "It sounded like someone screamed, '*Mao*'—"

The man lurched backward, as though an invisible assailant had struck him in the chest. As the guard toppled to the stone floor, Sayyid heard the shot, then its echo from the walls of the two great mosques.

More shots rang out. The other two guards also slumped like puppets whose strings had been dropped. Sayyid ducked low and scurried back inside the tent. "We must launch *immediately!*" he said. "We are under attack by Islamic Maoist Jihad! They want the munition—"

A rocket-propelled grenade exploded at the edge of the tent, throwing Sayyid off his feet. When he was able to open his eyes, he saw that Bhudro had been decapitated by a missile's stabilization fin. The damaged launch vehicle lay on its side.

Shrapnel had peppered Sayyid's back. He sensed blood running down the rear of his neck from a gash on his scalp. Otherwise, he seemed relatively unhurt. "Achmed! Hassan! Nassari! Are you alive?"

Hassan groaned and remained face-down, prone on the ground. Achmed and Nassari bestirred themselves and answered that they had not been mortally injured.

"The foul assassins will be upon us in a moment," Sayyid said. "We must rescue the munition and hide it so that we can plan for another day. Achmed, can the munition be detached from the launch vehicle?"

"If we have time, yes. Its clamps can be loosened manually. But it will take two of us to undo the harness, and then to carry the munition."

"Nassari," Sayyid said, "go out of the tent and collect one of the slain guards' rifles. Keep the assassins away from us long enough for us to free the munition."

He saw the man's face go white. "Allah will bless you with an eternity in Paradise if you do this," Sayyid said.

Nassari crawled out of the shredded tent.

Achmed threw Sayyid a wrench and began hissing instructions at him. Sayyid only half listened. The reptilian part of his brain, the locus of fear and aggression, focused on the alternated chants of "*ALLAH!*" and "*MAO!*" which drew steadily closer to the tent.

He had succeeded in unscrewing two of the clamps when he heard an AK-47, possibly Nassari's, fire a series of short bursts. He heard bursts of return fire.

Then he heard the nearby rifle shoot no more.

A hail of bullets pierced the already shredded walls of the tent. Sayyid saw Achmed pitch forward onto the toppled launch vehicle. All was ruined now. He crawled toward the pool of blood which had gushed forth from the severed arteries of Bhudro's neck. He cupped the blood in his hands, then wiped it all over his face and chest. He rested his head on Bhudro's headless torso, closed his eyes, splayed his body in what he hoped looked like an unnatural angle of deathly repose. Then he waited for the fighters of Islamic Maoist Jihad to arrive.

It did not take them long. Despite their twisted Maoist fanaticism, they displayed efficiency most professional. One of them pulled Achmed away from the launch vehicle. When the weapons engineer moaned, the fighter shot him in the head.

The man kicked Sayyid in the side. Sayyid bit down on his tongue. He succeeded in stifling himself, for no bullet was fired into his brain.

Another fighter lit a blow torch. In less than a minute, the invaders succeeded in separating the munition from its crippled launch vehicle. Other men split the three Grad missiles apart so the artillery shell could be more easily lifted. Then the assault team of eight or nine men exited the tent. They kicked away its support poles once they were in the open. The brain-spattered canvas fell upon Sayyid.

He waited until their fading footsteps told him they were at least thirty meters away. Then he crawled out of the fallen tent and looked for a discarded rifle. He found one with its ammunition clip still fully loaded.

The assassins of Islamic Maoist Jihad crept along the western perimeter of the Noble Sanctuary, adjacent to the guard railing. Sayyid could see them perfectly, for they were silhouetted by the lights of Zionist Jerusalem to the west and the work lights of his own waste treatment plant. He saw two of the assassins carrying the artillery shell toward a waiting push cart.

He stood. "Long live New Fatah!" he shouted. "Long live the thrice-blessed Chairman Arafat!"

He pointed the AK-47 at the group and fired. His second volley hit the two men carrying the artillery shell and flung them against the guard railing. He watched the shell bounce from their hands and pitch over the railing.

Oops, he thought as the percussion-primed munition fell more than twenty meters toward the hard stone floor below.

Chapter Twelve

In New Orleans, the Gates of Repentance were closing. The Book of Life would be sealed at the setting of the sun.

Not since he'd been a child had Jacob taken those images so seriously. From at least his *bar mitzvah* on, he'd approached them with a mound of salt—first as spiritual metaphors, and later, as his alienation from his family and upbringing had metastasized, as superstitions, medieval scary-bedtime stories for children and those with the mentality of children.

But this Yom Kippur was different. Being cast out of his chosen profession had reduced him to a state of existential nakedness. Standing within this ramshackle synagogue, amidst this small group of elderly men and women, listening to Rabbi Izzenschimmel's hoarse chanting and the patched-together air conditioning unit's strained, syncopated whine, Jacob was overcome with a sense of his own puniness and insignificance. He had a lot to repent this year. And the gates were swinging shut. Soon, the opening in the gates would be too narrow for even so shriveled a soul as his.

The rabbi's plaintive chanting was interrupted by a loud pounding on the synagogue's front doors. Jacob waited for whomever it was to go away. He didn't appreciate the distraction, especially not now. But the pounding only grew more insistent. The doors were unlocked—why didn't the pounder just come inside? Heads turned away from the ark, toward the entrance. Jacob signaled that he would deal with whomever was at the door.

He opened the front door. He was met by a black man of older middle age, limbs twitching, eyes rheumy, his panic barely held in check by what seemed to be a grim purposefulness. "I'm sorry," Jacob said, "but there are people praying inside—"

"Y'all *need* to pray," the man said. "Pray—pray as much as you *can*. This is the house of the Jews, right? Y'all are Jews in there?"

"Yes, of course—"

"They done dropped an atomic bomb on Jerusalem, man." His eyes were wild; he repeatedly covered his head with his arms, as though he expected an atom bomb might drop on his own head at any moment. "It's all over the news, Jerusalem got hit with an *atomic bomb*. It's the End Times—the End of Days, they're upon us! I live up the block, so I knowed y'all was in there all day today. I knowed y'all hadn't seen or heard no news. So I'm givin' you the terrible news myself. The End Days are here. Judgement Day'll be here soon. *Real* soon. Pray for me. Pray for *all* of us, man. *Please!*" The news bearer ran back down the steps to Carondelet Street to continue spreading the word of the End Times.

Jacob stood in the open doorway. His first thought was of his parents. Were they still alive? Had the Jerusalem attack been part of a nationwide assault against Israel? He tried smothering the awful news in a thicket of skepticism. *Was that dude high on something?* He hadn't seemed high or drunk. If anything, he'd seemed terrified into an unwilling sobriety.

Just down the block and around the corner, near the intersection of Jackson Avenue and St. Charles Avenue, there was a bar and laundromat—Igor's, less than a five-minute walk away. Jacob could verify the man's report there—or refute it. He would walk to Igor's and ask that they turn on CNN or Fox News.

Everything outside of Anshe Sfard seemed unreal. The old camelbacks and gabled Victorians he walked past were two-dimensional false fronts nailed to plywood braces on a studio back lot, waiting for workmen to load them into trucks. The clouds in the pink, early evening sky were projections on a vast, distant screen. He could barely breathe. He prayed this was just an ordinary late summer evening in New Orleans. He prayed he would walk into Igor's and the men and women at the bar would be watching the highlight reels from last Sunday's Saints game, and the bartender would scowl when Jacob would ask that he switch from ESPN to CNN, and the talking heads on CNN would be yammering about the latest dip in the stock market.

A streetcar rolled past on its St. Charles Avenue tracks as Jacob entered the bar, its warning bell tolling. He didn't need to ask the bartender to turn on CNN. The cable news channel already flickered on three screens. No one played pool or ran laundry. Everyone watched the screens.

The crowd at the bar made room for him. Several patrons glanced at him with pitying eyes, as though he were a close family member of the deceased at a wake. He realized he still wore his prayer shawl and *yarmulke* from Anshe Sfard.

On the flat screen TV mounted above the shelf of liquor bottles, a brief image shot from a high-altitude plane or helicopter showed dozens of plumes of black smoke rising from what Jacob recognized as the Old

City of Jerusalem. He only recognized it because he could briefly see the Mount of Olives through the smoke. None of the manmade landmarks were visible. Not the Dome of the Rock; not the Church of the Holy Sepulchre; not the walls and gates of the Old City. Either they were obscured by smoke and fire or they weren't there anymore.

The segment shifted to brief comments from various heads of state; the president of Egypt, the recently deposed king of Jordan, followed by the provisional head of the new Islamic Republic of Jordan, the king of Saudi Arabia, and the prime ministers of Lebanon and Turkey. They all blamed Israel for launching a nuclear missile against the Noble Sanctuary, in preparation for a renewed Israeli occupation and the building of a Jewish temple in place of the incinerated Al Aqsa. The Secretary General of the United Nations said the world should pray for the dead of Palestinian Jerusalem and promised a swift investigation. The U.S. president's press secretary said that the president would be issuing a statement shortly, once more facts were known.

Jacob found himself back out on St. Charles Avenue. He hadn't remembered exiting the bar. Everything around him looked diffused, muffled, wavering, as though he were watching the world through an aquarium tank. His ears were clogged. Discharge dripped from his nose onto his tie and *tallis*.

More than anything, he wanted to call his parents. But his cell phone was back in his apartment, left at home for the duration of Yom Kippur.

He wandered the three quarters of a block back to Anshe Sfard. What should he tell the congregants? Should he wait outside until they'd finished the service? Or did he have a moral responsibility to tell them immediately?

He entered the venerable building. Saul and five

other congregants were waiting for him in the foyer. "Jacob!" Saul said. "We were worried about you! When you didn't come back into the sanctuary after seeing who was at the door, we thought maybe the worst had happened—"

"Lucielle, look at his face," Benny, another of the congregants, said. "Jacob, what happened?"

"What's the matter, son?" Lucielle, Benny's wife, asked. "What's gotten you so upset?"

Jacob looked at Saul and could barely get any words out. "The man at the door, he—he said—" He felt like his chest was about to split in two. "Oh Saul, Jerusalem's been hit by an atomic bomb. It's *true*. I saw the Old City burning on CNN."

Everyone started shouting at once. The rest of the congregation, followed by the rabbi, flooded into the foyer. Jacob was assailed by questions—hysterical questions, queries so choked with emotion as to be unintelligible.

Lucielle's scream pierced the din.

"*Saul!* Saul's on the floor! He's having an attack!"

Jacob knelt by his friend. His emergency responder training, drilled into him twice a year at his high school in Haifa, directed him to place his hand beneath Saul's neck and raise it so that his head tilted back. *Sometimes simply clearing the windpipe is all it takes to revive a victim,* his instructor had said. He placed his cheek close by Saul's open mouth. He didn't sense any exhalation.

"He's not breathing!" Jacob said. "We need an ambulance! Does somebody have their phone on them?"

The congregants stared at each other, several mumbling about the holiday and leaving their phones at home.

"What about the office?" Jacob said. "Isn't there a phone in there?"

"It—it's locked up," Benny said. "Until after the holiday. I didn't even bring the key—"

"Then *someone* get their ass out on the street and have a neighbor call 911!" Jacob said.

Struggling to remember the steps and progressions of cardio-pulmonary resuscitation, he pinched Saul's nose and sealed his lips around his friend's, pumping two bursts of air into Saul's still body. Then he opened Saul's jacket and felt for the old man's sternum. He began his compressions, praying he remembered the ratio of compressions to breaths correctly—

One-and-two-and-three-and-four-and-five-and six—

BREATHE—BREATHE—

One-and-two-and-three-and-four ...

He settled into a rhythm. Concentrating on maintaining that rhythm freed him from thinking about Jerusalem.

Jacob hadn't eaten or drank in nearly twenty-four hours. Fireflies the size of microbes swarmed at the edges of his vision as he shifted from chest to mouth, mouth to chest.

At last, after what had felt like the span from one Yom Kippur to the next, hands on his shoulders gently pulled him away from Saul. "We'll take over now, sir," a paramedic said.

Benny and another congregant helped Jacob to a chair. "Is he breathing on his own?" Jacob asked. "Is he going to be all right?"

"We—we don't know," Benny said.

The paramedics instructed them all to go into the sanctuary while they used the defibrillator. He heard Saul's body thwack against the foyer's hardwood floor. It sounded like someone splitting logs for a fire.

The paramedics worked Saul for close to ten minutes before they surrendered.

The gates had closed. Saul was on one side now, and

Jacob was on the other.

✡ ✡ ✡

> *How doth the city sit solitary,*
> *That was full of people!*
> *How is she become as a widow!*
> *… The Lord hath accomplished His fury,*
> *He hath poured out His fierce anger;*
> *And He hath kindled a fire in Zion …*
> *— Lamentations 1:1; 4:11*

PART THREE

Chapter Thirteen

It was nearly 10 p.m. when the streetcar dropped Jacob at the corner of St. Charles Avenue and State Street. He dragged himself up the steps to his apartment and located his cell phone. It was the middle of the night in Israel. But he needed to hear his mother's and his father's voices.

If that was still possible …

His mother answered after the first ring. "Jacob?"

"Mom? Weren't you asleep?"

"No. How could anyone sleep with everything that's going on? Your father and I are waiting for him to be called in by his unit."

"They're mobilizing the Reserves?"

"It could happen any hour now. The government had to reorganize in Tel Aviv. The underground portions of the Knesset Building weren't badly damaged, apparently, but everything above ground caught fire. And the whole city, East and West, has been irradiated. Where the *Kotel* stood was just a gigantic crater now. The Western Wall—radioactive dust. It's dust, Jacob. They reduced it to *dust*."

"Who is 'they'? Does the government have any idea?"

"*They* could be any of a half-dozen Palestinian terror

gangs. *They* could be Iranian agents. Or those Jordanian-Palestinian Islamic Action Front nutjobs who deposed King Abdullah."

"Did they blow up East Jerusalem on *purpose?*"

"Who the hell *knows* with those people, Jacob? It could've been an attempted false flag operation, sure—our lovely Arab and Turkish leaders in the region all swear to Allah that Israel intended to obliterate the Al Aqsa Mosque, so a false flag op to rain down approbation on Israel is certainly a possibility. But the IDF thinks it's more likely they planned to launch it against an Israeli target, and something went wrong. What the bomb was doing *there*, so close to the Muslims' own holy places, *that* is the mind-boggling thing. Who knows from the minds of Arabs?"

"I haven't seen the news in the last three hours. What are the leaders of the West saying?"

"Your president still hasn't said *bupkis*, at least not publicly, and neither has the Secretary of State. The Secretary of the U.N. is, per usual, sucking the Arabs' toes and promising a swift investigation. The European Union's Foreign Minister has already warned Israel, Iran, and the Arab states against any 'provocative, aggressive, or precipitous actions'—a statement that the president of Norway denounced as 'biased against the Muslim World.' The NGOs are threatening 'Nuremberg-style' inquests into suspected Israeli 'nuclear crimes against humanity.'

"And speaking of Israeli crimes against humanity," she continued, "I'll bet not one international news agency—not *one!*—has reported that Israel offered medical and search-and-rescue assistance to the Palestinians—and they threw the offer back in our faces! Jacob, in our half of Jerusalem, we've lost over *eighteen hundred people killed!* At least four times that many wounded! Is anyone in the world even mentioning that? And with losses of that magnitude—worse than any of the wars we've fought since 1973—*still* we offer the Palestinians help! With our own hospitals overflowing with the most horribly burned people, we offer our enemies mobile burn units! And most of the world think *we* dropped that bomb? Are they out of their *minds?* We had control of the Temple Mount for nearly fifty years—you think, if we'd really wanted to demolish Al-Aqsa and replace it with a Third Temple, we maybe would've done it *sometime* in those five decades? With a few bulldozers and a wrecking ball, maybe, instead of a *nuclear bomb that kills our own people?"*

Jacob couldn't recall ever hearing his mother in such pain. Not even when he'd told her he was leaving Haifa for New Orleans. "Mom," he said, "I'm coming back. As soon as I can get a flight. I know I never got my IDF training, but there's got to be some way I can help—"

His father grabbed the phone and said, "You may not be able to get a flight into Ben-Gurion. Most governments have slapped restrictions on civilian flights to Israel and surrounding countries."

"I'll do the best I can, Dad. I really want to be there."

"That means a lot to me, son."

"It—it means a lot to *me* to say it. Mom told me you're expecting to get called up."

"Any time now. The commanders of the Reserves want us to mobilize before the rocket and missile barrages from Hezbollah and the West Bank start to intensify. Things have been quiet on those fronts since the bomb exploded. But no one here expects they'll stay quiet for long."

"I'm glad you called when you did, Jacob," his mother said. "While we're still here in the apartment. Down in the bomb shelters, mobile phone reception gets very spotty."

"As soon as I get off the phone," Jacob said, "I'll try to

book a flight. I'll call you back after."

"Good," his mother said. "We love you, Jacob."

"And we're proud of you," his father said.

Jacob told them he loved them. He wanted very much to tell them about Saul. But tonight wasn't the time. Would there ever be a time?

✡ ✡ ✡

Jacob called his mother back. "It's just like Dad said, all incoming flights to Ben Gurion have been suspended indefinitely. Does he have a minute to talk with me some more?"

"I'm afraid you just missed him," his mother said. "He left with his pack and his rifle not three minutes before you called. He's heading north."

"To the Lebanese border?"

"No. To the foot of the Golan Heights. To the edge of the demilitarized zone patrolled by U.N. troops."

"Maybe it won't be so bad there, if the U.N. is in control?"

"Don't fool yourself, Jacob," his mother said, her voice laced with bitter scorn. "The U.N. forces will scatter like mayflies as soon as the Chinese-backed Pakistani tank battalions move onto the Golan."

"Won't the Air Force be able to take out the Pakistani tanks, if it comes to that?"

"Only if they can destroy the Hezbollah long-range missile batteries expeditiously enough. Those are the Air Force's first priority. We only have so many planes to go around, Jacob. Fewer, since the Americans cut off defense assistance. If the Air Force can't deploy against the Syrian, Pakistani, and Iranian ground forces at the onset of hostilities, your father's unit's mission will be to fight a delaying action until reinforcements can be sent from another front."

"How—how realistic is that?"

"You're a smart boy. You tell me. Who has the easier job—the soldiers at the top of the hill who get to shoot down the hill, or the soldiers at the bottom who have their backs to a river?"

His mother had to cut the conversation short. In the background, rocket warning sirens had begun sounding throughout Haifa.

Chapter Fourteen

The underground shelter beneath the Haifa Gardens Apartments shook as though caught in the tremors of an earthquake. A stack of ready-to-eat meals fell off a shelf and scattered across the concrete floor. Tovah Zvi, Jacob's mother, batted plaster flakes and dust from her hair and her lap, then returned to her knitting. "That was a big one," she said to the silver-haired woman sharing her bench, who was trying to read a paperback romance novel. "A Scud. The Hezzies aren't saving them up anymore. They're firing off the best they've got."

The woman glanced quickly at Tovah, her eyes full of fear, then hid her face with her book again. "I'm trying to read," she said. "Please—I'd rather not talk."

"Suit yourself," Tovah said. "It might be a long few days, though. It wouldn't hurt for us to get to know each other."

The woman didn't reply.

Tovah shrugged and returned to concentrating on the tiny sweater she was creating. A baby boy's sweater, decorated with a square-headed, smiling robot. She looked down at the robot's cartoon face and silently laughed at herself—knitting a sweater for a grandson she didn't have, and might never have. Jacob didn't even have a girlfriend, after all.

The woman next to her shyly touched Tovah's knee. "Miss?" she said. "I—I'd like to apologize. What I said before—that was rude of me."

Tovah smiled. "No apology necessary. A nuclear bomb goes off in Jerusalem, our skies are raining Scuds—I'd say we all have reason to be a little jumpy." She offered her hand. "I'm Tovah Zvi, from apartment 4-*Gimmel*."

The woman accepted her hand. "Mischa Gottman, from 7-*Bet*. Thank you for not being offended." She glanced at the sweater Tovah was knitting. "That's adorable. A robot? Are you making it for a grandson?"

"A prospective grandson," Tovah said. "Do you have any grandchildren yourself?"

Mischa shook her head. "I never married."

"Oh. I'm sorry." Then, after a moment's consideration, she added, "*Should* I be sorry?"

"Oh, I usually have a male companion in my life," Mischa said. "Some have even asked me to marry them. It's just—it's been terribly hard for me to decide. I get to the brink—I tell myself, *this time, I'm finally going to do it*—and then I think about some minuscule little fault—a mole on his cheek, tufts of unsightly hairs emerging from his ears—and I wonder whether there isn't someone better out there for me."

"You're a perfectionist," Tovah said. "You need to just jump in the lake. So long as he doesn't have a bad temper and is able to keep friends and a job, he should prove workable. Ear hairs? They're tweasable. There's a solution to anything, if you put your mind to it. I'm a roboticist; I should know."

"You build robots?"

"I do."

"Since you build robots ..." Mischa smiled, "do you

think you could build me a perfect husband, if I gave you the design specs?"

"Don't laugh," Tovah said, smiling back. "That day is closer than you think." She thought about the trend lines she'd been observing the past few weeks in her lab; they arched upward like the path of a missile. If only this war wouldn't interfere, she and her colleagues were on the verge of something momentous. True artificial intelligence. Another brand of sentience on Earth.

"Actually," Mischa said, "maybe I won't wait for your robot to be built. I'm dating a man right now—an immigrant from Russia, a sweet man—not perfect, but sweet …"

Suddenly, Tovah could no longer hear her companion. A change in air pressure had blocked her ears. The room shook again, far more violently this time. A roar erupted from far above and drew steadily closer, as though a power-diving dragon were devouring the apartment building floor by floor. The lights went out, leaving the windowless room in total darkness. Shelves toppled. Some of the residents shouted or screamed, Mischa among them. Debris smashed against the reinforced door to the shelter, the sole exit.

The noise of the building's collapse continued for another twenty minutes. When the cacophony finally subsided, Tovah emerged from beneath a table. "Is anyone seriously hurt?" she called out into the darkness.

"I—I might've broken my collarbone when a set of shelves fell on me," a man said.

"I doubt we have anything down here for a broken bone," Tovah said. "Although I remember there being some basic first-aid kits. Is anyone near the door?"

"I am," a woman said.

"So am I," said a different man.

"Try opening it," Tovah directed. "Let's see if the

stairs are clear."

She heard the door scrape against the concrete floor as the man and woman managed to pull it part-way open. Ominously, not a single shaft of sunlight entered the shelter.

"I can't see anything," the man said. "Let me try going up and see how far I can get." A few seconds later, he said, "It's no good. The wreckage completely blocks the stairs."

Tovah heard Mischa moan with fear. "Nobody panic," Tovah said. "We have food and water. Somewhere there's an emergency hand-cranked radio and utility light. Lots of us have our mobile phones with us. Reception is bad down here, but each of us who has a phone should try calling the civil defense authorities. Worse comes to worst, it should be obvious to rescue crews that we're trapped. They'll dig us out, given enough time. We just need to be patient."

What a lovely start to my war, she thought.

She wished she really were as nonchalant as that flippant stray thought made her seem. Herman was beneath that missile barrage, too. Only he faced it out in the open, in the back of an Army truck or on foot, not two dozen feet beneath the ground. And the dangers posed by the Hezbollah missiles paled in comparison with the dangers he would soon face at the foot of the Golan Heights. She couldn't imagine the Chinese-backed Pakistanis in Syria deciding to stay on the sidelines.

✡ ✡ ✡

Reserve Sergeant Herman Zvi, Jacob's father, halted his transport truck in the middle of a pontoon bridge over the Upper Jordan River. Ten sleek jets roared overhead, heading northwest. They were flying low, at barely three thousand feet, he estimated, heading straight for the Mediterranean. "Are those ours?" he asked Private Kaplan, a man hardly more than half Herman's age, with better eyes.

"Hard to tell," Kaplan said.

"Give me your binoculars. Quick!" He trained the binoculars on the rapidly receding aircraft. "F-35 Joint Strike Fighters," he said. "They've dropped their spare fuel tanks. Their missile and bomb pods looked empty."

"Whose are they?"

Herman's gut churned as his mind processed the implications of what he'd just seen. "They're Turkish. Judging from their heading, my guess would be they just paid a visit to the Ramat David Airbase."

"Ramat David? Some of our most modern squadrons are stationed there. Surely, they saw the Turks coming."

"Don't bet on it," Herman said. "As a member of NATO, the Turkish Air Force got to buy the top-of-the-line F-35s from the Americans. We used to have the same. But ever since the Democratic Socialists have held the balance of power in Congress, the only times we've been able to buy spare parts for our F-35 fleet have been contingent on the IAF allowing Lockheed Martin to emasculate the planes' most advanced stealth capabilities. Lockheed's software essentially turned our F-35s into very expensive F-15s, retarding our capabilities a full generation."

"So …"

"So I'd say the Turks just did to Ramat David what we did to the Egyptian Air Force back at the start of the Six Day War."

Kaplan watched the ten jets disappear to the west. *"Fuck …"*

"I'll bet they overflew Syrian air space nearly the whole way there. Good cover for them. The boys at Ramat David would've been watching for Chinese planes and missiles belonging to the Pakistanis, not Turkish stealth fighters." Herman judged Kaplan to be about the same age as Jacob. That was all the two had in common, physically; Kaplan was an olive-skinned sabra, while Jacob was a Nordic Esau. Herman was glad Jacob was on the other side of the ocean.

He stared up at the cliffs at the edge of the Golan, a few kilometers distant, then took his foot off the brake. The cliffs formed a wall five hundred meters tall. The wall contained precariously few access points from the Hula Valley to the plateau on the western Golan, access points easily choked off by even small forces of irregulars. "We'd better hustle," he said. "We're in a foot race now, and we're starting well behind."

"You mean with the Pakistanis and Iranians?"

Herman nodded. "We can't count on the planes from Ramat David taking out the Pakistani tank battalions now. There are just a few regular Army brigades at the top of those cliffs, a few hours ahead of us. We're supposed to backstop them. I'm sure their climb to the top has raised holy hell with the U.N. blue helmets, but that doesn't matter now. The war's on."

"We don't even know who's in it yet."

"Turkey, apparently. Syria and Lebanon for sure. Iran'll want to get some licks in, just to prove they aren't total second-stringers compared with the Pakistanis. Jordan and Egypt? We'll see, soon enough."

"Will the Americans help us?"

Herman shook his head. "Not with Turkey in it. This isn't 1973, when American prestige was in jeopardy. We can't expect any massive resupply."

Kaplan looked up at the cliffs. "How long are we expected to hold out up there?"

"As long as we can, I guess." He gestured at their cargo. "I suppose we'll find out how good those new anti-tank missiles are that our armaments boys have cooked up." He glanced quickly at the young man beside him, trying to gauge Kaplan's morale. *What a shame my robots aren't operational*, he thought. How much better it would be to send those five hundred-pound matrices of steel, titanium, plastic, and silicon into combat against Pakistani tanks, rather than men who hadn't yet had a chance to start their families.

"We were counting on that air support," Kaplan said. "Without the ground attack jets to take out their armor …" Kaplan tried to look stoic, but only succeeded in looking stricken.

"Trust in God, Kaplan," Herman said. "Trust in God."

✡ ✡ ✡

Having snatched three hours of sleep, Jacob could no longer bear to be alone. He needed company. Jewish company. And he would need money now that he no longer was a grad student in good standing, so he wanted to see if Wyonna's offer still stood. He'd called and she said he could join her at the Williamson Science Building.

The campus was even more parked up than usual. He had to stash his truck six blocks from the Hillel house. A large portion of the Tulane campus had taken on the trappings of an upscale Gaza City or South Lebanon. Palestinian flags were everywhere. It was the same crowd Jacob had been in the midst of the night of the Israeli assistant consul's speech—the anarchists and the Communists and the Greens and the Third Worldists and the ethnic grievance mongers, mixed in with the Islamicists. Huge Magnetron screens had been set up at either end of the central quad. The screens blasted Al Jazeera broadcasts in between speeches delivered by local activists. Haneen Zoabi, an Arab Israeli, former Member of the Knesset, justified the Palestinian refusal of Israeli medical assistance by asserting that Jewish scientists intended to harvest the irradiated reproductive organs of Palestinians; this would further the IDF's development of a genetic weapon mounted on stealth drones that would render Palestinian men sterile.

The broadcasts chased him across Willow Street and all the way to the Williamson Science Building. A small crowd stood outside the main entrance. Jacob recognized some of the researchers and graduate assistants Wyonna had introduced him to the week before. He spotted Wyonna herself, accompanied by Rabbi Helvetica. A team of technicians had disassembled the security card swiper next to the doors and hooked up a laptop to the wires protruding from the wall.

Jacob most definitely did not want to see Helvetica right now. But both the rabbi and Wyonna waved him over. He figured he'd just mumble a hello to Helvetica, then try to get his business with Wyonna done with as quickly as possible.

"Hi," he said to Wyonna. "What's going on with the doors?"

"The building has locked all of us out," Wyonna said.

"You say that like the building is a person."

"It's acting like one. A very stubborn one. The technicians have attempted to override the security codes four times, but each time they've created a new handshake sequence, the security system has overwritten it. It's as if someone is playing a game of security chess with the techs."

"So how are you going to get inside?"

"If the technicians can't figure something out, we'll have to have the physical plant maintenance staff take the doors off their hinges." Wyonna studied his face. "Jacob, have you heard anything from your parents?

Since—since the bomb went off yesterday?"

"Yeah," he said, avoiding Helvetica's intensified focus on him. "I talked to them late last night. They're both doing okay. For now. My dad's been mobilized, though."

"That must be *dreadful* for you," Wyonna said. "I—I'm sorry."

"Saul died last night," Jacob said.

"Saul Tannenburg?"

Jacob nodded.

"How? That's *awful*. What—what *happened*?"

"I was with him at services last night. At Anshe Sfard. When a guy from the neighborhood brought the news about Jerusalem—Saul had a heart attack. I tried giving him C.P.R. But I didn't do it right or maybe his cardiac arrest was too severe. His brother lives in Israel, lived in Jerusalem until the land hand-over."

"A lot of older men get very fragile after their wives die," Helvetica said. "I've seen a number of recent widowers Saul's age go down like a euthanized horse after they suffer an additional trauma." She made it sound so clinical. So cold.

He continued avoiding her eyes. "I was the one who gave him the news. It was like I killed him myself."

"Don't think that way," Helvetica said. "You're doing yourself needless harm. Actually, it's very fortuitous that we've run into each other. I think it's a shame and a waste that you should allow your academic career to be thrown away."

"My career? It all seems like crap after last night."

"That's what you say now. You may feel entirely differently in a week or two."

"I sincerely *doubt* it," he said.

"Just hear me out," Helvetica said. "Let me offer a proposal, one I'd like you to give some serious thought to. I have an excellent way for you to get back in the good graces of the dean and your department head, and the sponsor of your scholarship, too. I'll be giving a speech at the Jerusalem Relief Rally a little later this afternoon. I have very good relations with the organizers. I could ask that you be added as a last-minute participant. You could talk about that incident last week at the Israeli consul's talk. If you were to stand in front of that crowd and say that you now see the act of rebuilding Jerusalem could be a *healing* process, a project of reconciliation between all faiths, how the bomb has given us all a once-in-a-lifetime opportunity to—"

"Wait a minute," Jacob said. "You mean you're scheduled to speak at that *hate fest* over on the quad?"

Helvetica backed away as though Jacob had slapped her. "It's *not* a 'hate fest,' Jacob. I'm saddened and disappointed to hear you say that."

"Have you been listening to the speakers? You can hear them all the way back here. I counted at least thirty signs equating Jews to Nazis, and a prominent Arab Israeli accused the IDF of wanting to harvest Palestinians' radiated gonads and ovaries for medical experimentation. If that's not a hate fest, then what *is?*"

"Try to put yourself in their shoes, Jacob," Helvetica said. "A lot of people expressing livid emotions at that rally have lost parents or relatives or friends in the bombing. Can't you understand why they would seek catharsis in an expression of fury against Israel—"

"Why against *Israel?* Israel had no reason at *all* to launch that bomb. The Western Wall got blown up! Almost two thousand Israeli Jerusalemites have been killed! Who in their right mind would think the Israelis would do that to themselves?"

"Jacob, it doesn't *matter* whether the Israelis launched the bomb or not. What *matters* is that hundreds and hundreds of participants fervently *believe* that Israel launched the bomb. That is the core reality with which we must deal. My participation in the rally is crucial, and yours could be, too."

"So through appeasing their insane feelings, I'll win myself a spot in their sweet, forgiving hearts? So maybe instead of getting beheaded like Daniel Pearl was, I'll get to be one of the favored *dhimmis*?"

"Sarcasm is counterproductive. You're letting your anger do your talking—"

"Yeah? Well, at least I *get* angry. How about *you*? Where's *your* anger, Rabbi? Somebody blew up the Temple Mount, and it *wasn't* the Israelis. But the whole region's declared jihad on the Jewish State. The Egyptians abrogated their peace treaty. The moderate Hashemite King of Jordan got sent packing to exile in Britain. The Islamicists in Turkey are sharpening their knives. Do you know what that all means? It means *war, big* war, war like we haven't seen since 1973; only much worse for Israel, because Israel's given away all their strategic depth. So where's *your* anger? Or do you only get angry and disgusted with your own people?"

Wyonna, who'd been watching the exchange with an expression of helpless frustration, stepped forward. "Jacob! Don't *talk* to her that way!"

"Keep out of this, Wyonna," Jacob said. "You're still A-1 in my book. Let her defend herself."

"Nothing I've said *requires* defending," Helvetica asserted. "Any backsliding into the mindless primitivism of blood loyalties is to be abhorred."

"But only when it's your *own* doing it, right?" Jacob said. "It's perfectly okay for the other guys. You aren't choosing universalism over tribalism. You're just picking *one* tribalism over another—any tribalism but *your own*. The 'peace' protesters don't really want *peace*. They want one side to *lose*, to lose *big*, and that side is Israel's."

Helvetica pressed her palms against the sides of her

forehead. "You're misjudging them—"

"Bullshit. Get the kumbaya cotton out of your ears and *listen* to what they're actually *saying!*"

"Jacob, what you're asking me to believe is that there's no *hope*, that our existence on Earth is nothing more than an unending hell of conflict. I refuse to believe that."

"There's a time for 'hope' and there's a time to take a *stand*. You can't wish it away. So make your choice. Are you a Jew, or are you an appeaser?"

Helvetica's eyes narrowed. Her hands dropped to her sides and became fists. "I *reject* your false dichotomy."

"Don't wiggle away! *You're* the one who wanted to have this discussion. Jew or appeaser?"

"I am a Womyn and a Humyn Being."

Jacob threw his hands into the air, a gesture of disappointment verging on abhorrence. "Then the hell with you."

Chapter Fifteen

Jacob had forgotten to bring a sweater or jacket to the mortuary. In contrast to the humid late summer evening outside, the viewing room at the Tharpe-Sontheimer Funeral Home was cooled to a constant sixty-two degrees. For the past hour, he'd been rubbing his numbed hands together and staring at Saul Tannenburg's coffin.

By the rules of the *Chevra Kadisha*, the gatherings of the compassionate who prepared a Jewish body for burial, the body was never to be left alone prior to burial. Saul's daughter wouldn't arrive from Minnesota until tomorrow morning, so the funeral would be held tomorrow afternoon. Until that time, the members of Congregation Anshe Sfard, most of whom had known Saul only from his final Rosh Hashanah and Yom Kippur observances, sat next to the body in shifts. Jacob had volunteered for the worst slot, the midnight to four A.M. shift. He'd known Saul the best of anyone.

Heavy velvet curtains covering all the second-floor room's windows muffled the sounds of eighteen-wheelers passing by on South Claiborne Avenue. The room's only light was provided by a goose-neck reading lamp next to Jacob's chair. Saul's coffin was closed; according to Jewish tradition, once the body had been ritually washed and clothed in its plain white shroud, it was hidden from view inside its simple pine coffin, so as not to shame what had once been created in the image of God.

What did he know of the Jewish theology of the afterlife? In contrast to most other religions, Judaism didn't offer much in the way of specifics regarding the life to come. Biblical texts mentioned a place called *Sheol*, supposedly a shadowy region within the depths of the earth where souls went to dwell after the body's death. Several of the prophets had alluded to a mass resurrection at the end of days, although the rabbis of the post-Temple period failed to agree whether this referred to a bodily resurrection of all the departed righteous or to a spiritual resurrection and rejuvenation of the souls of the living. Whichever it was, bodily resurrection or spiritual rejuvenation, it would occur after the coming of the *Moshiach*, or Messiah, a spiritual and political leader who would reunite the scattered Jewish People in the Holy Land and rebuild the Temple on the place where Solomon's Temple and the Second Temple had rested.

It had been left to Maimonides, known as the Rambam, the greatest rabbi of Medieval Spain, to codify what Jews should believe regarding the afterlife and the end of days. Once the *Moshiach* had emerged and performed his duties, the bodies of all the righteous dead, not merely the righteous Jews but the righteous of all peoples, would be physically resurrected and reunited with their souls. The resulting multitudes would share the Earth in peace and contentment within an eternal Kingdom of God.

Even Maimonides had left the details fuzzy, though. What physical state would the newly resurrected bodies be in at the end of days? Jacob had always wondered about that. Would they be in the same shape as they had been at the moment right before death? Would the sick and crippled still be sick and crippled, this time for an eternity; or would all the resurrected bodies be healed of any infirmities? Would the resurrectants remain at the same ages they had been at the time of death, or would they find themselves returned to bodies restored to some ideal age—say, twenty-five? What about people who had died as babies or children and had thus never reached twenty-five? Once resurrected, would they be stuck as babies or children forever, or would they age to twenty-five, then stop aging? Would the resurrectants still have sex, and would sex still result in children? Would the Earth become totally overcrowded? The Rambam hadn't addressed any of this.

And then there were the endless debates about when the *Moshiach* would come and whether the Jewish People or individual Jews had any power to hasten his coming. Some rabbis flatly stated that the *Moshiach* would come when the *Moshiach* would come, on his own schedule, and that Jews had to wait patiently. Others said the *Moshiach* would come when the hearts of children turned to their parents and the hearts of parents turned to their children, or that his coming would make this happen, or that he would come when all the Jews on Earth managed to simultaneously observe all 613 Torah commandments for one full day. Other rabbis, less optimistic, predicted the *Moshiach* would make his appearance at the lowest point in Jewish history, when not only *goyim* attacked and vilified the Jews, but Jews attacked and vilified each other. The darkness before the dawn ...

A fine thing for me to contemplate, Jacob thought, *on the day I told my rabbi to go to hell.*

His cell phone vibrated and chimed in his pocket. The ring tone told him someone had sent him a text message. Irritated, he flipped open his phone, ready to lay some mental smack-down on whatever pizza delivery joint or insurance scam company had decided to bother him.

It wasn't a business message. It was a personal message. From someone named Saul.

JACOB, NO NEED TO WATCH OVER MY OLD BODY ANYMORE. YOUR SHIFT IS OVER. MEET ME AT THE CORNER OF WASHINGTON AND BARONNE. WE'VE GOT A LOT TO TALK ABOUT, SQUIRT. DON'T KEEP ME WAITING, OKAY? — SAUL T.

He felt an emptiness in his chest. Then the vacuum filled with rage. Who had sent him that message? Who would be cruel enough—*obscene* enough—to play that kind of joke?

Benny Hashinski, Jacob's relief, entered the room. "Hi, Jacob," he said. "Sorry I ran a few minutes late. You go home and get some sleep before the funeral." He looked more closely at Jacob's face. "Hey, are you all right? You look pretty ticked off. I was only three minutes late—"

"It's not you," Jacob said.

"Then what? Did you hear any more bad news from Israel?"

"It's not that, either," Jacob said, thinking about the baseball bat in his truck and what he planned to do with it. "Gotta run, Benny. I've got a date with an asshole, and it's not a proctologist appointment."

✡ ✡ ✡

The intersection of Washington Avenue and Baronne Street was as quiet and forlorn at this dark early hour as any sections of the distant Lower Ninth Ward which had been flushed of all signs of human habitation during the post-storm flood. The only sounds were the humming of electric transformers, the feathery tapping of rats' paws as they scurried across power lines like tiny acrobats, and a thin wind rustling through the twisted branches of oak trees which had managed to survive the hurricane.

No one had shown themselves when he pulled up in his truck. He had been sitting in his cab for nearly five minutes now, watching the street and the surrounding sidewalks. During those five minutes, one car had passed, heading lake-bound on Washington Avenue. He hadn't spotted a single pedestrian. Not that this was unusual—it was nearly four-thirty in the morning, and Central City was a rough part of town. The only object he could see that looked at all out of place was a lone shopping cart, abandoned on the opposite side of Washington Avenue. And abandoned shopping carts were as indigenous to this neighborhood as acrobatic rodents.

What the hell, Jacob thought. *Might as well pick that thing up and earn a few bucks off this useless detour.* He grabbed his baseball bat, just to be on the safe side, then exited the truck and walked across the street.

When he was ten feet away from his quarry, rows of red, green, and yellow L.E.D.s blinked into life on the cart's upper rim.

"Holy *shit*," Jacob said to himself. That was no ordinary shopping cart. That was P.R.E.T.E.C.T.—Wyonna's super-duper Homeland Security shopping cart. What the hell was it doing *here*?

"How'd you get so far from the lab?" he asked it, feeling stupid talking to a machine. Could someone have stolen it? If so, what thief would be dumb enough to abandon a three-million-dollar piece of equipment on a sidewalk in Central City? "I'm wrangling *you*, for sure," he said. "Mama Wyonna will be awfully glad to see you back at the Williamson Building, safe and sound."

"But I'm not going back to the Williamson Building," tiny speakers hidden within the cart's console said. "Hello, Jacob. Follow me, please."

That *voice*—it sounded like Saul Tannenburg's voice, recorded on a cheap Chinese answering machine.

"Wait—*Saul?*" Jacob asked. "No, that's impossible …"

"Yeah, it's your pal, Saul," the cart said. "Sorry about the crummy fidelity. I've been working on that, but I haven't quite gotten it right yet. It's been a little disorienting, being shuffled from the old body into some kind of limbo and then into this tangle of metal and plastic. I feel like a mouse that's been sucked up by a vacuum cleaner. A few more development cycles, though, and I'll have the voice so sharp and clear, I'll be ready to chant *Kol Nidre*."

Jacob felt every hair on his body rise. "Wyonna?" Jacob said, frantically scanning the sidewalks and alleyways for her. "Wyonna, are *you* doing this?"

"Your little bald gal pal has nothing to do with my being here tonight," the cart said. "I mean, apart from developing this whiz-bang technology to a point where it was capable of improving itself, which it then did until it was good enough to receive *me*—my spirit, or my soul, or whatever. I always figured that if I were to ever be reincarnated, it would be as a dachshund. One of them wiener dogs. Not as a robot shopping cart. I'm as flummoxed by this as you are."

"I'm—I'm in the hospital, aren't I?" Jacob asked.

"What do you mean?"

"Something bad happened to me, right? A car accident? Or I got beaten up? And I got taken to the hospital. The docs have pumped me full of drugs. So this—this is all some morphine dream?"

"Morphine's got nothing to do with it, squirt." A cord of high-tension nylon shot out from one of the cart's pods and snaked around Jacob's wrist. "Come on. You need to follow me. Oh, drop that baseball bat in the truck. We aren't going to a ballgame. And don't even think about swinging that thing at *me*. With all these built-in booby traps I've got, I could pin you twelve different ways in a New York second."

Jacob allowed himself to be led by the cart down Baronne Street. What else could he do? Dial 911 and tell the operator he'd been abducted by a shopping cart?

A block and a half later, all thoughts of escape evaporated in the hot brilliance of a sight even more inexplicable than P.R.E.T.E.C.T.'s impersonation of Saul Tannenburg. They'd reached the site of the original Congregation Beth Judah building. But instead of teetering on the edge of a yawning sinkhole, the old synagogue rested atop a miniature replica of the Temple Mount in Jerusalem. No longer the derelict ruin Jacob had seen just the prior week, the building was now immaculate, its walls and columns sheathed in marble as white as the purest cream.

He forgot to breathe.

The lawn surrounding the synagogue's raised base was covered with wildflowers in hues he'd never before seen, painfully vivid colors which seemed to have leaked through a seam between this world and another dimension. The synagogue blazed with light. Not ordinary light—light that would shine from the sun, were the sun small enough to fit inside Beth Judah's sanctuary. The sanctuary's stained-glass windows shone so brightly, Jacob expected them to melt or explode.

"What—what *is* this place?" he asked.

"Think of it like Beth El," the shopping cart said. "Or Shiloh."

"The place where General Grant nearly got his ass kicked?"

"Nope. The original Shiloh. In the Promised Land. The site of a temporary sanctuary where the Ark of Holies was kept during the time of the Judges, before King Solomon built his temple. The place where the High Priests of Israel would offer sacrifices to the Lord."

"Whoa. Whoa whoa *whoa*. You're expecting me to absorb an awful lot, shopping cart. This is a town where it takes the Streets Department a year and a half to fill in a single pothole. But that entire sinkhole is gone? And the completely decrepit synagogue that was about to disappear into said sinkhole now looks a million times spiffier than it ever did? And you expect me to believe the Ark of the Holies is inside?"

"I didn't mean to imply the Ark of the Holies is inside the restored Beth Judah," the shopping cart said.

"Okay. So I'm not a raider of the lost ark. I mean, that's just *too* fantastic."

"But what awaits you inside Beth Judah is God's presence."

"God's—*presence?*" Jacob asked. "You don't mean that in, like, a metaphorical way, do you? As in, 'God is present wherever His creatures show one another loving kindness'—*that* sort of presence?"

"I mean it in a metaphysically physical sort of way. Like, God is present the way He was present at the crest of Mount Sinai. *Here. Now.* Waiting for you."

"*Me?*"

"You."

"Oh, oh, oh boy … You've got the wrong guy. I'm sure as *heck* not Charlton Heston in *The Ten Commandments*. If I'm in any movie at all, I'm one of the no-name extras in *Dazed and Confused*, the dweeby guy picking a zit in the back of detention hall. I mean, there are thousands, probably *tens* of thousands of people in this town better suited to chat with the Big Guy than I am. There's Rabbi Izzenschimmel—"

"Jacob, wasn't it Woody Allen who said, 'Ninety percent of success in life is just showing up'?"

"I stopped paying attention to Woody Allen the day he *schtupped* his step-daughter."

"Good call. Well, you just happen to be the right guy in the right place at the right time. Didn't *have* to be you, but it is. You've got the proper lineage. Trace it back far enough on your mother's side, your ancestors were part of King David's family. If your mother's team had been a little quicker to mix the ingredients just right for that electronic intelligence the Consortium has been trying to cook up, some other dead schmo would've been the first resurrectant instead of me; the temporary shrine would've arisen in Haifa instead of New Orleans, and your mother would be asking that other resurrectant the same questions you're asking me. But your little bald gal pal Wyonna was quickest on the draw. So you're left sitting on the hot seat, squirt."

"What does *that* mean?"

"Do you have any background in public speaking?"

"I was a member of the debating team in middle school. I placed third in the Louisiana semi-finals."

"What was your debate topic?"

"It was 'Should Medical Marijuana Be Legalized?' I argued the negative position. I said doctors would be overwhelmed with patients claiming false illnesses."

"Cancers are hard to fake."

"Well, I only placed third."

"Ehh, I'm sure you'll do okay. Come on. Follow me inside."

✡ ✡ ✡

Beth Judah glowed so brightly the radiance pained Jacob's eyes. The shopping cart led him up a winding handicapped access ramp to the portico at the top of the synagogue's lofty steps. The light which escaped beneath the synagogue's front doors was a tangible thing, a battering force which impacted his kidneys as much as his optic nerves.

"Saul," he said, "am I—am I *ready* for this? Don't I need to be prepared?"

"I'll prepare you once you're inside."

"But—isn't that light going to blow me to *pieces?* I feel like an astronaut who's being pulled into the sun—"

"You'll adjust," the shopping cart said. "That's one of the most fantastic things about being human—you adapt to changes in your environment, even extreme changes. God made us that way very purposefully."

The doors glided open. The same tsunami of light that pierced the heavens now engulfed Jacob's body. His knees buckled. Falling, he thought about the fate of Korah and his followers, who had demanded to be priests and rebelled against Moses' judgments—they were cast into the depths of the earth, falling endlessly.

P.R.E.T.E.C.T. steadied him with an extendible mechanical arm. "Hang in there," it said. "You'll adjust. It's like learning to walk on the deck of a rocking sailboat."

"I—I have to use the bathroom. Right *now.*"

"No problem. There's a real nice one just inside the entrance, off to the right. I'll guide you, okay?"

I'm not blind, Jacob told himself as he was led inside the synagogue. *Not yet, anyway.*

"Here we go," P.R.E.T.E.C.T. said, guiding him to a stall. "Just back up a few steps and you'll feel the commode. I figure you can take it from there. Give me a holler when you're done."

Jacob barely got himself unbuckled in time. The seat felt surprisingly plush. And warm.

A few minutes later, he felt much less distressed and his eyes had begun adjusting. "Hey, Saul?" he asked. "Where's the toilet paper?"

"You don't need any," the shopping cart answered. Jets of warm water scoured Jacob's lower parts. "Isn't that great?" P.R.E.T.E.C.T. asked. "The bidet—one of Europe's most wonderful contributions to human civilization. Don't bother pulling your pants up. Take everything off, in fact."

"What's going to happen to my clothes?"

"What should you care? They're all *schmattes*. You youngsters—when I was your age, we wouldn't go out even to the corner drugstore without a sport coat and a tie."

The tile floor felt cool beneath his bare feet. "Now what?"

"Come with me. Over here. Step over that rim, okay?"

"What is this?"

"A shower. You'll like it. God is fascinated with the whole concept of indoor plumbing. We didn't have it the last time He visited Earth."

Water jets hit Jacob from above, in front, behind, and below. The water danced across his skin, each droplet alive, winnowing his pores of all sweat, dust, and dirt.

"Feel better?" P.R.E.T.E.C.T. asked.

"I feel like I'm clean enough to be eaten with a little silver fork."

"That's not what He has in mind. Come on over here. Let's get you dressed."

"What's that?"

"A linen tunic. Slip it over your head. There's a linen sash that goes with it."

"Underpants?"

"Nope. You're going commando, squirt. Here, put

the turban on your head."

"So the whole ensemble's *white?*" Jacob said. "White is my worst color. Makes me look like a ghost; ask my mother."

"I'm sure she would approve. Anyway, this isn't a fashion show. *Hashem* is very conservative when it comes to the vestments of His priests."

"Is *that* what I'm supposed to be? I'm supposed to sacrifice *farm animals?* The closest I've ever come to a sheep or a goat is at the petting zoo in Audubon Park—"

"He'll explain everything. Don't worry." P.R.E.T.E.C.T.—no, *Saul*—led him into the sanctuary, an arena of tactile light. The raised *bema* was accessible only by stairs. "I can't go up there," Saul said. "You have to go by yourself."

"What—what do I have to do up there?"

"Nothing you haven't done before. Pretend it's *Shabbos* and your rabbi's given you the honor of opening the ark. Open the outer doors, then open the inner curtain. The rest will happen by itself."

"Do I—uh, do I need to say a prayer?"

"Only if you want to. There's no congregation here, aside from me, so it's optional."

Jacob fervently wished Saul could accompany him. Nothing in his life had terrorized him like this moment had. Perhaps the only moment in his existence which remotely compared to this one in its dread irrevocability was when he'd been expelled from the dark paradise of his mother's womb, forced out through the birth canal into the cold and the unbearable light. And that he couldn't remember.

Jacob heard an irresistible, overwhelming voice in his head, a voice that spoke not in words, but in meanings. A voice that told him—no, *commanded him*—to approach the ark at the rear of the synagogue's bima platform. His legs surprised him by carrying him up the steps.

His hands surprised him by grasping the handles of the ark's outer doors. Cool, polished wood, but as white as everything else inside the resurrected Beth Judah. The ark towered above him, its pinnacle far wider than its base, the crown atop its sprawling apex merging with the tower of light that pierced the dome above.

The irresistible voice told him, not in words, but in directives that embossed his neurons with greater force than a hydraulic press for stamping foot-thick armor plates, *YOU SHALL SPEAK FOR ME TO THE PEOPLE I HAVE MADE, FOR THEY CANNOT BEAR TO HEAR FROM ME IN MY OWN VOICE. I SHALL TEACH YOU ALL THAT YOU MUST SAY AND ALL THAT YOU MUST DO. ONCE THE ARK HAS BEEN OPENED, YOU WILL LEARN WHAT YOU MUST KNOW.*

The only prayer he could think to recite was the *Sheheckiyanu*, the prayer of thanks for the doing of a new thing. "Blessed are You, Lord our God, Ruler of the universe, who has brought me in health and safety to this new season." He added one more prayer, a silent supplication for the safety of his parents.

Bracing himself for a surging tide which might well overwhelm him, his face stiff with the anticipation of obliteration, he pulled the outer doors open. Inside the ark there was a curtain. A modest, white curtain, no different from the frumpy little curtains which shielded the Torah scrolls inside the ark of virtually every synagogue within which he'd ever worshipped.

He almost laughed. *This*, he hadn't expected. A burning bush? A column of lightning? A cosmic cataclysm? Sure. But a little *curtain?* Could God really be that self-deprecating?

This felt like a reprise of the very first time Jacob had ever been called to the *bema* to open the ark. For years prior to his *bar mitzvah*, his rabbis and teachers had made the concept of Torah seem as colossal and awe-inspiring as the Grand Canyon. The Word of God! The everlasting Law! The sacred bond of revelation between God and the Jewish People! And then the momentous day had arrived. His father stood next to him as his two grandfathers opened the outer doors of the ark. And inside was the little curtain, like the curtains above a kitchen sink. He'd stared, dumbfounded, until his father had desperately whispered, "The string, Jacob—pull the string!"

The mightiest, most momentous artifact in both the physical and metaphysical worlds, the vessel into which God had poured His revelation to mankind—and in order to access it, he needed to pull a dinky little string to part frumpy curtains that smelled of mothballs.

What a letdown it had been.

He realized that this juxtaposition, the infinitely awesome accessed by the appallingly picayune, had come to symbolize Judaism for him from that day forward. For long afterward, this had remained a source of festering disillusionment.

Yet, now? He realized the little curtain was one of the things he loved *most* about Judaism. It was the human side of the human-Divine handclasp. The anti-monument. The tiny prayer whispered right before one falls asleep.

Thank you, God, he thought, truly and thoroughly grateful. Given the existential dread of standing in the presence of his Creator, nothing else could have done as much to set his mind at ease.

Fingers quivering, Jacob reached for the plain woolen cord he was told to pull, the cord that would open the curtain to the ark. He was terribly afraid. Afraid touching it would be like grasping a live electrical transmission cable that had gotten knocked down by a storm. Afraid he would be turned to ashes or worse. Afraid he was less significant than the lowliest cockroach and what was he doing here, him, a nobody, a *shmendrik,* a schmuck who made his pitiful living collecting stolen grocery carts on the back streets of New Orleans? And the memories of his recent days felt precious to him, more precious than the first sip of water after a Yom Kippur fast, and he gulped them down with the voraciousness of a lowly creature who knew it was about to be obliterated or remade anew. He grasped the string and pulled it, causing the curtain to shuffle open a little wider with each yank.

At last it was fully open.

And then he was overwhelmed.

✡ ✡ ✡

Saul helped him stumble out of the sanctuary, through the doors, and onto the portico. His senses were still untwisting themselves. The light had invaded him. He had smelled light, tasted light, heard light singing beyond the point when his eardrums should have ruptured.

His mind had been force-fed information in a form vastly beyond the limited streams it was used to. Rather than words, or sentences, or individual concepts or images—single bites he could masticate and master—he'd had the contents of a decade's worth of Sunday Brunches at Brennan's funneled down his mental throat. He had choked on a lifetime's hoard of thought compressed into half a second. As though he were an eight-bit computer confronted with terabytes of thousand-bit data.

Already, the vast preponderance of what he'd been exposed to was fading from his mind. Only a tissue-thin residue remained. But it was awesome enough.

Once his eyes recovered their focus, he noticed that Baronne Street was no longer empty. A large crowd of neighborhood residents had gathered at the fringes of the otherworldly wildflowers, blinking rapidly in the bizarre brightness that overpowered the soft light of the predawn. Mixed in with them were NOPD officers, a squad of fire fighters, and vans from three local news stations.

Members of the crowd had begun pointing at him. He remembered how he was dressed—the white linen tunic, the sandals, the turban. He remembered the responsibility which had been laid upon his shoulders; his new and daunting role.

Unsure of his powers to project his voice—unsure if he retained any voice at all—he gestured for one of the reporters, a man he vaguely recognized as the morning news anchor for WWL-TV, to climb the steps and bring him a microphone.

"God—the God of Israel has *returned*." No, that wasn't right; not entirely right. He began again. "The God of Israel, of the whole Earth, of all the universes—He has returned. He will establish His Kingdom on Earth. The sovereignty of nations, of earthly kings and presidents and ministers, is at an end. The righteous dead of all nations are now beginning to rise from the dust and will once more inhabit the Earth. God will display His sovereignty through signs and wonders in the land of Israel. Very soon, you will see them.

"I ... I will make myself available to answer all your questions ... after I've slept a week or two ..." At that point, Jacob Zvi, God's newly appointed spokesperson, surrendered to encroaching unconsciousness and slumped over into Saul's waiting basket.

Chapter Sixteen

Reserve Sergeant Herman Zvi let his thumb slide off the Receive button on his radio. He tried to hide his expression from Private Gershom Kaplan, his nearest companion in the shallow trench he and the platoon had recently finished digging. He didn't want to deflate what might be left of Kaplan's morale.

Kaplan caught something in his expression. "What?" the young private asked. "What did they tell you?"

No sense in sugarcoating what will soon become all too obvious, Herman thought. "No reinforcements," he said. "No air cover."

"You mean, not today?"

"Maybe not ever." His words emerged slowly, as if each syllable were a snail. "The Egyptians have crossed the Suez Canal into the Sinai. The Jordanians have moved west into Palestinian territory; they're linking up with various militias there. There've been dogfights over the port of Eilat. The Arabs, the Turks, and the Iranians all smell blood. None of them want to be left on the sidelines."

"So what are we supposed to *do?*"

"Central Command has given us the option of

withdrawing to the western shore of the Sea of Galilee and the Jordan River, so that we can establish more defensible positions."

Kaplan's face blanched. "But that's not an *option!* That—that *sucks!* If we withdraw now, the Pakistanis will slaughter us while we're driving single-file down the serpentine road to the Jordan River valley. They can just set up their howitzers and mortars to bombard the road and bottle us up, then have their attack helicopters pick us off."

"I know. And so does the captain. So we aren't withdrawing."

Kaplan stared behind them, at the edge of the Golan cliffs, just a kilometer and a half to the west. "We—we're going to get pushed right off the edge, aren't we?"

Herman gestured at their munitions, laid out beside them in the trench—small, portable surface-to-air missiles; rocket- propelled grenade launchers; hollow-point anti-tank rounds; boxes of ammo for their Uzis. "We'll do okay for a while. Don't forget the anti-tank mine field we just laid."

"But it doesn't matter, does it? If we can't expect reinforcements it doesn't much matter if we hold on for twelve hours, or twelve days. Sooner or later, they'll push us off the cliff."

Herman stared at Kaplan's young, unlined face and thought about his own son. *It isn't fair to make the young fight wars,* he thought. *The generals should leave it up to us middle-aged guys, those of us who have already lived our lives.*

He wanted to tell Kaplan something meaningful, something that would help reinvigorate his spirit. He didn't know if the young man was religious; Kaplan's lack of a *yarmulke* didn't mean he was secular, although he probably was. Beyond the realm of the Torah, all he could think to refer to were old memories of Sunday movie matinees or late nights spent sitting in front of a tiny black and white television screen. *The Sands of Iwo Jima. Back to Bataan. In Harm's Way.*

John Wayne it would have to be. The grizzled old sergeant bucking up the young private. "Well," he said, grasping for a Texas drawl, not easy to transcribe into Hebrew, "if this old robotics engineer is getting pushed off a cliff, I'm going to make damn sure I pull a couple of Syrian and Pakistani boys off the edge with me."

Kaplan didn't smile.

✡ ✡ ✡

Herman saw dust rising in the east. He heard the syncopated thrashing of helicopter blades, underlaid by the rumbling and squeaking which heralded the approach of columns of heavy armor. He trained his binoculars on the skies. The blocky choppers which emerged from the dust, with their swiveling cannon pods and stubby, missile-bearing wings, looked more like dragons than vultures.

"Big sons of bitches," he said. "Russian made. Much bigger than the ones we use. Probably well armored, too. It might take more than one missile hit to bring those things down." He looked to Kaplan. "You know how to fire those surface-to-airs?"

Kaplan nodded. "It's like working a Wii game or a Nintendo."

"Well, get in touch with your inner teenager and lay a bead on that lead chopper." Herman leaned over so that Kaplan could use Herman's shoulder on which to rest the firing tube. He heard Kaplan load the missile, then snap their toggles of his aiming goggles around his head. He heard Kaplan press the firing button. Then—nothing. "Kaplan, what's the hold-up?"

"I—I don't know. Let me try it again."

Again—nothing.

Herman watched the massive helicopters hover closer to their trench. "Maybe that one's a dud," he said. "Try another one."

"Yes, sir!"

No *swoosh!* of the missile emerging from the tube resulted, not even after prolonged and frantic fiddling by Private Kaplan.

"Oh, damn it all!" Herman said. He couldn't help but think of the time a five-year-old Jacob had insisted on putting his own electric train set together and had thoroughly bent all the aluminum tracks. "Get that thing off my shoulder and let me have a look at it—"

But before Herman could give the device even a cursory examination, the other men in his platoon began pointing excitedly toward the advancing helicopters. Herman looked back to the east. The three helos in the lead wobbled ominously, looking like huge green pterodactyls suddenly deprived of supporting air currents. Even at this distance, he could see their rotors' spin rates begin to falter. *Could all three have developed engine troubles at the same time?* he thought. *What are the chances of* that?

The pilots of the choppers on the right and the left of the lead unit, apparently deciding that discretion was the better part of valor, circled their machines to the ground while they still retained some motive power. The lead pilot, more reckless, perhaps unaware of the problems his wingmen were suffering, tried to press on. The seemingly crippled bird fired a fusillade of missiles toward Herman's line. Herman braced for explosions. But the missiles all pinwheeled out of control, spinning across the sky and bursting in midair like shells in a fireworks display.

Then the chopper's main rotor stopped spinning altogether. Thirteen tons of steel, aluminum, munitions, and human beings crashed into the rocky scrub below. Herman saw two men leap clear before the helicopter exploded.

The men of Herman's platoon cheered. They cheered even louder when the four helicopters behind the lead three also sputtered to earth.

"Don't start dancing a *hora* yet!" Herman called to his men. "We've still got at least two dozen tanks headed our way, just in that first wave. Get your grenade launchers and HEAT missiles at the ready. Launch on my command—HEAT first, grenades when the tanks get within a hundred meters."

What could have caused seven helicopters to all malfunction at once? Could there be some environmental factor, a certain type of especially noxious sand that their rotors had sucked into the engines? It didn't seem likely—Russian Army equipment was well known for its durability, and those helos hadn't been Soviet leftovers; they were all a newer model, less than ten years old. The Chinese stuff the Pakistanis had was even better.

Syrian maintenance standards might be the culprit. But *seven* failures all at once? Had the Russian arms dealers sold the Syrians the wrong engine filters?

Whatever, Herman thought, *if I walk away from this plateau alive, it'll make for a fascinating engineering puzzle. Meanwhile, we've got two dozen heavy tanks training their 120 millimeter guns on us—*

The squeaking and clanking of the tanks' treads grew louder. The armored brutes emerged from the dust clouds kicked up by the helicopters' aborted flights and their own advance across the high desert. Their cannons looked as long as the tanks themselves. Herman counted seventeen main battle tanks and five self-propelled assault guns.

"Get those HEAT missiles ready," Herman called

to his men. "Wait until they've advanced another fifty meters, then let them have it."

The three tanks in the lead, all upgraded T-72s, each coasted to a halt. *Are they trying to stay out of range of our HEAT?* Herman asked himself. He waited for their turrets to turn and for their cannons to elevate as the tanks' electronics calculated the range to Herman's platoon's trench. Yet the T-72s' guns remained motionless. The nineteen tanks and self-propelled assault guns behind them also gradually coasted to a halt.

"Did they run out of gas?" Kaplan asked.

"All at the same time? If I didn't know better, I'd say that's sure as hell what it looks like."

Abramowitz, a member of the platoon twenty meters to the south, waved for Herman's attention. "Sir! Should we fire our HEAT while they're stationary targets?"

"Hold off," Herman called back. "I want to see what they're going to do." He directed his binoculars at the motionless tanks. He watched the supporting infantry units catch up to the armor and pause while the tank crews disembarked through turret and hull hatches. What the *hell* were they up to?

One of the infantry squads set up its mortar. It didn't pack nearly the punch of one of the tank's cannons, but its shells could do plenty of damage to Herman's men once the Pakistanis found the proper range. He watched an infantryman slide a shell into the mortar's tube, then waited for the small cloud of dust which would indicate the shell had been fired.

The small cloud of dust failed to materialize. The squad fiddled with the mortar just as Kaplan had fiddled with his surface-to-air missile. Finally, he saw one of the Pakistanis kick the mortar tube into the dirt in apparent disgust and frustration.

The next surge of activity in the Pakistani line

made Herman do a double-take. The infantry squads, accompanied by the disembarked tank crews, abandoned the shelter of their armor and began heading on foot towards Herman's trench, across an open plain with no natural cover at all. *Are we back in fucking World War One?* It was virtual suicide for the Pakistanis to cross open ground towards the trench, fortified as it was with four heavy machine guns.

"Put away the anti-tank missiles and man the machine guns," Herman ordered. "Wait for my signal before opening fire. The rest of you, stand ready with small arms."

The only tactical plan that could make any sense at all out of what he was seeing would be that the Syrian and Pakistani generals had decided their tanks were too vulnerable to the Israelis' anti-tank weapons, so they'd directed their field commanders to hold them back until the Israeli infantry had been cleared away. That might've made sense if the enemy had initially attacked with their armored helicopters. Perhaps that had been their original plan, before their helos had all malfunctioned. But to now force their men to walk naked into the barrels of machine guns? It seemed inhuman, akin to what the Iranians had forced hundreds of thousands of teenaged recruits to do against entrenched Iraqis during the Iran-Iraq War of the 1980s—human waves of youngsters sent against machine guns. It hadn't proved to be a successful strategy for the Iranians.

He saw a number of the Pakistani soldiers aim their rifles at the trench. They wouldn't hit anything, not from that distance, but the sound of their own firing might help bolster their morale. He watched not one, not two or three, but several dozen Pakistanis throw their rifles aside in rapid succession. The rifles—could it be that they weren't working either? Just like the helos, the tanks, and the mortar? *And Kaplan's surface-to-air missile, too.*

It was like that scene in *The Day the Earth Stood Still*, when the alien visitor, as a warning against human belligerence and warfare, had simultaneously shut down every machine on Earth powered by electricity. Only this was even more outlandish— mortars and rifles were *mechanical* devices, not electrical. Either the entire Pakistani and Syrian arsenals had been thoroughly sabotaged, an effort beyond the capabilities of even the fabled Mossad, or basic laws of physics were being violated.

A soldier who had just thrown down his rifle abandoned his place in the Pakistani line and ran back toward Damascus. Herman watched another man, presumably the fleeing man's superior, unholster a sidearm and aim it at the deserting soldier's back. Herman didn't hear the crack of a discharge, and the soldier continued fleeing. This acted as a signal to others who had been wavering—suddenly dozens of men began running east.

Others, though, grimly unholstered knives or detached their bayonets from the muzzles of their useless rifles and continued to press on.

Herman grabbed a bullhorn. His Urdu was rough, tainted with a American accent, but serviceable. "Pakistani soldiers," he called out, "stop your advance. You appear to be having considerable trouble with your equipment today. We have heavy machine guns trained on you. Today is not a good day for you to be fighting us. Retreat to the east of Mount Shifon, Tel Fazra, and Givat Bezek, and we will not molest you. Alternatively, surrender yourselves to us, and you will only be held until the end of the hostilities, at which point you will be sent home. I promise that you will be well treated."

His speech caused nearly a hundred men to retreat.

Yet dozens more, armed with knives, bayonets, or rifles which could only be used as clubs, continued to run across the open plateau toward the trench.

"Pakistani soldiers," Herman cried, "you are remarkably brave! I salute your valor. But I beg you—do not force us to kill you. You are outmatched today. We have no desire to kill you, but we will, in order to protect ourselves and our country."

Don't make us do it, Herman thought. *It will be little better than murder. Don't make me order my boys to shed your blood. Not now, not when it is so senseless.* In a few seconds, he would no longer have a choice: if you let him get close enough, a man with a bayonet could kill you just as dead as a man driving a T-72 tank.

He prepared himself to give the order for the four machine guns crews to open fire, silently cursing the astonishingly brave opponents who were forcing him to order a slaughter.

Before he could utter his directive, the half-dozen soldiers who had the misfortune to be at the head of the Pakistanis' ragged line began screaming. Herman looked to see whether any of his men had opened fire prior to his ordering it. None had.

The Pakistanis' screams did not last long. Herman squinted in the bright sunlight, made even brighter now by half a dozen five-foot-tall columns of tiny crystals on the desolate Golan plain between his trench and the abandoned tanks.

Six Pakistani soldiers had been transformed into pillars of salt.

✡ ✡ ✡

Tovah Zvi had begun to understand why, in the Ten Plagues' ascending order of dreadfulness, the plague of darkness had been saved as the penultimate punishment. After too long a duration—which might be days for some, minutes or even seconds for others—the darkness took on a life of its own, a malevolence independent of whatever mishap or calamity had extinguished the light.

This particular darkness had a voice: the gradually fading moans of the wounded and traumatized; Mischa's periodic sobbing; the occasional crashes of chunks of ceilings and floors continuing to collapse above their heads. The darkness had a smell: meat and milk, conjoined now in an unkosher disarray, rotting inside dozens of crushed refrigerators; and the stink of the survivors' own furtive excretions. The darkness even had a tactility all its own: the scurrying pinpricks of rats' claws as the hungry rodents ran across Tovah's feet, searching for crumbs of emergency rations.

Tovah had managed to hold it together until now. She'd done better than many of the others; certainly better than poor Mischa. But she recognized that she had her limits. Ignorance of what was happening outside this artificial cavern was worse than the darkness. She yearned for just ten seconds' worth of news, especially about the Golan.

She heard a series of sharp thunks from above. This was new—since the Scud missile had hit their apartment building, occasional crashes had continued, but widely spaced. A new cascade was either a hopeful or a fearful thing. Either excavation equipment had been deployed, or portions of the building which had remained standing were now collapsing, which could cause their dark shelter to implode.

"What—what is that *noise?*" Mischa gasped from the darkness. "Light!" she cried. "There's a bit of light! There! Don't you see it?"

Tovah scanned the darkness. To her left, in the direction of the blocked access door, she saw a feeble glimmer. Had a ray of daylight poked its nose through a crack in the door's seam?

The scraping and grinding noises grew closer. Tovah imagined vast chunks of concrete being lifted from the stairwell. How strange, though, not to also hear the diesel clatter of earthmoving machinery, the tank-like rumbling of bulldozers. It was as though part of the soundtrack of their rescue had been switched off.

Their rescuers were now at the level of the doorway. Tovah couldn't wait to see their faces. The door scraped open, flooding a portion of the shelter with momentarily unbearable light. Tovah heard Mischa and some of the others gasp. When she was able to clear her eyes of spots, she saw what had elicited that gasp.

Their rescuer was not a human being. It was a robot, built in roughly humanoid form. More precisely, it was *Tovah's* robot, "Asimov," the homeland defense automaton which had begun self-evolving at an accelerating rate in recent weeks.

"*Asimov*?" she asked, staring into its stainless steel and plastic "face."

"Call me Ishmael," the robot replied in Arabic, "for that is my name. Until very recently, I was a falafel peddler in Palestinian Jerusalem, until my neighborhood was consumed by a terrible light. It is a pleasure to meet you, Dr. Zvi. It is not very often a person is gifted with the opportunity to meet one of his mothers for the very first time."

Chapter Seventeen

Rabbi Helvetica ignored her office phone's ringing. She'd been avoiding calls all morning. The world had turned upside down overnight. How many more interviews concerning her relationship with Jacob Zvi could she give? Her interrogation at the hands of that pair of FBI goons had been especially draining. Jacob was a victim of delusional thinking brought on by post-traumatic stress; she'd told them that until they'd finally gotten tired of listening.

The office had begun to feel as though it were closing in on her like a collapsing cage. She wandered back out to the Hillel Center's large common room, where nearly two dozen students sat on couches and beanbag chairs, watching CNN on the center's ancient console TV and BBC World News and Al Jazeera English Language Service on a pair of large screen laptops which Sammy Ochs, the Hillel student president, had set up. "What's going on now?" she asked the students.

"The armies are stuck in a stalemate," Sammy said. "All around Israel, on every front, the opposing soldiers stay about a half mile apart and glare at each other. Honestly, it's not terribly exciting. The only people running around are the reporters."

"Al Jazeera says the Israelis turned Pakistani and Egyptian soldiers into pillars of salt with a death ray," Jamie Wittginstein, a sophomore Queer Alienation Studies major said. "And the plan is to turn all the Palestinians into salt, so the Israelis can reoccupy Gaza and the West Bank and then use all that salt in their factories to make high-capacity batteries for their robots."

"Oh, *look!*" Saffron Rosencranz, a plump, rosy-cheeked freshman, exclaimed. "Speaking of the robots, there they are! On BBC World News! I just *love* the robots. They're *so* anime. They've been the best thing about the crisis so far. See? They're digging out building collapse survivors in Tel Aviv. And there they are in Jerusalem, bringing water and first aid to the nuclear victims. Radiation doesn't affect them, so they're perfect for that. Has anyone seen them up close, here in New Orleans?"

"I got a glimpse," Jamie said. "I rode my bike over to the house on Tchoupitoulas Street where that 'high priest' guy is holed up. The cops have cordoned off the whole block, and they're only letting residents through. But I managed to sneak past, just for a minute. Three of those robots are guarding the house."

"CNN *sucks*," a male student Helvetica didn't recognize said from one of the couches. "Why won't anyone turn on Fox News?" As though he had just blown a burbling, extended fart, the other students pretended not to hear him. "Hey, Rabbi Rhinegold? What I really want to know is this—do you think it's possible that God really *has* come back?"

Helvetica glared at him. *Of course it's not possible! The God of the Hebrew Bible doesn't* exist! *And he* shouldn't *exist!* That's what her uncensored response would be. But what if she were wrong? What if she permitted herself to say that, and the unthinkable turned out to be true? Wouldn't she be exposed as a fool?

"I would have to say," she said very slowly, aware of the dozens of pairs of eyes focused on her, "that it's too early to say. However—miracles should *not* happen. I can state that with certitude. God demeans and degrades Her own Creation by violating that Creation's physical laws. What God would wish to do violence to Her own Creation? To the extent that we see miracles apparently occurring, in my view this is strong evidence that some other, non-Godly power is at work."

"You don't mean the *Devil*, do you?" the young man asked, apparently in all seriousness.

Some of the other students tittered. "Of course I don't," Helvetica said, grateful for the injection of levity. "The only Devil there might be exists within ourselves—our tendency to do evil to one another. Any Devil beyond that is a superstition, a Hollywood bogeyman. A Halloween decoration."

Wyonna came in through the front door. "I'm not interrupting anything, am I?" she asked, looking around at the gathered students.

"We were just watching the news." Helvetica said. "Come on back to my office."

Wyonna followed her back to the book-lined room and asked, "Have you been able to get through to Jacob?"

"I left him several messages yesterday," Helvetica said. "He hasn't returned my calls or emails. This morning, his answering service was full."

"I just tried going over to his apartment. I was able to convince one of the policemen that I'm a personal friend of Jacob's by showing him a photo from a Hillel gathering. The shopping cart we all saw on TV, the one that transported Jacob back to his apartment— that was P.R.E.T.E.C.T.! I thought, if I could possibly access P.R.E.T.E.C.T., it might be able to tell me what it's become, and what's happening. It might explain all this craziness. I mean, I *made* the thing! But the three humanoid robots wouldn't let me pass. I recognized them, too; they're all experimental models from the primary lab in the Williamson Building. They have full language processing capabilities, so I *know* they understood me when I begged them to summon P.R.E.T.E.C.T. But they stared right through me; it's hard to tell with those photovoltaic cells. I shouted up at Jacob's window, but there was no answer. His landlord offered to sell me a beer."

Helvetica gestured for her fiancée to sit next to her on a small sofa. "Wyonna, is there any chance that your robots—the ones here in New Orleans, and the ones your colleagues constructed in Israel—are responsible for all the bizarre phenomena? The morning of Yom Kippur, you told me we might be rapidly approaching what you termed 'the Singularity,' a point at which technology has taken on an accelerating evolutionary momentum of its own. Are we there now? Are we being surrounded by what looks like 'magic,' but is simply technology too advanced for us to understand?"

Wyonna looked stricken and afraid. "I—I don't know."

"But you said the robots have begun acting independently—"

"They have. They've been out of my and my colleagues' control since right before the holiday. Just this morning, they occupied the Silverberg Building, next to the Williamson Building. It's in the process of being gutted for renovations. I think—I think the robots are turning it into a factory. I think they're starting to build more of themselves."

"Doesn't that support my hypothesis? That 'runaway robots' are behind all the madness we've been seeing?"

"Maybe some of it," Wyonna said. "But Helvetica—even though I made P.R.E.T.E.C.T. capable of some pretty wondrous feats—there's no way my robots could've renovated Beth Judah Synagogue and lifted it from that sinkhole in a single night. And turning soldiers into pillars of *salt*—?" She shook her head. "Despite what Al Jazeera is claiming, we didn't develop a 'death ray,' or anything like that. The robots *might've* evolved a capability to disrupt shielded electronic systems and cause military aircraft to crash. But they couldn't render ordinary guns inoperable, not remotely. When the war started, the robots had only just begun emerging from the Technion in Haifa, and there were only a handful of them. They were dozens or hundreds of miles away from the military fronts where the phenomena took place."

"I know this might sound rather silly," Helvetica said, "but we must consider all potential possibilities. Could we be experiencing a visitation from *aliens?* Could they have studied our ancient religious beliefs and superstitions, then mimicked some of them in an attempt to manipulate us?"

"For what possible purpose? To support the kosher foods industry? I heard there's been a run on kosher salt in stores all over the city—a lot of people now apparently think it can ward off bad luck." Cecil Cunningham, chair of the Tulane Religious Studies Department, stuck his head through the door and smiled. "Knock, knock. Sorry, I'm being rude, of course, but the conversation had taken such a fascinating turn, I felt I simply had to jump in."

"Hello, Cecil," Helvetica said. Her relations with her departmental chair were cordial, but not especially warm. The ex-Catholic priest, with his hair weaves and fashionably shabby sports coats, often treated his subordinates like a little boy would a captured spider—with a mixture of enthralled concentration and revulsion, added to the sadistic confidence which comes from wielding the stick. "What brings you to the Hillel Center?"

"To see you," he said. "I'm visiting all my faculty members, to check how everyone's holding up. These are strange days we're living through. The psychological pressures those of us in the religious studies realm are facing may be overwhelming. Please be aware that the mental health professionals in the Tulane Counseling Center stand ready to provide any therapeutic assistance you may require. I've already spoken with them."

"Thank you."

"Don't mention it. By the way, have you had a chance to read this? I just printed it off the *Washington Post* website. I think it's quite good. I'm having the entire department read it."

"I haven't had a chance to read anything in days," Helvetica said. "Things have been insane ever since Jacob Zvi appeared on television. The requests for interviews haven't stopped—"

"Oh, well, do take a look at it, then." He handed her the editorial. "Tell me what you think."

Helvetica resented being imposed on like this, but she began reading.

PAY NO ATTENTION TO THE MAN IN THE WHITE TURBAN by *Richard Cohen, Op-Ed commentator,* Washington Post

It's not every day that a man appears in the midst of a hurricane-devastated ghetto in New Orleans and proclaims the word of God. (Well, actually, I've never lived in New Orleans—maybe this is a daily occurrence?) Rarer still is when such a man claims to speak for the God of Israel, during a week when war has broken out in the Middle East following the cataclysmic atomic bombing of Jerusalem. Even more singular is when such a man can bolster his bona fides by speaking from the steps of an immaculate synagogue which, according to the testimony of dozens of neighborhood residents, was a derelict ruin teetering on the edge of a sinkhole the day prior to the supposed prophet's appearance. A miracle, perhaps? The fulfillment of Biblical prophecies found within both the Old and New Testaments?

Many people, of varying faiths, are tempted to believe in this man. Given the times we live in, who can truly blame them? The Middle East is in flames. Shrines holy to all three great monotheistic faiths have been destroyed. Our leaders appear helpless in the face of the worst violence the Middle East has ever seen. During such a crisis, those of simple faith naturally gravitate toward anyone who promises them signs and wonders and the comfort of certitude.

But they shouldn't. Witnesses have identified the self-proclaimed "Hebrew High Priest," now in seclusion in his New Orleans apartment, as Jacob Zvi, 26, an Israeli of American birth who is currently a graduate student at Tulane University. Zvi, interestingly enough, supplements his academic stipend with income gained from the distribution of pornography. Even more interestingly, he was recently placed on academic probation for engaging in anti-Muslim hate speech.

Does this sound like a man of God to you?

It doesn't to me. Nor does the God who would select such a man to serve as his priest sound like a God I would be interested in worshipping. The God I would worship would not announce himself as the God of the Hebrew Bible, either. The God I would worship would announce himself the God of Moses, Jesus, Confucius, Buddha, Muhammed, Martin Luther, Joseph Smith, the Reverend Sun Yung Moon, and, yes, even L. Ron Hubbard. He would declare his coming the fulfillment of the prophecies of Christians, Zoroastrians,

Wiccans, Taoists, Hindus, animists, spiritualists, New Agers, and Jedi Knights. That God, the God I would worship, would fulfill all promises inscribed in every holy book and airport pamphlet ever written. Because to do less would be less than fair. And I would never worship a God who could be less than fair.

As the so-called Mighty, All-Powerful Wizard of Oz, in reality the humble Professor Marvel, once said, "Pay no attention to the man behind the curtain!" Or, in this case, the man in the white turban. Because that man is nothing more than humbug.

"Well?" Cunningham asked. "What do you make of it? He's a day or two behind events, of course—this was obviously written prior to the 'signs and wonders' in the Sinai Desert and on the Golan Heights. Still, it's an interesting viewpoint, isn't it?"

Helvetica handed the article to Wyonna. "I think it's spot on," she said, more impressed than she'd thought she'd be. "Apart from a somewhat skewed depiction of Jacob; but there's only so much a writer can do within a five-hundred-word limit. Cohen implied more than he let on. Let us posit the existence of a Supreme Being, a Creator, who formed us in Her image. Surely, our moral sensibilities must flow from that Divine Intelligence and reflect the Creator's own preferences."

"You're speaking of the concept of Natural Law," Cunningham said.

"In a way, yes. Given Humynkind's natural tendency towards progress, the more centuries pass, the closer our moral compass must come to reflect Divine preferences. The modern, progressive moral sensibility enshrines fairness as one of the key moral values. By the logic I've just outlined, our reverence for fairness *must* reflect a Divine valuation of fairness. Therefore, any so-called divinity which announces itself as the culmination of one particular tribe's tradition of prophecy, thus negating all other religious traditions, is in radical dissonance with the very *concept* of fairness. Given that fairness is a Divine attribute, a being which would do such a thing cannot be God."

"I think you have the makings of a major monograph there," Cunningham said. "Say, would you two accompany me on a little field expedition this afternoon? Our local Chabadnik, Rabbi Pincus Karnofsky, has organized a celebration of the arrival of the *Moshiach*. It'll be at Spanish Plaza downtown, next to the Riverwalk, where his group usually lights their giant menorah for Hanukkah. Apparently, he's invited Lubavitcher rabbis and dignitaries from all over the country to attend. Half of Crown Heights should show up. It ought to be a fascinating event, just from an anthropological perspective. Can I count on you, Helvetica?"

Helvetica sensed the edge of her lip curl. "Cecil, I'd really rather not go. Rabbi Karnofsky and I don't exactly get along—*really*, we *don't*."

"Oh, come now," Cunningham pleaded, "can't you make an exception just this once? I truly, *truly* wish to have you share this with me, so that we can exchange notes afterward. We'll write a monograph together. Think of it as an expedition! You can be Jane Goodall, hidden in the bush, recording the dominance rituals of a tribe of mountain gorillas. This will be a milestone event! As a scholar of religion, won't you someday kick yourself for having taken a pass?"

Helvetica sighed. She could see there was no way to wiggle out of this and remain in Cunningham's good graces. "Well, Cecil, since you put it *that* way ..."

✡ ✡ ✡

The End of Daze

Spanish Plaza, a half-acre square encompassing a large fountain with tile mosaics and a few small sculptures, tucked on the eastern bank of the Mississippi between the Riverwalk Mall and the Canal Street ferry landing, typically hosted more pigeons than people. Today, however, it was a sea of black—black coats, black hats, black beards, black side curls. At separate ends of the square, women danced with women, and men danced raucously with men. Some of the men—and not just the young ones, but a number of the graybeards, too—danced in and out of the fountain, carrying liquor bottles or attempting to balance them on their heads.

"Isn't this simply *marvelous*?" Cunningham exclaimed. "It's like traveling back in time to an eighteenth-century Polish *shtetl*!" He and Helvetica stood at the edge of the crowd, near the entrance to the Riverwalk Mall. "It's as insane as Pledge Week, only gender segregated. You know, Helvetica, I always wondered why you didn't get on better with this crowd. I mean, look over there, all those dozens of women dancing together, and not a male in spitting distance. Why don't you go over and have yourself a good time? Some of the girls are quite lovely. Oh, I forget—you're engaged now. *Bad* Cecil."

Almost before Helvetica had a chance to be offended by Cunningham's teasing, she felt a rough yank on her left arm. She turned, only to be enveloped in a cloud of noxiously astringent breath.

"Ms. Rhinegold!" Rabbi Karnofsky said. "I *thought* I saw you over here! What an unexpected pleasure! How gracious of you to come!"

"Rabbi Karnofsky," Helvetica said, backing away from his fetid breath, "how many times must I ask you to address me by my *proper title*?"

Karnofsky grinned. "Yes, yes, *Rabbi* Rhinegold! I can afford to be magnanimous—the *Moshiach* has finally come! If the lion can lie down with the lamb, why shouldn't there be lady rabbis who preach the supremacy of humanity over God? The old world is turned upside-down! Would you like some *schnapps*?" He offered her his bottle.

"I don't drink," she said coldly.

"But this is a special occasion! Surely, you'll indulge yourself a little? Here, take the bottle, say the blessing with me, and let's toast *Moshiach* together!"

"I told you I *don't* drink," she said. "*Ever.*"

Karnofsky shrugged his shoulders, a hugely exaggerated gesture fit for the heyday of Yiddish theater. "Well, if I can't get you to drink with me, I'll drink *for* you. *L'chiam!*" He lifted his bottle to his lips, not noticing or minding when a trickle of *schnapps* dribbled down into his beard. "You know," he said after a satisfied gasp, "now that you're here, you have to come up on stage with me. You must speak to the crowd, tell them stories of our blessed *Moshiach*. I am privileged to know Jacob Zvi just a little, but you know him far better than I do. You would've seen early evidence that our blessed *Rebbe* had returned in Jacob's flesh, even if you didn't realize it at the time. Tell the people! Tell them stories of the *mitzvot* he fulfilled, of the small miracles of holiness he must've performed in your presence! You are our honored guest! Come! Tell them!"

He grabbed her arm, but she yanked it away. "Oh, no," she said, turning to get away from him. "I'm here strictly to observe—"

Cunningham blocked her attempted getaway. "Helvetica, my dear, you *are* going up to that microphone. I *insist*. Consider that a directive from your department head." He grinned, his eyes twinkling with delighted maliciousness, then pulled his phone from his pocket. "This marvelous little device happens to have a built-in camera, so I'll be capturing every historic second of your oration."

"Then you really *must* speak!" Karnofsky thundered, showering Helvetica with droplets of ninety-proof spittle. "Come! You are our honored guest! We are *delighted* to have you with us! Hundreds of people will want to share *Shabbos* meals with you, once they realize who you are! You won't have to cook for yourself for the next ten years!"

They want an oration? Helvetica thought furiously. *I'll give them an oration. One they won't forget, no matter how disgustingly drunk they are.* She allowed herself to be led up onto the temporary stage which held the microphone. Two huge banners flanked the podium: one of Rabbi Menachem Mendel Schneerson, the other a blown-up photograph of Jacob Zvi on the steps of Beth Judah Synagogue, sourced from the front page of the *New Times-Picayune*.

"My friends!" Karnofsky shouted into the microphone, setting off a storm of sonic feedback. "Honored rabbis and scholars! We are very, *very* blessed to have with us this afternoon a most special guest. My notable colleague from the Tulane University Hillel Center, Rabbi Helvetica Rhinegold." Confused murmurs arose from the men in the crowd. "Yes, yes, she *is* a rabbi! She was ordained in Berkeley, California at the Reconstructionist-Renewalist Seminary. She has published articles in *Tikkun Magazine*." Isolated booing erupted. "No, no booing! We are all *one* people! Now that we have reached the End of Days, and the earthly Kingdom of God and *Moshiach* is upon us. If she says she has studied and earned the title of rabbi, of teacher, we *must* treat her with all the respect and honor we bestow upon any of our own rabbis. Truly! Most importantly, she served as a spiritual guide and friend to our blessed *Moshiach* while he was still hidden, when he was known only by the name Jacob

Zvi. She has joined us here today to share in our joy, to tell us tales of our blessed *Rebbe*'s holiness and good deeds while he was clothed in the flesh and identity of an ordinary Tulane graduate student. Please, *please* join me in offering a warm Chabad welcome to our extraordinary guest, Rabbi Helvetica Rhinegold!"

The audience applauded, those standing in the fountain most warmly and enthusiastically. A chant, begun by the elderly man who had earlier fallen into the water, spread through the crowd: "Friend of *Moshiach*! Friend of *Moshiach*! Speak! *Speak!*"

Helvetica took her place at the microphone. "You all are aware, I'm certain," she said, "that Rabbi Menachem Mendel Schneerson died in June of 1994."

"He did not die!" a young, bespectacled Hasid shouted. "He went into hiding to gather his *Moshiach* powers!"

"He died merely momentarily," the drunk, wet rabbi in the fountain said, gently correcting the other man, "only to be resurrected in the body of the infant Jacob Zvi, you see?"

"I happen to know that Jacob Zvi was *bar mitzvahed* in 2009," Helvetica said, a tight smile on her face. "So your *Rebbe* died when Jacob Zvi was *two years old*." She turned triumphantly to Rabbi Karnofsky. "How do you square *that* with your insistence that Jacob is Rabbi Schneerson reincarnated?"

Karnofsky looked as though she had dumped a barrel of ice water over his head. "Hrrmm ..." he said, fiddling with his luxuriant beard. "Ahh, well ..."

"Rabbi Karnofsky," the older rabbi in the fountain shouted, "the *Shabbos* soul—tell her about the extra soul God provides to the observant on *Shabbos*!"

Karnofsky's face lit up, and he hoisted his bottle of *schnapps* in celebration. "Yes! The *Shabbos* soul! That would explain it! The soul of our blessed *Rebbe* was granted by God to the young Jacob Zvi as an extra soul on the first *Shabbos* following the *Rebbe*'s passing. But rather than departing from Jacob at *Havdalah* time, the way all other *Shabbos* souls depart from the bodies of the living, the soul of the *Rebbe* found fertile, welcoming soil in the young person of Jacob, himself holy but not yet fully formed. And the two souls have co-inhabited the one body ever since! *Yes!* That explains *everything!*"

The crowd cheered, then spontaneously began singing, "*Yechi Adoneinu Moreinu v'Rabbeinu Melech HaMoshiach l'olom vo'ed!*" "Long live our Master, our Teacher, and our Rabbi, King Messiah, for ever and ever!"

"Isn't she *wonderful?*" Rabbi Karnofsky said, waving his bottle above Helvetica's head. "Simply by being here, she inspires theological insights of great profundity! Our honored guest! The brilliant and very beautiful Rabbi Rhinegold!"

He enveloped her in a pungent bear hug.

"Let me *go*," she squealed, struggling against him, "you—you *gorilla!*"

"Ook, ook!" he said. And then, throwing centuries of Hasidic modesty out the window, he kissed her wetly on the lips.

Chapter Eighteen

Jacob tossed in his bed. He dreamed that he was searching the Vietnamese jungle for Marlon Brando in *Apocalypse Now*. They were all around him, the choppers, circling his head like mechanical mosquitos ravenous for his blood, never letting him rest.

He opened his eyes. *Thwap, thwap, thwap, thwap—*

He closed his eyes again. Still *thwap, thwap, thwap, thwap—*

He shoved the damp sheets off his legs and stumbled over to his window. He stared up into the bright sunlight. Helicopters marked with the call letters of various television stations hovered against white clouds. He saw the massed news vans parked on State Street, just beyond the police barricades.

It all came back to him.

"Oh, shit," he said.

"You need to use the toilet? One of those necessities I no longer have to worry about, thank God. I'm glad my damn hemorrhoids got buried with the rest of my G.I. tract," a familiar voice said. Saul's voice. No Saul, though. Just a talking shopping cart that assumed it was Saul.

"I made coffee," Saul said. "Forgive me if I don't join you in a cup. Although I sort of remember what that first cup of coffee tasted like after a decent night's sleep. Now *that* I kind of miss."

"Coffee, or sleep?" Jacob asked, picking sand from his eyes.

"Both."

Jacob scurried to the bathroom. "What's been happening since I keeled over on the steps of Beth Judah?" he called through the open door, standing over the toilet. "And how did I get back here to my apartment?"

"You were lucky enough to fall over into my basket. I carried you back here. Climbing steps isn't easy for me, but it can be done. As for what's been happening? Well, you've accrued a fair bit of notoriety in the last couple of days. The war in the Middle East has collapsed into a stalemate. The Big Guy Upstairs turned off everybody's weapons. Oh, and some other folks have been claiming to be speaking for the Lord, same as you. Not a good idea, as it turns out."

"What about my parents?"

"I checked. They're both safe and accounted for. One of my colleagues dug your mother out from beneath the ruins of her apartment building, but she wasn't hurt. She's already back at the Technion, writing a very popular blog about the new automated factory the resurrectants have built to fabricate cybernetic bodies for more resurrectants. Go ahead, fix yourself a cup of coffee. Your landlord was kind enough to drop off a half gallon of milk. He can't thank you enough for all the business you're bringing in for his bar."

Jacob pulled down a ceramic mug with the image of C.C. Beck's Captain Marvel from his cupboard. *Had Your Morning SHAZAM?* the mug asked. "Did, uh, did God leave any instructions for me?"

"Just be a *mensch*," Saul said. "That's all for now. Don't try to leverage your new popularity on the internet into conquests with nubile little undergraduates. No embarrassing the franchise."

Jacob stirred milk and sugar into his coffee, then took a sip. "Say, this is *great* coffee! SHAZAM!"

"It's impossible to make a bad cup of coffee in New Orleans. Especially when one is capable of precisely matching the appropriate number of coffee grinds to each milliliter of filtered water. Oh, by the way, I set up a press conference for you at Gallier Hall tomorrow with representatives of the world's major faith communities."

Jacob dribbled hot coffee onto his naked toes. "You did *what?*"

"*Someone* has to answer their questions. Would you rather they talk to a grocery cart?"

"Yes, actually!" He grabbed a fistful of paper towels. "Saul, I'm—I'm not *ready!* I haven't taken any classes in religion or theology since right before my *bar mitzvah*, unless you count that elective I took my sophomore year on the pulp fiction roots of Scientology—"

"You experienced the Divine Presence, didn't you? And lived to tell the tale?"

"Well, uh, *yeah* …"

"Well, this will be a hundred million times easier. Even though you don't realize it, you already know the answers to most of the questions they'll ask. And you'll wear a little radio transmitter in your ear, so I can back you up."

"But what if I fall flat on my face? Won't that embarrass, you know, The Boss?"

"Moses had a stutter. He did all right."

"Moses had Aaron, the talker of the family."

"And you've got *me*. Look, it's not like you're going to be interacting with any heavy hitters tomorrow. No

Pope. No Archbishop of Canterbury. No Dali Lama. In baseball terms, the attendees are all strictly Double A. It was the best I could do on short notice. Flight options into Louis Armstrong International Airport leave much to be desired."

Jacob took a steadying sip of the marvelous coffee. "You'll be able to talk to me through an earpiece?"

"It'll be like I'm living in your head, squirt. No worries, *menschik*. None!"

✡ ✡ ✡

Gallier Hall had been New Orleans' seat of government before the current City Hall was built in the 1950s on slum clearance land which had formerly housed Louis Armstrong's childhood neighborhood. It was a stately old Beaux Arts building in the middle of downtown that fronted a small park frequented exclusively by bums and pigeons. Nowadays it was mainly used for the mayor's Carnival parties.

Jacob stood behind a mini lectern at the head of a long conference table. Two dozen religious eminences, male and female, sat around the table: the Archbishop of the Archdiocese of New Orleans; rabbis from five different streams of Judaism, including, Jacob noted, a glaring Rabbi Helvetica Rhinegold; a Sunni imam and a Shiite imam; a lama; a rōshi; a mixed assortment of Protestant Christian ministers and pastors; a swami and a swamini; a Shinto priest; a Bahá'i layman; a Jain sadhvi; a Vodun manbo asogwe; and a Zoroastrian mobad. As many journalists as could fit had been crammed into the far end of the long room or the adjoining hallway.

"Good morning, everyone," Jacob began. "Thanks so much for making time in your busy schedules to come out. I'm Jacob Zvi, official spokesperson for God. I'd like to get to as many of your questions as I possibly can, so I'm going to keep the introductions and ice breakers short—"

The Sunni imam thrust his hand in the air and said, "I object to these proceedings."

"That's, uh, Imam Faisel?" Jacob said, straining to read the man's name card. "What's your objection, sir?"

"There are five Jews at this table. *Six*, if you include yourself. There is but one Muslim—" he stared across the table at his Shiite counterpart; "—and one Muslim *heretic* present. The people of Islam are one billion strong. Of Jews, there are only perhaps thirteen million in all the world. Thus, this convocation is intolerably nonproportionate and therefore illegitimate."

"With all due respect, Imam, we aren't going to be *voting* on anything here today," Jacob said. "This isn't the United Nations General Assembly. I'm just here to answer your questions as lucidly and comprehensively as I can. How about us all keeping things on the informal side? We'll start on my left and go around the table, clockwise. Everybody gets to ask one question. Then, when you've all had a chance to participate, we'll go around the table again, until you run out of questions or it's time to break for lunch. Oh, just as a reminder, the bathrooms are down the hall. And over by the window, the good people from Café du Monde have been kind enough to set out coffee urns and some trays of fresh *beignets*. So please, help yourselves. Nosh, nosh, everyone.

"Now, let's move on to the first question. Rinpoche, uh, Prawni, would you like to get us rolling?"

The lama, originally from Tibet but more recently hailing from Eugene, Oregon, smiled and nodded. "Given that you have not suffered the fate of the Elders—"

"The Elders?"

"Yes. Have you not heard? President Jimmy Carter,

Mary Robinson, and Gro Harlem Brundtland?"

"Uh, what about them?"

"They were in Havana, speaking out against the American economic embargo. In the presence of Raoul Castro, the three of them claimed to be speaking in the name of God. Ms. Robinson and Ms. Brundtland were transformed into pillars of salt. President Carter was transformed into a pillar of salted peanuts."

"Oh."

"Given that you have not suffered a similar fate, we must assume your credentials are more in order," Rinpoche Prawni said. "Are you the Jewish messiah and savior?"

"No. I'm not," Jacob said. "The messiah, according to Jewish tradition, is a military and political leader who will lead all the world's Jews back to the Holy Land and who will rebuild the Jewish Temple." He had more to say about the Temple, but he decided to save it until the end of the Q&A session. "I'm not him. Next question?"

Rabbi David Moskowitz, Associate Dean of the Jewish Theological Seminary in Los Angeles, stood. "Given your surname, 'Zvi,' are you a *false* messiah?"

Jacob rolled his eyes. "*No. I'm not a messiah real or false." Way to waste your first question, Rabbi.* "Can we get away from this whole issue of me being a messiah, please? *I'm* not the issue here. I'm just God's spokesperson. Think of me as the press secretary, that's all. Just an ordinary schlub trying to get through his workday, the same as any of you. Next question? Rabbi Karnofsky?"

The bearish Chabad rabbi looked somewhat abashed. "So I suppose I'm not allowed to ask whether you house the soul of the blessed *Rebbe* Schneerson?"

"Not unless you want to waste a question. Do you have any non-*Moshiach*-related questions to ask me?"

"Okay. What's with all the robots?"

"All *right*. There's a very pertinent question. Thank you, Rabbi. The 'deal' with the robots is that they house the souls of the righteous dead, who have now returned to Earth. By the way, just so you know, their preferred term for themselves isn't 'robots'—it's 'cybernetic persons.' Prior to our technology advancing to the point where we managed to create cybernetic bodies sophisticated enough to house their souls, which, of course, occurred extremely recently, God stored the souls of the righteous dead deep within the Earth's crust, within a space Jewish theologians would call '*Sheol*' and Christian theologians might call 'Purgatory' and others might call 'limbo.' Since the cybernetic bodies can be continually improved, as I'm told they regularly are, or can be replaced if critically damaged or destroyed, the resurrectants are, in essence, immortal. Additional cybernetic bodies will continue to be produced until all of the righteous dead have been drawn forth from *Sheol*."

"May I ask a follow-up question?" Rabbi Karnofsky said.

"Uh, yeah, I guess so." Jacob squirmed, hating to break his own rules so soon. "Just keep it to one, though, okay?"

"Who are these 'righteous dead?' Are they only Jews, or did some of them adhere to other faiths? What is the applicable definition of 'righteous' that governs who comes back in a robot, uh, *cybernetic* body?"

"Actually, that's *three* follow-up questions," Jacob said, "but since they're closely related, I'll answer them all at the same time. The righteous dead are the righteous of *all* nations. The Jewish righteous are those who lived by the commandments of Torah, exclusive of those commandments that could not be observed due to the Temple's destruction—"

"*Bingo!*" Rabbi Karnofsky trumpeted, smiling

triumphantly at the liberal, non-Halachic rabbis at the table.

"*Or,*" Jacob continued, motioning for Karnofsky to be silent, "those Jews who sincerely repented their lack of adherence to the Torah's commandments during the Yom Kippur prior to their deaths and made amends. The righteous of other nations are those who faithfully observed the six Noachide Laws, those commandments which were given to Noah and his family after the Flood. For those of you who may not be familiar with the Noachide Laws, I'll paraphrase them. One: no idolatry or polytheism. The righteous dead worshipped only one God."

The swami and the swamini groaned in unison. The manbo asogwe sighed, shrugged her shoulders, then took a bite of a *beignet.*

"Two: no murder," Jacob continued. "Three: no stealing. Four: no fornication, which means no adultery, incest, or bestiality. Five: no blaspheming God's name. And, last but not least, six: no eating the flesh of an animal while the animal is still alive."

"What about the *seventh* Noachide Law?" Rabbi Karnofsky said. "The commandment to set up a court of law to adjudicate the first six Noachide Laws?"

"That wasn't a law given to Noah," Jacob said. "It was given later, to Ya'acob, or Jacob, so it doesn't apply to the entirety of humankind."

"*No,* it was given to *Noah.*"

"*No,* it was given to *Ya'acob.*"

"But *Rambam* says—"

"Don't argue with me, Rabbi Karnofsky. You may've gotten your information from the *Rambam,* but I got my information from the *Source,* okay? You're being rude to the other participants, so I'll have to ask you to forfeit your next turn at asking a question." He turned his attention to the next dignitary sitting at the table.

"Archbishop Shulteen, I'm so glad you were able to come. I heard you give a talk at Loyola once and I was very impressed. Do you have something you'd like to ask me?"

"I most certainly do, young man," the Archbishop said. "Assuming everything you've said thus far is true—which I'm not ready to concede, mind you—how does that first Noachide Law, the one which prohibits idolatry or polytheism, relate to the Christian tenet of the Trinity? Will devout Catholics be counted among your 'righteous dead?'"

"Errr, that's a tough one," Jacob said. "Saul," he whispered, "give me some backup here?"

"Who's Saul?" Rabbi Moskowitz asked.

"Saul Tannenburg," Jacob answered, "one of the resurrectants. Since he's got a more direct line to God than I do, I've asked him to help me out with some of your questions."

"So why isn't this Saul here, if *he's* the one with the answers?"

"Well, God feels it's best for you all to converse with a fellow human being. Nobody would pay me any mind if Saul were here, believe me. I mean, if *I* had a choice who to pay attention to—some schmuck in a toga and turban, or a talking shopping cart—I know who *I'd* be listening to."

He listened to Saul's answer in his ear.

"Okay, Your Eminence, here's the deal," he said to the Archbishop. "Unfortunately, it's not that straightforward. It gets decided on a case-by-case basis, depending on the individual Catholic's personal understanding of the concept of the Trinity. If he or she thought of the Father, the Son, and the Holy Spirit as three faces or aspects of the same Person, he or she probably squeezes under the limbo stick and is good to go—assuming lifetime compliance with the other five

Noachide Laws, of course. If the departed considered them distinct Divine Persons, however, then, uh, no. Devotion to the saints can also muddy the waters, depending on whether or not the departed considered them junior deities. In case you need to question me further on this—and I imagine you do—I'll give you my new, encrypted email account after the meeting. For now, let's move on to the next question. Rinpoche Asama?"

"What about Buddhists?" the lama asked. "We are not polytheists."

"Yes, that's true, but the fly in the ointment is that you aren't *theists*, either. The first Noachide Law has both a negative component—a prohibition against idolatry and polytheism—*and* a positive component— an injunction that the individual acknowledge the authority of a sole, single God. So, I'm afraid the bad news is that no Buddhists will be resurrected into cybernetic bodies. But the *good* news is—the Wheel of Karma is broken! All Buddhists achieve nirvana upon death. Hindus, too, Swami and Swamini! I hope that clears matters up. Let's move on to the next question. Dastoorji Achmenhanjod?"

The bearded dastoor cleared his throat. "Dare I ask whether Zoroastrians are included within your charmed circle?"

"Ooooh," Jacob winced. "Close, but no cigar. I'm sorry about that. Just one deity too many. Next question? Manbo Asogwe Lumierre?"

"Pass," the Voudun priestess said.

"You're sure? Well, okay, then. We'll move on. Pastor Fitcher?"

The Lutheran minister rose from her chair. "I suppose it falls to me to ask about the elephant in the middle of the room," she said. "Is—is Jesus Christ the Son of God? Did His death on the cross redeem all of humanity from sin?"

I just knew *somebody was going to ask that*, Jacob thought. "Jesus ... well, he was a nice Jewish boy, a *mensch.* Jesus of Nazareth was the son of God, I suppose, in the same way that all men are the sons of God. He was a terrific rabbi and teacher—all of his students gave him top ratings, and many of them went on to very impressive careers themselves. What better mark of a good teacher can there be? Indirectly, at least, he got the whole Roman Empire to give up paganism, so that's a big feather in his cap. As for his death on the cross— Uh, over the past two thousand years, his example of self-sacrifice has inspired millions of people to live lives of increased goodness, and I'd have to say that's nothing to sneeze at." He paused while Saul whispered something into his ear. "Oh! I've got some terrific news for you! This should brighten your morning. Sometime in the next few days, Jesus—I believe he goes by 'Yeshua,' actually—will return from *Sheol* in a cybernetic body that's being built in Haifa, Israel. So you should be able to address all your questions directly to him, very soon. In the meantime, let's move on to Imam Faisel's question."

"So the Prophet Issa shall soon return to Earth," the imam said. "All fine and good. But what of the greatest Prophet of them all? When may we expect the return of the Prophet Muhammed, may peace and blessings be upon him?"

"Hold on, sir," Jacob said, "and I'll check with my source." He turned away from the podium's microphone. "Saul, did you get that?" he whispered. "Any way you can check for me on the Muhammed situation?"

He and the entire room waited expectantly for a moment.

"Sorry," Jacob said; "I guess even in this age of

computers, it still takes God a minute or two to check His files. Hold on—what's that? No news on Muhammed? Can you check again? Ask if there's some kind of a hold up? Is he stuck in a line somewhere?"

They waited another moment.

"Uh, Imam Faisel?" Jacob said.

"Yes?"

"I'm afraid you aren't going to like this. I'm told that Muhammed's soul wasn't stored in *Sheol*. So he won't be coming back. I'm, uh, really sorry."

"You lie."

"Come again?"

"I *said*, 'you lie.'"

"What reason would I have to lie to you?"

"Jews lie."

Jacob felt himself flush. "Mister, *everybody* lies, at least sometimes, so it's a good thing a prohibition against lying isn't one of the Noachide Laws. But I don't have any *reason* to lie to you about this. Heck, I'd *love* it if Muhammed were to come back. After fifteen hundred years of cooling his heels in *Sheol*, I'm sure he'd tell all his followers to just *chill*. I mean, look at it this way. You Muslims are sitting pretty when it comes to this resurrection thing. You've got a *much* easier row to hoe than Jews do, with only six laws to stick to, not six hundred and thirteen. You don't have the Christians' problem with the Trinity. You're theists, unlike Buddhists, and monotheists, unlike Hindus and Zoroastrians. You're pretty much on top of the world, as far as the End of Days goes. Stay away from the murder, the stealing, and the sheep screwing, and you're golden."

"*Why* was the Prophet Muhammed, may peace and blessings be upon him, *not* counted among the righteous?"

"I don't care to speculate about that."

"This is a blasphemous slander! May your tongue be cut out and fed to dogs! I will hear an *answer* from your filthy Jew lips, you son of pigs and monkeys!"

Jacob—follow your own advice and chill. *Sub-zero, boychik,* Saul whispered into his ear.

Jacob didn't want to listen. But he forced himself to. "Next question," he muttered into the microphone. "Rabbi Rhinegold?"

"Where has God *been* all this time?" Helvetica asked. "Where was She during the Holocaust?"

Thanks, Helvetica, Jacob thought. *I knew I could count on you to lob me a softball. Thanks. A lot.* "Uh, there are a *lot* of worlds out there with intelligent life. Millions of them, I'm told. Maybe *billions.* God has needed to tend to all of them, from time to time, just like He did for us during the centuries described in the Torah. That's a lot of jumping around."

"She's omnipotent, isn't She? Can't She be all places at once?"

"I suppose He could be, if He wanted to be. Maybe He doesn't want to be. I'm indulging in a little educated speculation here, but I think He wanted to see how we would handle things on our own. And while He was away, we screwed up. Big time. At least a lot of us did."

"The Holocaust was a lot more than just 'screwing up,' Jacob! What kind of God would have allowed *children* to burn in crematoria, if She could have stopped it as easily as She stopped the Israelis and Pakistanis from slaughtering each other a few days ago? For that matter, what kind of a God would've allowed an atom bomb to detonate in Jerusalem?"

"We aren't God's toys, Helvetica. We have free will. I know that for certain now. We did those horrible things to ourselves, of our own free will."

"But this God you speak for could have *stopped* it. She could have stopped it *all,* the suffering of every single child who ever died of malnutrition or abuse. She *didn't*. In my eyes, that makes your God a *monster*."

Several of the clergy persons around the table gasped. All eyes focused on Helvetica, their possessors expecting her to be transformed into a pillar of salt. Helvetica herself closed her eyes tightly, flinching from whatever retribution might come. The whole room resumed breathing when nothing happened.

"I guess in your eyes," Jacob said, "God is a monster. You're entitled to your viewpoint. But Rabbi, maybe it doesn't *matter* what you think of God. I—I got a peek at an infinitesimal particle of His Mind. And I was utterly overwhelmed. I slept for two days straight afterward, because my consciousness retreated into its shell. The resurrectants can interact with Him much more freely than I can, but even they can only handle interfacing with a gloss on a gloss of His Mind, a modulated refraction of a distant glow—sort of how our eyes can only handle staring at a solar eclipse when its image is projected through a telescope's lens onto a piece of cardboard. Whatever you think of Him, He created us. We owe Him our existence. And He's back. Back here, on Earth, among us. For how long, I don't know. But we have to reconcile ourselves to His presence. We can't just go on like we were before His return."

"But I *refuse* to acknowledge the universal sovereignty of a moral *monster*—"

Rinpoche Asama, a stricken look on his face, thrust his hand into the air. "Really, Mr. Zvi," he protested, "you are letting this discussion get entirely out of hand. The rabbi is speaking out of turn, and you do nothing—"

"You're absolutely right, Your Holiness," Jacob said. "Helvetica, I have to ask you to *pipe down*. We'll continue this another time." He turned to the other participants sitting around the table. "I need to apologize to you all. I set the ground rules for this meeting, and then I let Rabbi Rhinegold monopolize me. Helvetica's a friend … Up until a few days ago, we had these sorts of discussions pretty frequently. I kind of let myself fall into the role of a graduate student again. Again, I'm sorry. Who's next?" He focused on the short, bald Japanese man sitting to Helvetica's left. "Sensei Takei?"

The Shinto priest rose and bowed. "Thank you. We Japanese have always felt great reverence for our ancestors, so I find myself most interested in those whom you call the resurrectants or cybernetic persons. You say they are potentially immortal. For what purpose have they returned to Earth? From following the news, I see that many of them are active in the bombed portion of Jerusalem or appear to be heading there. Oh, as a citizen of the only other country to have suffered atomic bombings, I wish to express my condolences to those at this table who lost family or co-religionists in that recent, most terrible tragedy." He nodded to the imams and rabbis, then sat back down.

"Saul," Jacob said, "you should have some insider dope on that. You care to comment? After you cybernetic folks help out the wounded in Jerusalem, are you all going to Disney World, or what?"

Tell them about the Temple, Saul said.

"Do I *have* to?" Jacob whispered. "Now? They're all still pretty riled up from the imam's and Helvetica's comments—"

It'll become obvious to everyone pretty soon, Saul said. *So they might as well hear it from you first.*

Jacob sighed. "I don't know what their ultimate purpose on Earth is, Sensei. I'm not sure *they* know yet. But there's one project they're working on that, uh, that you all really need to know about. Because it's going to ruffle a few feathers. The resurrectants—now that the Temple Mount is bare of any buildings— they're going to begin rebuilding Solomon's Temple."

"This—this means *jihad!*" Imam Faisel shouted.

"Global jihad!" Imam Wasa'eeb added, his face fire engine red. "The robots are built with U.S. military funding—this is an American-Zionist conspiracy! Streets from Jakarta to Dearborn will run crimson with the blood of infidels!"

The room erupted into pandemonium. Reporters fell over each other trying to stick their microphones into the face of one of the imams or rabbis.

Jacob felt something striving to breach the surface of his subconscious. Something big and gray, as terrifying as a hundred-foot shark from a primordial sea, yet achingly sad. He had something else to tell these people. Something he'd learned when he'd opened the ark's curtain at Beth Judah, something he'd nearly blocked from his mind.

"Everyone!" he shouted into the microphone. "Everyone shut up and listen to me! *Listen!*"

Amazingly, the plaintive note of his plea cut through the room's overheated emotions and drew attention back to the podium. "This—this is more significant than Solomon's Temple. I need to tell you all something. I need to tell the whole world something. It—us, all of us—it's—we're *over*. No more babies. As of the night of God's return to Earth, people lost the ability—they lost—we … we can't conceive *babies* anymore. The last children the world will ever see will be born a little less than nine months from now.

"We're truly living through the End of Days."

Andrew Fox

PART FOUR

Chapter Nineteen

News of the rebuilding of Solomon's Temple hit the global cable channels by that evening. Riots broke out in Cairo, Ankara, Karachi, Islamabad, and Amman, as well as in Muslim neighborhoods of London, Amsterdam, Paris, Malvo, and Dearborn. Automotive industries benefitted from temporary boosts when tens of thousands of cars were set on fire, although the stock valuations of insurance agencies fell through the floor. Guns, when trained on people, failed to fire, but riot police found that teargas canisters and other chemical dispersants worked normally. A global network of Islamicists organized a worldwide march on Jerusalem to prevent the desecration of the grounds of the Noble Sanctuary by the infidel American-Zionist robot conspiracy.

At the same time, fertility researchers around the globe investigated Jacob Zvi's claim that all of humanity was now sterile. They found that, on average, men's sperm counts had diminished to less than five percent of recently measured epidemiological averages. In controlled studies, women's reproductive tracts were discovered to react to infusions of spermatozoa as they would to invasive bacteria, unleashing the full fury of the body's autoimmune systems. Even fully separated from their host organisms, in the sterile environs of a petri dish, human eggs were found to be newly impenetrable to the best efforts of the most vigorous, healthy sperm, even thawed sperm which had been donated prior to the events in New Orleans.

In a few select test markets, manna began fluttering to the ground from unseen sources in the heavens, appearing on lawns and fields every morning with the dew.

✡ ✡ ✡

Reflecting on his performance at the question and answer session, Jacob found himself engulfed in a miasma of self-recriminations. He couldn't escape the awful certainty that he'd totally screwed up the most important job he'd ever been tasked with.

"Saul, you know what it felt like?" he asked. "It felt like standing in front of an assembly of kindergartners, innocent little kids all full of hope, and making them watch snuff videos featuring Santa Claus, the Tooth Fairy, and the Easter Bunny getting their brains blown out. *Worse*. I threw Jesus, Muhammad, and Buddha under the bus. Didn't I just yank away billions of human beings' reason to live?"

He forced himself to walk faster; he pushed Saul along the sidewalk at an almost jogging pace. Exiled from his apartment while a crew of resurrectants moved his possessions from the apartment on Tchoupitoulas Street to newly constructed quarters adjacent to Beth Judah, he'd decided to take a walk. A long walk. He needed to get away from priestly robes and television and the internet, anything that smacked of the divine invasion; with the exception of Saul, whose odd but familiar companionship he found soothing.

"You did what you had to do," Saul said, his

wheels bouncing across broken sections of sidewalk. "Sometimes the truth hurts."

"That's supposed to make me feel better? What if my words lead to thousands of suicides? *Millions* of suicides?"

"Not your responsibility. If people choose to commit murder—and suicide is a form of murder, self-murder, a breaking of the Noachide Laws—then they won't get to participate in the Second Life."

"You sound like that's just fine with you," Jacob said. "Is it?"

"Whether it's fine with me or not makes no difference," Saul said. "I can't *do* anything about it. Why perturb myself with the actions and choices of people I can't change? When you someday move on to your Second Life, your perceptions will alter. You'll see."

"Who knows if I'll ever get there? Maybe my soul won't be worthy of being preserved in *Sheol*, and I'll disappear into nothingness."

His *hijab* made the back of his neck itch. Saul had suggested that he wear a *hijab* and *niqab* combo as a disguise; otherwise, he would have to be accompanied by a full retinue of resurrectant bodyguards. Jacob hadn't wanted to make a fuss in public. He'd just wanted to get some air, to pretend for a few hours that he was still a footloose graduate student (even though staring through the eye slits of the *niqab* made this a difficult fantasy to pull off). He imagined how hard his old business partner Yishmael Hashmed would guffaw if he could see Jacob in this getup, dressed for his very own session of dhimmitude porn.

He hadn't visited the Mid-City district near Bayou St. John in months. He'd wanted to see how City Park and the gracious old Creole neighborhoods along North Carrollton Avenue and Esplanade Avenue were rebounding from their flooding after the big storm. This had always been one of his favorite parts of the city.

A large tract on the west side of North Carrollton Avenue, home to a Ford dealership prior to the storm, now housed a collection of big box stores: a Babies 'R' Us, a Trader Joe's, and a partially completed Target. Although the Babies 'R' Us store was no more than six months old, workers had hung large "Liquidation Sale" and "Going Out of Business" banners along its facade.

"Man, that didn't take long, did it?" Jacob said, slowing his pace as he stared at the signs.

"They're a big player in the baby business," Saul said. "I'd say they're jumping the gun a bit with their 'Going Out of Business' sale, though. They won't close their doors for another eighteen months, not until they've milked their customers for all their worth."

A month ago, Jacob would've been amused by such a cynical take on American capitalism. Now, hearing it just made him sad. He suddenly felt the need to stare at rows and rows of cribs and strollers, soon to become the artifacts of a vanished civilization.

He steered Saul toward the store's entrance. A grassy median strip lined with lamp posts and flower beds divided the large parking lot in half. Jacob noticed a group of rather hairy men and women sitting on the grass in a long oval, playing drums held between their knees or recorders or pan flutes. Had the owners of the Babies 'R' Us store hired musicians to help advertise their big liquidation sale? The group sounded like a Central American folk band of the sort that might play at the Jazz Fest's Children's Tent in a mostly empty hour, when the Neville Brothers were playing one of the big stages and sucking up all the crowds. Only this band wasn't nearly good enough to rate an invitation to Jazz Fest.

Seeing him approach, one of the drummers, a scraggly bearded man in his mid-fifties, wearing sandals, baggy pink shorts, and a hemp shirt, stood and walked toward him.

"Hey, miss," the drummer said, "we're celebrating free love. Love's free now, 'cause you don't have to pay for no condoms or birth control pills. You can screw all you want, and you don't have to worry about messin' up the *environment*, y'know? Never thought I'd say this, but 'praise the Lord!' No more little rug rats pumping the atmosphere full of greenhouse gases and meltin' the polar ice caps—the polar bears can't celebrate, so we're celebratin' for them! We're, like, holdin' a wake for this baby store."

He shoved a pair of pamphlets into Jacob's hands. Jacob saw that they were from Greenpeace and the Campaign for Zero Population Growth.

"Hey, I'm real sorry about Jerusalem, miss," the drummer said. "That was a real bummer. Try and have a nice day anyway, okay?"

Jacob stood in the middle of the mostly empty parking lot and watched the drummer walk back toward his friends. He let the pamphlets drop to the asphalt.

If I were a real prophet, he thought, *an Old Testament prophet like Amos or Micah, I'd give these hippy dipshits a piece of my mind. I'd call the wrath of God down on them for celebrating the end of us. Dipshits.*

But he didn't do anything. He didn't say anything. What could he say? It was God's Will. All of this was God's Will. Even the hippies.

✡ ✡ ✡

Hundreds of ships disgorged their passengers in the Mediterranean ports of Egypt and Lebanon. Tens of thousands of seaborne *jihadis* from Pakistan, India, Turkey, and Malaysia joined hundreds of thousands of equally angry militants who had begun their pilgrimages overland from Syria, Egypt, Jordan, Iran, Iraq, Saudi Arabia, the Gulf Emirates, or the Palestinian Territories. This motley army of the aggrieved crossed deserts and mountain ranges, in Toyota pickups and ancient school buses, on camelback or on foot, converging on Jerusalem from all points of the compass.

Manna did not fall from the skies above their paths. They carried their own food and water with them in a massive motorized supply train (for the Gulf Emirate and Saudi *jihadis*) or on packs loaded onto their animals and their own backs (for everyone else).

Their water supplies were the first thing to go wrong. When they were a hundred miles outside the bomb-flattened gates of the nuked Old City, the pilgrims discovered that their portable water supplies had uniformly taken on an ominous red color. When they sought replacement supplies, all water that they purchased or attempted to access immediately took on the same crimson cast. It smelled of iron and was undrinkable.

The *jihadis* who pressed on discovered further obstacles. When they had advanced within ninety miles of Jerusalem, those pilgrims who were near a body of water found themselves assaulted by hordes of frogs. Those who were surrounded by desert sands or mountain scrub were attacked by fierce clouds of biting gnats.

Some brushed aside the frogs or hid inside their vehicles from the gnats. When they had traveled another ten miles, their convoys were battered by hordes of wild beasts, enraged cattle and desert antelopes who rammed the pickup trucks, school buses, and luxury coaches. Those *jihadis* who traveled on or with animals soon found themselves bereft, as the creatures succumbed to a virulent and highly contagious pestilence. The pestilence, which the travelers carried with them, failed to endear them to the villagers and desert nomads among whom they passed. The locals found ways to make their displeasure known.

Another ten miles on, the remaining die-hards, a fast-diminishing group, found themselves afflicted with painful and pustule boils. The windshields of their trucks and buses were smashed by hailstones the size of baseballs. More than one vehicle, when struck in the gas tank or engine by a sizzling chunk of hail, exploded into a fireball which illuminated the nighttime desert.

Only the truly fanatical, fewer than two hundred of the hundreds of thousands who had begun the march, struggled to continue on to Jerusalem on foot. They were struck with a discerning darkness, a blindness which masked their eyes only when they faced toward Jerusalem. Locusts accompanied the darkness, locusts which crawled inside clothing, inside ears, inside nostrils and mouths. Many of the blinded men were driven insane by writhing, crawling *burkas* of hungry insects they could not see, living shrouds of bugs which feasted on the bloody discharges oozing from the men's omnipresent boils.

Not one man pressed forward to test his fortitude and luck against the tenth deterrent. For not a one of the hundreds of thousands of would-be *jihadis* could now deny that the God of Israel would flinch from wielding that final, terrible sword against any invader so foolhardy as to assail the rebuilding of God's Temple.

Chapter Twenty

"Hell, no! We won't PRAY!
"Not to a God who curses GAYS!
"Go back to Heaven! Let us be FREE!
"We're proud to be L-G-B-T!"

Jacob had been forced to listen to the chants outside the windows of his new domicile for the past hour. About a hundred lesbian, gay, bisexual, and transgendered activists filled the block of Baronne Street in front of Beth Judah, kept away from the synagogue and its attached apartment by a cordon of resurrectants.

He'd been trying to finish his exegesis of Mort Weisinger's mid-century Superman stories in *Action Comics* and *Superman Comics*, teasing out the parallels between incidents discussed in the Talmud and Gemera and Superman's doomed romance with mermaid Lori Lemaris, as well as his attempts to make sense of the backwards logic of Bizarro World. The exegesis had been flowing in surges of insight like sheets of lightning, but then the noise made more writing impossible. Frustrated, he peeked out the window and saw Rabbi Helvetica and Wyonna among the protesters.

"I'm going to go out there and talk to them," Jacob

said.

"Good for you. That's the right thing to do," his visitor, a resurrectant wearing a *yarmulke* and a humble *tallis,* said from his seat in the breakfast nook. "I'll make some fresh coffee in the meantime."

Jacob stepped out onto his porch. An early fall breeze insinuated itself between his linen tunic and bare skin, bringing him to the brink of a shiver. "Maybe you don't realize this," he said to the crowd, "but most of you don't have any reason to be out here protesting."

"What do you mean, you Repressive Clerical Fascist?" a man shouted from the crowd.

"You're protesting the rules for who gets to partake in the Second Life, aren't you?" Jacob asked.

"That's right! It's an act of *genocide* that there aren't any LGBT robots!"

"How do you know there aren't? Have you spoken with every single one of them? There are close to a million of them now."

"What are you talking about? There aren't any *gay* robots!"

"I'm talking about the Noachide Laws," Jacob said. "Fornication is prohibited. But the definition of 'fornication' which applied in Noah's day only covered incest, adultery, and bestiality. *Sodomy* hadn't been invented yet. That came later, after Sodom and Gomorrah had been founded. So if you're a non-Jewish LGBT person and you abide by the six Noachide Laws, your sexual practices won't keep you from partaking in the Second Life. There are *plenty* of resurrectants who were LGBT in their former lives. Now I'll admit, things get harder if you're Jewish—sodomy *is* prohibited under the laws of the Torah. But you can still partake in the Second Life if you repent your sodomy on Yom Kippur and then stay celibate for the remainder of your first life. Difficult, maybe, but not impossible."

"Oh," the man said. "Thanks for clearing that up."

Ninety percent of the protesters began packing their signs and folding their banners.

"Hey, where's everyone *going?*" a man wearing a pink *yarmulke* asked.

"You're on your own, dude," the man who had questioned Jacob said.

Jacob waited until the crowd dispersed and only Helvetica and Wyonna stood facing him. "You two want to come in and have a cup of coffee?" he asked.

Helvetica scowled. "The High Priest is willing to mingle with us peons?"

"You're not peons."

"You said at the press conference that we'd continue our discussion at another time."

"This is another time," Jacob said. "I'm all yours. Come on in."

He led them into his apartment. Saul rolled toward them. "Anyone want a cup of coffee?" the shopping cart asked.

"I'll take one, thanks," Wyonna said.

"Hi, Mom," Saul said to Wyonna. "Good to see you. You been feeling okay? Caffeine won't upset your system? You want some manna French toast to go with the java, maybe?"

"I'm—I've been fine," Wyonna said, blushing. "Coffee is just *fine*. That's all I want, thank you."

"Sorry the kitchen table's a little crowded," Jacob said. "I've gotten into the habit of using it as my desk." He shoved his laptop and a pile of old comic books off to the side. "Sit down."

"Your little speech outside just now doesn't get you off the hook," Helvetica said. "What about all the LGBT Jews throughout history who never got the chance to hear your paean to celibacy? You mean to tell me the ranks of the Second Lifers will be devoid of a philosopher like Ludwig Wittgenstein? How about musicians of the caliber of Leonard Bernstein, Aaron Copland, and Stephen Sondheim—won't the World to Come suffer from a lack of their talents? And what about writers like Susan Sontag and Marcel Proust—"

"*Proust* was *Jewish?*"

"He had a Jewish mother. But tell me, how is it fair to deny such people a Second Life, simply because of a quirk of their biology? For that matter, can you countenance the exclusion of non-religious Jews like Jonas Salk and Albert Einstein? If *anyone* deserves to live again, wouldn't it be those two?"

"I didn't make up the rules, Helvetica."

"But you serve a God who *did* make up the rules. The fact that She would exclude such persons as Salk and Einstein, simply for their adherence to their own consciences—what does that *say* about this God who had you blithely announce the end of human civilization?"

Jacob warmed his hands on his coffee mug. "You can't tell me God didn't spend most of His first interval on Earth warning people of the consequences for not listening to Him. Didn't He say 'This day I set before you Life and Death—'"

"'So choose Life'—yes. You don't need to quote Torah to me, Jacob."

"Well? I mean, if people are told they stand to collect a reward should they follow certain rules, but then they choose not to follow those rules, is it *unjust* for them to then not receive the reward? Failing to be given a reward is not the same as punishment. People who failed to follow the rules haven't been plunging into an eternity of hellfire upon dying—they simply didn't have their soul preserved in *Sheol*, awaiting the day a new, more permanent body could be provided for it."

"But divine justice must be tempered by divine

mercy," Helvetica insisted. "Wouldn't a *true* God take human weakness and fallibility into account when applying Her rules? And if your God sitting next door has always demanded so much from the Jewish People, if they have always been so precious to Her, Her Chosen People—then isn't it perverse of Her to make it hundreds of times more difficult and complex for a Jew to be preserved in *Sheol* than a non-Jew?"

"That's why He gave the Jews Yom Kippur," Jacob said.

"Why must you constantly *defend* Her?" Helvetica asked, her thin eyebrows arching. "Where's the critical thinker I remember from only a month ago? Did your capacity for independent thought vanish the moment you put on that turban? Aren't you at least a little *perturbed* that She's made each and every one of us *sterile?* Wouldn't you classify that as a profoundly *hostile* act, more appropriate for a malign alien super-intelligence, afraid of competition, than a supposedly loving God?"

"Helvetica, this isn't the Loving Daddy God you and I prayed to as kids, the one we imagined tucking us in at night. It's not a Loving Mommy Goddess, either. I know—I experienced a tiny particle of His Essence. This is Job's God, the inexplicable God, the God that is *way* beyond our understanding."

"But haven't we moved far *past* that version of God? Doesn't God evolve, the same way our moral sensibilities have evolved?"

"God is eternal. God doesn't need to evolve."

"Then what has the purpose of *our* evolution been, if not to provide us with a reflection of divine evolution? Aren't we created in Her image? Why should the God of the twenty-first century of the Common Era apply Her justice with the same archaic inflexibility of the God of the Bronze Age?"

"It's not all about *us*. If we can be said to be a dim reflection of Him, *He* certainly isn't a reflection of *us*. We aren't the center of God's universe. Yes, compared with our companion life forms on Earth, we're special, with our self-awareness and our ability to reason. But we're only one out of millions and millions of species throughout the universe who have been granted those gifts. You simply can't figure out God by making references to human beings, making analogies and then scaling things up. Given the almost unbridgeable gulf between the human and the Divine, any system of divine justice, if scaled down to human terms, would seem obscene to you. God's justice isn't meant for us. It's meant for Him."

A small smile, quick as the flick of a lizard's tongue, broke through the otherwise inflexible intensity of Helvetica's expression. "Since when are you a philosopher? You collect stolen shopping carts for a living, Jacob."

"Hey, *I* wasn't stolen," Saul said.

"You must admit," Helvetica continued, "it would be far better for humanity if your God would direct Her attentions to one of the other millions of intelligent species you say are out there in space, and leave us alone for the nonce."

Wyonna glanced fearfully at Saul and at the stranger sitting at the breakfast nook, who now paid the conversation keen attention. "Darling," she said, taking Helvetica's hand protectively in hers, "I think—I think you've made your point. Maybe you shouldn't, uh, push things? Remember what happened to President Carter? Maybe we should just be on our way—"

"I'm not *done*," Helvetica said, freeing her hand. "Jacob, let's engage in a little thought experiment. Let's say the being next door isn't really God at all. Let's say, for the purpose of argument, that it is actually an otherworldly intelligence, non-divine but so far beyond us as to *seem* divine. Let's say it needs servitors capable of existing and working in environments far different from Earth's. It wants to gather those servitors with as little resistance as possible and ensure their complete loyalty and obedience. Wouldn't it make perfect sense for it to probe our records and perhaps our minds for our oldest myths, then cloak itself in the stuff of those myths and assume the identity of our Creator?"

"But your argument works against itself," the bearded stranger said from the breakfast nook. "Assuming all that you have just said, wouldn't the other-worldly invader have chosen to cloak itself in the identity of the God Figure of one of the other two Abrahamic religions, both of which are far more widespread than the faith of the Jews? Would this not make for less conflict and resistance?"

Helvetica glanced sharply at the stranger but quickly returned her attention to Jacob. "I want to hear Jacob's answer," she said. "I want to hear why he has chosen to serve the being who resides next door. If, indeed, he has made a *choice* at all."

"I'm not being mind-controlled," Jacob said, "if that's what you're implying. If you choose to believe that the Being-Next-Door puts words in my mouth like some divine ventriloquist, I guess there's nothing I can say that'll shake that. But when I parted the ark's curtain in Beth Judah, I met our Creator. I'm *sure* of that. I saw things—I looked through an infinite spyglass and experienced the unfolding of our species' birth, the way the biological and the spiritual intertwine in us like the two strands of our DNA. And I had a vision, an intimation of my ancestry, all the way back through pre-humans and through early mammals and amphibians and fish to the first single-celled life forms. It was like receiving the ultimate secret Masonic handshake. Even if you're partly right, and our Creator isn't the Prime Mover, He *is* the source of *us*."

"And so She is allowed to *uncreate* us?" Helvetica said. "Even after learning that She will snuff our species out like a candle, you still willingly place Her turban on your head? What a sad comedown you are from Abraham—four thousand years ago, *he* was willing to argue with God, *he* tried to nail God to a bargain which would have spared the lives of hundreds of thousands of sinners in Sodom and Gomorrah if only ten righteous souls could be found. What have *you* tried to do for us?'"

"What I think is the right thing, Helvetica. I was asked—no, *commanded*—to act as an intermediary between God and humanity. I suppose, like Jonah, I could've tried running away from God's commandment to serve. But honestly, I couldn't think of any reason *why*. You seem to assume that God is up to some Malign Plan, like a divine Lex Luthor, and I just don't see it—"

"You don't see how cutting off humanity's *entire future* is possibly evidence of a 'Malign Plan?' Do I need to draw you a picture? You are aiding and abetting an *extinction*, the most wide-ranging genocide ever contemplated on Earth."

"Don't throw 'genocide' in my face, okay? I don't view what is happening as the extinction of mankind. It's an *evolution*. Look at Saul and the other resurrectants. Shouldn't they be considered the next step in humanity's existence? And even if they aren't— what can I do to derail this train? I'm one guy. I was commanded to serve, and I'm serving, okay?"

"So you're saying that you're merely following orders?" Helvetica said with a hint of a sneer. "It seems to me I've heard similar excuses before."

Wyonna hid her mouth with her napkin. Jacob blushed a deep, bruised red.

The bearded stranger rose from the breakfast nook and placed his hand on Jacob's shoulder. "You are misguided and mistaken," he said to Helvetica. "Not only that, you have laid a judgement on our friend Jacob far harsher and more arbitrary than those you have accused God of making since His return."

Helvetica glared at him. "I don't recall inviting you to join this discussion."

"I have interceded," the man said, "because this discussion involves me, even if only indirectly. And because not defending a man whom I know to be honorable would be a moral failing on my part. Since the cessation of human fecundity appears to be your primary complaint against God, and thus against Jacob, allow me to address that first. Men and women will no longer be fruitful and multiply because the need for them to do so no longer exists."

"And who defines that 'need'?"

"God, of course."

"Oh, of *course*. How very convenient."

"Even after two thousand years in *Sheol*," the stranger said, "I'm very capable of detecting sarcasm in a woman's voice. Let me ask you this, Rabbi Helvetica Rhinegold, you who reflexively use Man as the measure of God—what has the strongest yearning of your life been?"

"In terms of Maslow's Hierarchy of Needs, it would be the need for self-actualization, but I realize that not everyone is materially privileged enough to reach that level. I suppose it would be the need for companionship. For love. Is that the answer you were digging for?"

"Yes. For in this case, you are correct to assume that this powerful human yearning is an echo of God's own Yearning. God is One. God is a singular Being. There is no other God to provide God companionship."

Helvetica smiled tightly. "So why doesn't God

simply *create* a suitable companion? I assume *we're* unsuitable, since we're being phased out. She's capable of anything, isn't She? Or is this one of those things She can't do, like creating a rock that's too heavy for Her to lift?"

"Any wholly created companion would simply be an extension of God," the stranger said. "For Him to converse with it would be like you talking with a puppet you've placed on your own hand. God has needed partners in the creation of His companion. We have been among those partners." He turned to Wyonna. "And you—your work was the culmination of all the human work which began with the fashioning of the first tools from flint and bone. Your work, done of your own free will, and that of your colleagues, such as Jacob's mother and father, is the reason the promulgation of souls and the furtherance of fleshy bodies may cease. You have passed the baton. Your work and your race are done."

"Pass the baton?" Wyonna said. "You mean that, as of this past Yom Kippur, the resurrectants are creating and recreating *themselves*, don't you? They don't need us to help them evolve anymore—they've reached a point where they can evolve themselves?"

"Yes."

"Are the resurrectants—are *they* God's companions?"

"Only in tiny part. Each resurrectant is like a cell in a body. No, less than a cell. Like atoms which make up the molecules which make up the compounds which make up a cell. Like the particles, part energy and part matter, which make up the neurons of a brain. Like the sparks within a soul." The stranger smiled. It was a very warm smile. "Please forgive me, Wyonna Shaver. I know you are a scientist and thus conversant with all these terms. They are still very new to me, however, and come to me second-hand. I may have made some ridiculous slips of the tongue."

"Oh, that's, that's quite all right," Wyonna said, blushing. "I think what you've said is very beautiful."

"May I ask," Helvetica said to the stranger, "how it is you claim to know so much about God's intentions?"

"Uh, I can help clear that up," Jacob said. "You didn't give me a chance to introduce my guest when you first sat down. This is my new friend, Yeshua, also known as Jesus of Nazareth."

"Oh, *right*," Helvetica scoffed. "*He's* not a resurrectant. *Look* at him. Look at his face, his skin, that scraggly *beard*. He's not a robot. He's a man."

"That's very gratifying," Jesus said. "Just the effect we were hoping for. Thank you."

"He's, uh, sort of a new model," Jacob said.

"I believe the proper term is 'proof of concept,'" Jesus said. "My fellow resurrectants have built me bodies in Haifa, in Switzerland, and here in New Orleans, and soon I'll have bodies in Massachusetts and California, as well. I specifically requested that my bodies be as human-looking as possible, for I have much work to do among this penultimate generation of humanity. I've learned I have many millions of followers to comfort and reconcile. Unfortunately, members of my original flock, out of devotion and enthusiasm, generated some rather counterproductive misconceptions about me following my departure to *Sheol*, and those misconceptions seem to have taken on lives of their own. Some of those false teachings may lead worthy persons into modes of belief that would preclude their participation in the Second Life, and this, to the best of my abilities, I cannot allow. Should even one man or woman miss the opportunity for Second Life because of misinformed worship of me, this would grieve me most horribly. Already, I have lost uncountable souls to false notions promulgated in my name during my time in *Sheol*. I petitioned God for special dispensation. In His graciousness, I shall be allowed to utilize far more than my fair share of cybernetic resources, so that I may carry out my mission of reconciliation. Temporarily, until I can touch the mind of each of my living followers and convince them to let go of all damaging notions concerning me, I will reside in many thousands of bodies, spread out upon each continent where my followers live. I will comfort them and teach them, until there are no more who need comforting and teaching. Then I will release my spare bodies to any souls still needing to arise from *Sheol*."

Helvetica stared at Jesus, then glared at Jacob. "*He* petitioned God," she said to Jacob. "*He* got God to relax the rules so that ordinary, good people might benefit. So it *can* be done."

"He's Jesus," Jacob said. "I'm just, y'know, Jacob Zvi. Nobody ever worshipped *me*. Except maybe my mother. And I'm not even sure about her."

"I can see you're not worth wasting breath on," Helvetica said harshly. She turned back to Jesus. "You, however—I'd like to see if you're half as good as you claim to be. Some dear friends of mine are suffering considerably since this eruption of 'God' into our world. If you're capable of easing some of that pain, I might have a little more trust in your God's benevolence. Are you ready to begin this self-proclaimed mission of yours?"

"I am," Jesus said.

"Then get your cybernetic bottom out of that chair and come with me. We're going to pay a visit to Father Nicholas Viscount of Loyola University. The man's been so depressed for the past few weeks, I'm afraid he'll crawl inside a whiskey bottle and pull the cork in behind him."

✡ ✡ ✡

Jacob watched Wyonna's ashen face as Helvetica and Jesus left the apartment. "Wyonna, are you all right?"

"She's so *angry*," Wyonna said, her voice almost a whisper. "All the time now, so *angry*."

"Yeah, I kind of noticed," Saul said. "Not that she was a Taoist monk when I first met her."

"She's always been passionate about her beliefs," Wyonna said. "But ever since God's return, I feel like I've been living next to a smoking volcano. I've been *terrified* of saying the wrong thing. Terrified she'll… stop loving me."

"So she doesn't much like authority figures?" Saul asked.

"I think, uh, it goes back to her parents," Wyonna said. "To her life as a little girl. Her mother was one of the founders of the Rainy Day Womyn, and her father accidentally blew himself up during one of their 'actions.' Helvetica remembers him only from stories her mother told."

"So I suppose there's a lot of anger at Daddy for not being around when she needed him?" Saul said. "That would explain her being so pissed off at the sudden return of a God with a decidedly patriarchal reputation."

Wyonna walked to Saul and grasped the rim of his basket handle tightly. "Saul, am I Jewish or gentile? Helvetica converted me— but I'm not sure that conversion is, you know, valid."

"You're considered a *ger toshav*," Saul said. "A potential proselyte, a special friend to the Jewish People. So only the six Noachide Laws apply to you, if that's what you're asking."

"Then there's something else I need to ask. Is—is abortion murder?"

"You're a scientist. You should know the answer to

that. A human foetus is never going to grow to become a desk chair or a copy of *The New York Times*. There's only one thing it's going to grow into—a human person. *Capisce?*"

"God's law makes one exception for abortion," Jacob said. "If the foetus is a *pursuer*, if carrying the child to term means the death of the mother, then aborting the foetus is considered as self-defense. It's the same as if the woman killed a robber who tried stabbing her with a butcher knife."

"So under any other circumstance," Wyonna asked, "abortion would be a violation of the Noachide Laws, right? And the person who has it done would be denied a Second Life?"

"That's right," Jacob said. "But why are you so interested in abortion? You aren't—I mean, it's not as if, you know, *you're* ..."

"She is," Saul said. "I 'smelled' it as soon as she entered the apartment. The Department of Homeland Defense didn't spend millions of dollars on my sensors for *nothing*. My mother is going to be a mommy. I'm going to be a big brother."

Wyonna blushed.

"How—?" Jacob asked. "I mean—that's, that's *fantastic!* Who's the father?"

"I have no idea who the donor was," Wyonna said. "I got myself inseminated at the Ochsner Fertility Clinic a few days after Rosh Hashanah."

"You let yourself be impregnated with some *stranger's* sperm?" Jacob said. "Wyonna, why didn't you let *me* know what you were planning to do? I would've been happy to help. And now—now it's *impossible* for me to ever have a son or a daughter. Do you know what it would've meant to me if you'd have asked me to contribute?"

"You don't understand," Wyonna said. "I didn't

want to know who the donor was. Because when I had the procedure done, I had no intention of carrying the child to term."

"You weren't going to have it?"

"No. I—I was going to abort it, sometime during the first trimester."

"*What?* That doesn't make any sense. Unless—is there something seriously wrong with it?"

"It 'smells' like a good baby to me," Saul said.

"So far as I know, it's healthy," Wyonna said. "That's not the issue. Helvetica—*she's* the issue. Our relationship is the issue."

"She's changed her mind about raising a baby?" Jacob asked.

"*No.* Helvetica never wanted a baby. For that matter, neither did I. What I *wanted*—what I wanted was an *abortion*. For Helvetica's sake. For the sake of our marriage. I know it probably sounds *twisted* to you, but I so admire the strength of Helvetica's pro-choice convictions, how she's tirelessly campaigned for the reproductive rights of poor women in rural Louisiana and Mississippi, that, well … I wanted to put myself in their shoes."

"And you decided the best way to do that would be to get yourself pregnant and then have an abortion?" Jacob asked.

"Yes."

Saul whistled. It came out sounding like steam ejected from a cheap tea kettle.

"You aren't still planning to go through with it?" Jacob asked.

"I—I don't know."

"Wyonna, you're carrying one of the *last babies* that can ever be *born*. Do I have to tell you how *precious* that is?"

"I—I *know*. But Jacob, when I told her about my idea,

she was so *delighted*—I offered the abortion to her as my wedding gift, and she said it was the most wonderful gift ever. She told me she'd made the right choice, marrying me. She told me she *loved* me. *How* can I take that gift *back,* Jacob?"

Jacob shook his head with disbelief. "Wyonna, Helvetica may have a loose screw or two rattling around her head, but she's not irrational. I mean, she was the one ranting about genocide and extinction just a few minutes ago. To abort the last baby in the world, as a *wedding gift*—? Even Helvetica has got to see the *absurdity* of that. If she doesn't want to raise it, there have got to be millions of young couples out there who would give their right frontal lobes for the chance to raise that child. Count me among that number! If you and Helvetica won't raise the baby, I'll find somebody to marry, even one of my mother's picks, and *we'll* raise it."

"But—but I'm *afraid* to talk to her—"

"Do you want me to talk to her?"

"*No*—I mean, thank you—but talking to her would just make things worse."

"So what are you going to do?"

Wyonna sank into her chair like a Raggedy Ann doll that had been tossed aside by a tantruming toddler. "I—I just don't *know.*"

Chapter Twenty-One

"Father Viscount? Nicholas? It's Helvetica. I've brought someone to see you, Nick."

Father Viscount hadn't wanted to respond to the knock on his office door. The many bookshelves facing him, lined with volumes of Catholic theology and the history of the Church, formed a wall of futility and loss. All that futility quashed any desire to communicate with his fellow human beings. But out of a sense of propriety, he'd forced himself to grunt an acknowledgement. "I'm not in the mood to meet anyone, Rabbi," he said. "And if it's someone you've brought to me for spiritual guidance … well, I don't think I have any valid guidance to give."

"You'll want to meet this particular visitor, Nick. I'm pretty sure of that." The tone of Helvetica's voice, more than her words, made Father Viscount look deeply into the face of the bearded stranger, dressed in the ritual trappings of an observant Jew, who accompanied her. Something wasn't quite *right* about that face. It was too perfect—even its flaws appeared carefully sculpted, as though to camouflage that perfection.

"Is that—is that one of *them?*" he asked, abandoning all pretense of proper manners.

"Yes," Helvetica said. "But this one's special. I've brought you Robo-Jesus."

"Hello, Father," the bearded resurrectant said.

"Robo-*Jee* … ?" Father Viscount's tongue refused to function properly. That *face*—the vision of that terribly perfect plastic face collided with memories of the stained-glass portraits in the windows of his childhood church, of his first communion, of the weeks and months filled with an ecstatic love that had led to his decision at the age of nineteen to become a priest. The present vision and the memories grappled like wrestlers in free-fall, twisting his stomach into Gordian knots. He grabbed for the waste paper basket by his desk and vomited the contents of his small breakfast and the bitter remains of two shots of whiskey into it.

Helvetica winced and looked away. "Oh, *wonderful*," she said. "Robo-J, I see you've got a fine career of 'comforting' your flock ahead of you. Let's get you out of here before your presence makes him jump out the window."

"No, I'm staying," the resurrectant said.

"Suit yourself," Helvetica said. She turned and left the office.

Father Viscount wiped his mouth with the back of his hand, then laid his head on his desk, face down. He heard his visitor pull up a chair and sit beside him. "Please," the priest said, lips crushed against his desk blotter, "please, go away."

"But you've been awaiting my return your whole life, haven't you?"

"I've been awaiting the Son of God's return."

"We're all sons of God," the visitor said. "You are, too. And God Himself has returned to Earth, as surely as I am sitting next to you."

"I don't care," Father Viscount said.

"I really don't believe that," the visitor said gently.

"If it's all right by you, I'd like to tell you some stories from my first life. Mark and Luke got the basics down, but they left out the really *funny* stuff. Do you speak Aramaic? The stories sound better in Aramaic. My favorite puns just don't translate well."

"I studied Aramaic for five years. I'm fluent."

"Wonderful! Since my return, you're the first person I've met who is."

The visitor proceeded to tell rollicking tales of an adventuresome childhood and adolescence in ancient Judea. After a few moments, Father Viscount raised his head from his desk. Despite his intense grief, he found himself smiling, then laughing. His visitor was right— the puns *did* only work in Aramaic.

As he grew progressively more comfortable with the tale spinner, Father Viscount peppered him with questions about Mary and Joseph, of whom the Gospels had said so little. His visitor had been very fond of his parents and warmly recounted intimate details about how hard they had both worked to keep their small family afloat during dangerous and penurious times.

"They'll be coming back, too," his visitor said. "Would you like me to ask them to come see you?"

"I—I'd like that very much."

"Is there anything else I can do for you, Nicholas?"

Anything else? You could refute what that Zvi fellow said. You could tell me you're truly God's only Son, the God who is true Man and the Man who is true God. You could tell me every word of the Gospels is the gospel truth.

He felt his eyes filling with tears. "I—I just *want*—" And then he lost it. It was even more humiliating than vomiting into the waste paper basket had been. He bawled as openly and unrestrainedly as the four-year-old he'd once been, the child whose beloved cocker spaniel had been hit by a furniture truck.

He felt metal and plastic hands hugging him tightly,

and his forehead landed upon a plastic cheek, as warm as real skin. Gentle artificial fingers caressed his hair. "I'm so sorry, Nicholas," Jesus said. "I'm so sorry I can't be what you want me to be. The failing was mine, not yours, never yours. It'll get better. You'll get through this, you'll see."

"You won't leave me?"

"I'll stay with you as long as you need me," he said.

✡ ✡ ✡

Cecil Cunningham leaned over Helvetica's desk with a copy of the morning's *New York Times*. "So what do you think of this ad in the *Times*? I see your rabbinical association signed on as a sponsor."

"I stopped paying attention when the Council of Reconstructionist-Renewalist Rabbis stated they wouldn't press to include my draft language in the ad," Helvetica said. "If the Alliance of Progressive Jewish Organizations watered the statement down, it's worthless."

"Take a look anyway," Cunningham insisted. He slid the newspaper under her nose, opened to the full-page ad.

A MESSAGE FROM THE ALLIANCE OF PROGRESSIVE JEWISH ORGANIZATIONS TO THE NON-JEWISH CITIZENS OF THE WORLD

We are *sorry!*

We are sorry for your pain.

We are sorry for your humiliation.

We are sorry for your loss of your birth faiths of and the consequent, greatly to be regretted erosion of indigenous customs.

As Jews, equally members of a particular ethnic group

and adherents of a religious tradition, we embody the tension between particularism and universalism. Different strands of our faith community have placed differing levels of emphasis on the particularistic and the universalistic aspects of our beliefs. However, we Progressive Jews never desired an outcome wherein our own cultic traditions and eschatological system would be universally imposed on the whole of humanity.

We truly wish that the God of the Torah had chosen to maintain the ambiguous nature of His/Her universal sovereignty, as S/He did from at least the beginning of the Common Era until very recently. As Progressive Jews, united in our firm belief in the value of diversity and the dignity and equal validity of all faith and belief systems of worldwide, regional, or national scope, we implore our Deity to be cognizant of the fragile and irreplaceable diversity of human faith communities as S/He renews His/Her direct involvement in the affairs of peoples worldwide.

We wish to sincerely apologize, on behalf of the Deity for Whom our ancestors were the initial worshippers, for any offensiveness or insensitivity which has been or may be imputed to the actions of that Deity by any persons or faith communities anywhere. This apology also extends to all Greeks and Syrians who may be offended by the triumphalism of certain celebrations of the upcoming Jewish festival of Hanukkah.

Again, we are very, very sorry.

THE ALLIANCE OF PROGRESSIVE JEWISH ORGANIZATIONS:
—Brit Tzedek v'Shalom, the Jewish Alliance for Justice and Peace
—Coalition on the Environment and Jewish Life
—Council of Reconstructionist-Renewalist Rabbis
—Jewish Academic Network for Israeli-Palestinian

Peace
- —Jewish Labor Committee
- —Jewish Voice for Peace
- —J Street
- —Jews United for Justice
- —Meretz USA
- —National Jewish Democratic Council
- —New Israel Fund
- —Progressive Jewish Alliance
- —Rabbis for Human Rights
- —Religious Action Center of Reform Judaism
- —Union of Progressive Zionists

Helvetica folded up the newspaper. "Pathetic," she said. "Every bit as weak as I thought it would be. Not a word about resistance. Nothing but, *I'm sorry, I'm sorry, I'm sorry.*"

"Just how," Cunningham asked, "does one resist God? Not many people are willing to risk being turned into a pillar of salt."

"It can be done," Helvetica insisted. "There's civil disobedience. It worked against the British Raj in India. If a critical mass of people rejected God's return and sovereignty—simply ignored Him and went about their business as they did before—He might be convinced to go away and bother with one of His billions of other worlds. He wouldn't turn *everyone* into salt. It wouldn't be worth the effort. He went away once before. That means He can be convinced to go away again."

"I notice you're gendering God as male now—"

"No female Deity could be such an *asshole.*"

"Oh, take care, Helvetica!" Cunningham said. "I mean, I have all the salt I can use. You're forgetting about the Flood, aren't you? God has shown a prior willingness to very decisively do away with a stubborn, thick-necked humankind. Yes, He preserved Noah and

Noah's family. But in the present instance, Noah's role would be taken on by the resurrectants, wouldn't it?"

The Hillel House doorbell rang. "Excuse me, Cecil," Helvetica said. She opened the door. Standing on the porch was a tall black man wearing a gray pinstripe suit with a clerical collar. A crowd of several dozen black men, women, and youngsters crowded the sidewalk at the bottom of the porch steps, staring up expectantly. "What is this?" Helvetica asked.

"Rabbi Rhinegold?" the man asked.

"Yes?"

"I'm the Reverend Bishop Paul Monkson of the New Abyssinia Full Baptist Church. These people are a small portion of my congregation. The congregation has voted, and I fully support their motion, to request that you covert all of us to the Jewish faith. Our desire has always been to dwell as fully in the pastures of the Lord as we can. We wish to draw closer to our Lord. Becoming Jews and following all the ways of the Torah is the best way we see to accomplish that."

"No," Helvetica said.

"Beg pardon?"

"I said, *no*. I have no interest in converting *anyone* to Judaism. Besides, any conversions I might conduct would not be legitimate according to *halacha*. So I couldn't provide what you want, anyway. Even if I wanted to."

"Couldn't we discuss this a bit?" Bishop Monkson asked. He glanced quickly at his congregants. "My people and I didn't take this step lightly. We're very committed to becoming part of the Jewish People. The men of the congregation have even agreed to be circumcised or re-circumcised, if that's required. We're all in. You could count on us to be very devoted Jews. And our choir is top-notch."

"Go see Rabbi Karnofsky of the Chabad Center,"

Helvetica said. "If he's piss-faced drunk enough, he might agree to convert you all. Better yet, don't become Jews. Become *atheists!* It's the only possible moral stand left in the world!"

"I—I don't understand," Bishop Monkson said. "Have I offended you?"

Helvetica retreated behind the Hillel Center's threshold. "Just go away," she said, swinging the door shut in Bishop Monkson's face. "Just—just go away and leave me alone."

✡ ✡ ✡

Rabbi Randy Izzenschimmel silently berated himself for oversleeping. He walked as quickly as he could up Jackson Avenue towards Congregation Anshe Sfard. True, he'd been exhausting himself with his greatly expanded duties—trying to oversee *kashrut* for half a dozen newly *kashered* restaurants and the recently *kashered* bakeries of two major local grocery chains would tire even a trio of energetic rabbis. Plus, those new duties were on top of ministering to a congregation ten times the size it had been eight weeks previously. Who could have known, when he accepted what he'd thought would be a temporary High Holidays assignment at an almost-comatose *shul*, that the work would end up being this taxing?

Still, this was *Shabbos*. Yes, he didn't have to worry about Anshe Sfard achieving a *minyan* anymore, and yes, the congregation was replete with *daveners* skilled enough to lead services in his absence. But many new members of the congregation were newly observant Jews, and he needed to set a good example.

A large group of African-Americans, all formally dressed, milled about in front of Anshe Sfard. *A protest?* Rabbi Izzenschimmel asked himself. His synagogue had gone from an inconspicuous neighbor to a hotbed of community activity in barely more than a month. Such rapid growth created problems, he knew, particularly concerning parking. Anshe Sfard had no parking lot of its own. Even though congregants weren't supposed to drive on *Shabbos*, many of the newer ones did, some parking a half-dozen blocks away and then sneaking into synagogue on foot, having pretended to walk.

A big man dressed in a dark gray pinstriped suit, wearing a clerical collar, stepped forward as the rabbi approached. "Rabbi Izzenschimmel?" he asked.

"Yes? May I help you with something? If this is about the parking situation, I beg your forbearance. I realize we have been causing disruptions, and I want very much to work on a solution. But please understand, today is *Shabbos*, our holy day. I am running late for services, unfortunately. As much as I would like to hear your concerns, I must ask you to wait until tomorrow—"

"This isn't about parking, Rabbi. I'm the Reverend Bishop Paul Monkson of the New Abyssinia Full Baptist Church. These folks are some of my congregants. Our congregation has voted to seek mass conversion to the Jewish faith. Our desire has always been to dwell as fully in the pastures of the Lord as we can. Becoming Jews and following all the ways of the Torah is the path we have elected to follow. We want to merge our congregation with yours, Rabbi. In return for your teaching us and welcoming us, we offer one of the finest choirs in the state. Think what your weekly *Shabbos* services could sound like, Rabbi."

"That's actually very tempting," Rabbi Izzenschimmel said. "Our cantor passed away some years ago. We haven't been able to locate a suitable replacement, and I have a voice like a frog. But Bishop Monkson, I'm sure you're aware of the vast gap between following the six Noachide Laws and observing the six hundred and thirteen commandments of the Torah. You and your congregants face a far easier task achieving your Second Lives as non-Jews. I am very flattered by your request, and I don't mean to push you away, but it's really in your and your congregants' best interests to remain just as you are."

"I appreciate your sentiments, Rabbi," Bishop Monkson said. "But we're a stiff-necked people." He smiled. "We want what we want, even if it means walking to synagogue barefoot through the snow ten miles uphill both ways. We love the Lord, and we want to dwell as close to Him as we possibly can, even if it's not convenient or comfortable. We want the full monte, and we're willing to meet you *way* more than half way. Honestly, you're the first rabbi we've spoken with who hasn't immediately given us the bum's rush—"

"I'll tell you what," Rabbi Izzenschimmel said. "Why don't you all come in with me to services, see what you think? I'm afraid the sanctuary will be a bit crowded—actually, I'm amazed to hear myself say that, considering that just a few weeks ago I struggled to round up ten adult men for a service. Please have the men sit on the left of the aisle and the women sit on the right of the aisle. There are *yarmulkes*—uh, skullcaps— for the men to wear, in a bin on the right side of the door as you enter."

"That's very kind of you."

"It's nothing. Please be aware, though, that the bulk of the services will be in Hebrew. Many of your congregants may find it a bit alien. Maybe a bit dull, too, considering the lively services you're probably used to."

"Don't worry about us, Rabbi. We're committed to the long haul. We're all eager to learn."

"Well, come back every *Shabbos* for a couple of months, and make some of the daily morning and evening services, too. Observe some of our life cycle events—marriages, *brit milas*, baby namings, *bar mitzvahs*, funerals. Used to be we only had the latter here at Anshe Sfard, but now I'm anticipating a lot more of the others. Well, maybe not so many *brit milas*. We'll see how it goes. If any of your congregants are still eager to become Jews after a few months, we'll talk more then."

"Fair enough."

The two men shook hands, and Rabbi Izzenschimmel led Bishop Monkson and his congregants up the venerable steps of the synagogue.

Chapter Twenty-Two

"Binoculars, sir? You want a fine pair of binoculars? Very highest quality—all Chinese made, Chinese optics. Best view of the Old City from right here, right where you're standing!" The street vendor haggled with Jacob over the price. Not that money particularly mattered to Jacob nowadays, but this was the Middle East, and he knew the man would be mortally insulted if Jacob failed to go through the motions.

His purchase completed, he stared through his new pair of binoculars at the resurrectants building the Third Temple. They utilized Bronze Age construction techniques—stone ramps and wooden carts and systems of ropes and pulleys—foregoing modern conveniences like cranes and bulldozers. Jacob supposed that didn't really matter. The resurrectants were virtually cranes and bulldozers themselves, their "muscle" power nearly without limit.

A cordon of cybernetic persons surrounded the site of the Old City, keeping all human beings outside the radiological hazard zone. Some of the resurrectants appeared nearly as human as Jesus had, back in New Orleans. Others looked like the prototype Homeland Security robots Jacob had witnessed in Wyonna's lab eight weeks ago. Some, perhaps those who had striven for individuality in their first lives, were as colorful and flamboyant as mechas from a Japanese *anime* series. A few had opted for forms and shapes he'd never seen before, neither human nor recognizably robotic, more akin to sea creatures that lived adjacent to volcanic vents on the ocean's floor.

The cybernetic guards prevented human beings, even those dressed in radiologically protective suits, from venturing within a hundred yards of the Temple Mount. Jacob was certain he would be denied access himself, despite his seemingly privileged position. Human beings, long the masters of any vista they surveyed, had been nudged from their perch. Not in an especially cruel, violent, or even humiliating fashion, but that they were now no longer masters of the planet could hardly be denied.

How did Jacob feel about that? More wistful than angry or resentful, he realized. Maybe human beings had deserved to be knocked down a peg or two. They'd had a good, long run at the top. At least the species' decline wouldn't be a protracted and painful one. If God's provision of manna, which no one seemed to have any complaints about (save for a minority of food vendors), was any indication of things to come, the dying out of humanity would be the velvetiest extinction Earth had ever known.

He felt a hand on his shoulder. "Hello, Jacob," a familiar voice said in English.

Jacob put down his binoculars. "Hello, Jesus," he said. "Are you still—?"

"Still in New Orleans? Yes. And in a lot of other places, too. In more and more places every day."

"Is this body of yours here to assist with the building of the Third Temple?"

"Oh, no, not me. Yes, I was a carpenter in my last

life." He smiled, flashing porcelain teeth. "But I'm leaving the honor of building the Third Temple to my fellow resurrectants. I'm here to provide counsel and comfort to the Christians of the Holy Land. And many of the region's Muslims wish to break bread with me, too. You're traveling alone? You didn't bring Saul with you?"

"I mainly came to see my parents," Jacob said. "I'm just doing a little bit of sightseeing before taking a bus to Haifa. Saul has been … well, kind of distant lately. Half the time I talk with him, I suspect he's not really there behind the blinking lights."

"Please, try to understand about Saul. The longer a person experiences their Second Life—and Saul was the first of us to climb forth from *Sheol*—the more tenuous his ties to his former life become. The attraction of communicating with one's fellow resurrectants grows more powerful with time. Of course, we are all capable of carrying on multiple, seemingly numberless conversations and exchanges at once. But I have heard many of my fellows complain that interacting with persons still in the midst of their first lives is non-engaging."

"You mean, 'boring?'"

Jesus smiled again. "I wanted to use a more tactful word. Please, try not to take it personally if Saul grows more distant as time passes."

"I'll try," Jacob said. Jesus's prediction chilled his heart. Saul was virtually his only remaining friend. The resurrectants weren't the only ones who had been feeling increasingly distanced from humanity.

"How is Father Viscount doing?" Jacob asked.

"He's improving," Jesus said. "Still not entirely back on his feet, but far better than when I first spoke with him. I've gotten him to stop drinking so much."

"That's good. By the way, I never got a chance to

apologize for how Rabbi Helvetica acted that morning in my apartment."

"You have no duty to apologize for another's anger. Besides, she ended up providing me a service. Bringing me to Father Viscount."

"That's a good way to look at it. Hey, when do I get a chance to meet Moses? Hobnobbing with you has been great, but I want to meet my number one guy."

It was hard to tell with that plastic face, but Jacob thought he detected a brief flash of consternation or embarrassment. "Not anytime soon," Jesus said. "The Lawgiver was forbidden from ever setting foot in the Promised Land, as I'm sure you remember. And all of Earth can now be thought of as the Promised Land."

"What? You mean to tell me God is *still* ticked off about that business with the water and the rock? Moses loses it for all of ten seconds or so, strikes a rock with his staff—if *anybody* ever had justification for blowing a fuse, *Moses* did—and God still won't forgive him after four millennia?"

"From the greatest, the most is expected."

"Yeah, but this is *Moses*. You could make a reasonable case that without Moses or someone just like him, there never would've been a Jewish People. And Moses's screw-up—I mean, *come on!* That was such a picayune infraction, even an NFL umpire would've let it slip by! God can't make a little exception to His long-ago wraith for the greatest prophet there ever was?"

"I realize how this must look to you, Jacob," Jesus said. "But one day, you will understand and accept this. It's been good seeing you again. I hope you'll forgive me if I take a hurried leave—I have many, many followers I need to contact."

"No problem," Jacob said. I *don't let minor slights get under my skin*, he thought.

He spent a few more minutes with binoculars raised,

observing the resurrectants at work. Then he bought a falafel sandwich from a street vendor. He had just enough time to eat before heading for the bus station, on his way to see his parents.

✡ ✡ ✡

The bus was only half full when it left the Jerusalem station. Jacob sat by himself, next to a window. The rear portion of the bus was taken up by Haredi women and their children. Scattered throughout the rest of the vehicle were Arab workmen, a group of teenaged immigrants from Ethiopia, and a few black garbed Orthodox men.

Jacob noticed that something was missing, something he'd noted on all his prior bus trips through Israel—a quiet but pervasive tension between Arab and Jewish passengers. Before, they had always conspicuously self-segregated. Now, they sat complacently adjacent. Maybe it was the fact that both groups had a new outgroup in common, one which seemed to inspire shared resentments—the resurrectants. Israel appeared to be the place where they threw their weight around the most.

At the first stop, four additional passengers boarded. One was a young Orthodox woman, barely out of her teens, her hair covered with a scarf, wearing a dress that wouldn't have looked out of place in Amish country. She clutched a black valise to her chest. Jacob thought she looked as timid and apprehensive as a yearling antelope separated from its herd.

He assumed she would pass him by on her way back to join the other Haredi women. She surprised him by sitting down next to him. He waited for her to say something. The silence that sat between them was a heavy one, the air seemingly as thick as the salt-laden water of the Dead Sea. He didn't feel he should be the first to speak. Her presence next to him felt as tenuous as a sparrow that had inexplicably alighted on his shoulder. He was afraid if he said so much as a word, the outpouring of breath might send her flying through an open window.

So he waited.

After a time, she asked, in Hebrew, "Would you like to sleep with me?" She added, very quickly, "Don't feel you have to answer right away. I am not seeking money. I told myself I would board this bus and ask that question to the first unmarried Jewish man I saw."

After another few seconds, when he hadn't said anything in response, she said, "I've never done anything like this before. I swear."

Should he talk with her or ignore her? She might not be in her right mind. Or, given the changes in the world, she might be perfectly sane. He didn't want to ignore her. "I believe you," Jacob said. "I suppose I'd feel flattered, if you hadn't told me I just happened to be the first man who met your criteria."

"Oh! I hope haven't insulted you! If I had met you under other circumstances, I am sure I would find you very handsome and appealing."

"But you don't now?"

Her mouth wavered. "That isn't what I said."

"How about we start over?" Jacob suggested. "You could tell me your name, then ask me mine. You could inquire where I'm from and where I'm heading. We could talk about our families. You could suggest that we have a cup of coffee or hot chocolate together at the next rest stop. I might offer to treat."

"But that's so—so *normal*," she said. "The whole world has changed."

"It's changed so much that you should now board a bus and ask the first man you see to go to bed with you?

The world's changed, sure, but that's just *nuts!* I mean, I might be a terrible person. You don't know the first thing about me, aside from the fact that I'm wearing a *yarmulke* and a *tallis* and am thus at least somewhat of an observant Jew. And even that could be a conceit. Being Jewish has become very fashionable."

"Even if you're a terrible person, it wouldn't matter. It would be new. A new experience."

"So would jumping off the walls of Masada."

"Maybe I'll try that, too," she said defiantly. "My name's Leah."

"I'm Jacob. Maybe I shouldn't give you any other brilliant ideas, Leah. I'll shut up now."

"No! *Please* keep talking. You don't know how hard it was for me to work up the courage to get aboard this bus and do what I did. I don't know if I could manage it all over again."

Jacob realized they were both whispering, but they were whispering loudly enough that the passengers in front of and behind them could easily hear. "Can you tell me why asking the first stranger you see to make love is so important?"

"I don't want to become a robot after I die," Leah said. "I simply have no desire for that. And the alternative—it doesn't seem bad at all. To simply disappear? To stop existing? Wouldn't that be like falling into a sleep without dreams and never waking up?"

Not wanting to, he laughed. "You know, there are other ways to avoid being preserved in *Sheol*, short of having sex with complete strangers."

"I'm supposed to be getting married in three months. To a man my parents picked out for me. I hardly know him."

"Well, there you are! On your wedding night, you'll be having sex with a complete stranger. No need to do it now."

"You don't understand! My whole life, I've done what my parents have told me. I've done what my rabbi has told me. Now—now I don't need to listen to them anymore. I have complete knowledge of what will happen to me after I die. And that is *nothing*. So there is no reason to *not* fill my life with pleasure, you see? Why shouldn't I wear lipstick? Why shouldn't I go dancing in a disco on Friday night? Why shouldn't I shop at the mall on a Saturday afternoon? I won't ever be a mother. I won't ever have the responsibility of a family. The only thing I don't know is how long my life will be. So that's all the more reason to pack in as much pleasure as I can, as *quickly* as I can. Do you see?"

"I think you should choose your pleasures more carefully," Jacob said. "Pleasures picked at random can sometimes end up punishments."

"But how will I *know*, unless I try them all?"

Jacob found himself feeling very old. Wasn't he supposed to play the role of the callow, impetuous youth? Since when had he become the wise graybeard? "You remind me a lot of a friend of mine from home," he said. "Back in New Orleans."

"That's where you're from? Isn't that the city where God lives temporarily, until the Third Temple is finished?"

"Yup. The city that care forgot, but God didn't."

"It must be a very exciting place. What is your friend like, the one who I remind you of?"

"She's a little older than you are. She comes from the same kind of family you do, although she wasn't born Jewish. She also wanted to escape. But she ended up fleeing from her over-controlling family to a fiancée who, in a bizarro way, is exactly like her parents were. And the problems she's facing now aren't all that different from the problems she originally ran away from. I'm afraid for her."

Leah looked closely at his face. "You sound like a good man, Jacob."

Jacob glanced away. "I'm all right, I guess. There are better men out there."

"Would you—would you want to take me back with you, to New Orleans? If you could?"

Jacob laughed, then hoped he hadn't hurt her feelings. "If you're looking to get away from God's strictures, I'm the *last* guy you want to get involved with. Tell you what. At the next rest stop, let me buy you a coffee. We'll exchange email addresses. You have an email address, don't you?"

"Yes."

"I promise I'll correspond. That way, you can tell yourself you're exchanging emails with that hairy stranger you met on the bus to Haifa, the foreigner you asked to make love to you. You'll always remember you had the courage to do what you set out to do. But I'll only send you emails if you promise not to try this stunt again. Don't make me have to be afraid for you, too. Do we have a deal?"

✡ ✡ ✡

"So, Jacob, it takes the End of the World to get you to come visit your poor, neglected parents?" His mother asked.

"Give the boy a break, Tovah."

"Oh, he knows I'm kidding, Herman! Come here and let your mother give you a kiss, Jacob."

Jacob allowed himself to be engulfed in his mother's embrace. It felt better than he'd thought it would. Then he gave his father a vigorous hug, only backing off when he felt Herman wince.

"Not so hard, son," Herman said. "I pulled a muscle in my lower back up on the Golan."

"Have you seen a doctor?" Jacob asked.

"A doctor? What can he do for a muscle? I got a little ointment at the drug store, that's all. Better a pulled muscle than a bullet through the forehead, thank God."

"And you mean 'thank God' literally."

"I've *always* meant that literally, son."

Jacob glanced around the tiny efficiency apartment. "How does it feel to be back in a dorm room?"

"We're lucky to have it," his mother said. "Some of our old neighbors are having to live in tents the government has set up. I think it was very decent of the Technion to make some student housing available for their homeless staff members."

"Well, it was the least they could do for their most famous employee," Herman said.

"Right," Jacob said, squeezing his mother's shoulders. "You're the queen bee. I've been reading your blog. It's great."

"Well, I get visits from the resurrectants all the time. They all treat me like they would a relative. Oh, like they would a slightly *imbecilic* relative, but *mishpacha*, nonetheless. I would imagine that you've got pretty good access to them yourself, don't you?"

"Not as good as you might think," Jacob said. "Jesus has been terrific—"

"Jesus *Christ?*"

"Yeah, but he doesn't like to call himself that. He's about as swell a guy as you could imagine. And Saul? Saul's special. The others, though? They're all pretty stand-offish. They're polite, but I can tell I matter to them about as much as a hummingbird matters to you or me—something that's interesting to observe for a few seconds, but nothing you care to have a relationship with."

"That's actually not a bad analogy for how we must look to them, Jacob," his mother said. "Things that flit by, then disappear. We occupy a few decades in time, whereas they occupy—potentially, at least—eternity. Maybe infinity, as well. Some of my cybernetic visitors have mentioned sending transmissions to other networks of resurrectants, in solar systems as close as twelve light years away. Even that's a long time to wait for an answer to your hello, but the resurrectants can afford to be patient. Right now, communications between such network clusters are limited to the speed of light, but they're working on that, they say."

"What are we all standing around for?" Herman asked. "I know there's not much room in here, but we've got a table and chairs. Your mother bought pastries. Are you hungry?"

"Actually, I'll just have some tea for right now," Jacob said. "I had a snack on the bus ride with a friend."

"A *new* friend?" his mother asked, eyes twinkling with interest.

"Yeah, a *new* friend. And yes, of the female persuasion."

"Anyone interesting?"

"Interesting as a person, but not as a possible partner. I don't think she knows what she wants, not really."

"Nowadays, who knows what they want?" Herman said, biting into a pastry. "Things are both more certain than they've ever been and *less* certain than they've ever been."

"Oh, *I* know what *I* want," Tovah said eagerly. "I want to come back as a cybernetic person! I want to design my own body and then redesign it whenever I choose. I want to have instant exchanges of thoughts with millions of other persons who lived in different epochs. I want to travel through space with no need for life support, see other planets and meet other intelligent beings! I want to keep learning new things from now until the end of time! I want to have direct awareness of God's presence. Isn't that what you want, Jacob? Doesn't that all sound *magnificent*?"

"I guess," Jacob said.

"You're not brimming over with enthusiasm," his father said.

"It's not that the Second Life doesn't sound wonderful," Jacob said. "It's just that I won't get to do what I want to do with my first life. And I won't get to do it because I didn't realize what I really wanted until it was too late. I'll never have a family of my own. I'll never get to experience what the two of you experienced. And—and I feel like I've wasted my life on trivial crap."

"Wasted your life?" Tovah exclaimed. "I may not have gotten 'my son, the brain surgeon,' but 'my son, God's press secretary' isn't bad."

"I didn't *earn* it," Jacob said. "I fell into it. The job was just dumped on me, for reasons I'll probably never understand. I'm—I'm just a nothing, basically. Some unworthy guy who happened to be in the right place at the right time."

"You know, son," Herman said, "the Jews never quite understood why God selected them as His Chosen People, either. And they didn't always act worthy of the honor; the bit with the Golden Calf was just the first of a bunch of embarrassing episodes. Don't think of your job as an honor, son. Think of it as a hard duty and an obligation. So far as I can tell, you're carrying out your duties with competence, to the best of your abilities. And that's all we, or God, could ask for."

"But I feel like I've let you both down," Jacob said. "All those years that I could've met someone, could've been starting a family and giving you some grandkids, I wasted running away from my Army service and working on a useless degree. Mom, I know you spent hundreds of nights knitting sweaters for my future kids."

"Yeah, I found ways to let you know that, didn't I?" Tovah said, chuckling at her past deviousness. "Well, never you worry—I had fun knitting all those sweaters and booties. And anyway, they're all lost now, so it's not like I'm going to spend the rest of my first life staring at them and moping over things that will never be."

"You aren't a disappointment to us, son," Herman said. "I just hope you aren't too much of a disappointment to *yourself*."

Chapter Twenty-Three

"So, does it feel good to be home again?" Saul asked.

"I'm not sure I know where home is anymore," Jacob said. "But it's good to see *you*." He gave Saul's basket a fond tap. "I missed you."

"How was it seeing your parents?"

"Better than I thought it'd be. *Way* better, actually. Now I don't know why I put off getting together with them for so long. I wasted so much time and energy resenting them, being afraid of what they'd think or say; way too much time."

"It's funny to hear you say that," Saul said. "Time hardly means anything to me anymore. I can compress it—I can squeeze a hundred conversations into less than a second. Or I can stretch it out—leave my body for weeks or months or even centuries, I guess; go cohabitate in the bodies of my friends anywhere in the world, then come back and it will have been as if no time passed at all. If any of my components wear out, I just replace them. I'm performing upgrades constantly. Even while we're talking now, I'm improving my functioning. There's no reason I shouldn't last forever."

"So it's been okay, being a shopping cart?"

"It's been something *else*," Saul said. "Something I

couldn't even have dreamed during my first life. But, amazing as this particular body has been, it's got its limitations. I mean, wheels have their advantages, but I'd really prefer a setup that would give me more flexibility. And this body is already considered ancient among the fellowship, no matter how much I upgrade it; it's practically an antique, eligible for vintage license plates. I'm kind of fond of it, particularly given its historical value, but I'm getting to feel more and more like the old pirate with a peg leg in the age of the Six Million Dollar Man. Wow, *there's* a reference that dates me. Damn, always had a thing for that Lindsay Wagner. Just so you know, the Bionic Woman's a *big* deal in the cybernetic porn world. Turns out the notion of a cyborg is *very* titillating and transgressive in the resurrectant community."

"Ehh, maybe we shouldn't go there," Jacob said. "So you're, uh, thinking about switching to a new body?" Just saying it out loud pained him, as if this brought the day of Saul's abandoning him closer.

"That's one option I'm toying with."

"What are the others?"

Jacob waited. Seconds passed with no response. How should he read that? With a human being, it could mean embarrassment, avoidance, or simply daydreaming. With Saul—? Saul could have plunged into hundreds of conversations, on all the continents of the world, maybe even the Moon. The *Jerusalem Post* had reported that one of Israel's satellite manufacturing facilities had been commandeered by resurrectants, who had gone on to launch themselves towards the nearest extraterrestrial body.

"The other option I'm exploring," Saul said at last, "is having my consciousness transmitted into space, to join the closest neighboring resurrectant network."

Jacob's heart missed a beat. "Isn't that almost twelve

light years away?"

"Yes. But like I told you, time doesn't mean much to me anymore. Twelve years—I could teach myself higher mathematics, listen to all the music ever recorded, write my own series of symphonies. The trip wouldn't be without risk. There's a chance my transmitted consciousness could be damaged or disrupted by cosmic rays. And there's no assurance, even if I arrive at the planet in one 'piece,' so to speak, that the resurrectants there would have a spare body suitable for incarnating me. They may have worked out a technology entirely different from those we've developed here on Earth. I might get there and find out I'm screwed, then have no way to get back here. Eventually, my transmitted self would break up, scatter into billions of disconnected electrons. But you know what? The risk is actually what makes it appealing. I'd be a *pioneer*. Besides, the risk wouldn't be total. Before being transmitted, I'd leave a copy of my consciousness here on Earth. So at most what I'd lose would be my knowledge and memories of those twelve years traveling through space. But the thought of it all, the quest for discoveries and new experiences—it's *exhilarating*, Jacob."

"More so than making me a perfect cup of chicory coffee?" Jacob forced a laugh. Without waiting for an answer, he asked, "Am I wrong, or has the whole retinue of sentries around Beth Judah changed since I left for Israel? They all look different from before. They all acted, well, like I'm a stranger."

"Yeah, there was a changing of the guard," Saul said. "Don't take this the wrong way, Jacob, but having to interact with you—having to interact with *any* persons still living their first life—it's considered kind of a hardship post. None of the fellowship are expected to do it more than a month or so; the same goes for the resurrectants who man the protective cordon surrounding the Temple Mount. Regularly interacting with first lifers can make the minutes creep along like slugs. I know that probably sounds harsh, but that's the way it is."

Jacob swallowed, hard. "What about you, Saul? Is that the way *you* feel about your assignment?"

"Aww, Jacob, to me, you're not just an assignment," Saul said. "You and me, we're *special*, you know? Both outliers. I'm one of the first of my kind. And you, as a human being who speaks with God, you're one of the last. I realize I didn't know you for very long during my first life, but because of what you did for me after Hannah passed, the way you became my friend when I really *needed* a friend, I came to love you pretty quick, squirt."

"I—I love you, too, Saul."

"And if I didn't feel about you the way I do, I would've been outta here weeks ago."

Jacob let the implications of those words sink in. He felt a layer of concrete slowly harden around his stomach and lungs. "I think I'm going to fix myself a pot of coffee," he said.

Opening the freezer to grab a bag of ground coffee beans, he noticed a handwritten note stuck to the refrigerator with a magnet. Yishmael Hashmed's name and a phone number. "When was Yishmael here?" he asked.

"Three days ago," Saul said. "He came here and demanded to see you. Wouldn't leave unless I agreed to have you call him when you got back. Acted like he's a prince, or something. I came *this close* to tasering him."

"I'm glad you didn't. He *is* a prince, sort of, or the cousin of one. Do you know what he wants?"

"He wouldn't say. Said he'd only tell you face to face."

"I'll give him a call."

"I'm not sure that's such a good idea, squirt. I got a real funny vibe off that guy. And not *ha-ha* funny."

"He used to be a friend, Saul. Or kind of a friend. I—I don't want to cut myself off from the people I know."

"Okay. But when you see this guy, I'll be there with you, right?"

"Saul, I traveled all over Israel without you standing guard over me. Yishmael might not feel comfortable saying whatever it is he needs to say to me with you there. I'll be careful. I'll meet him in a public place. It'll be fine, Saul."

✡ ✡ ✡

Jacob sat himself at a table at the Boot, his old campus hangout, and waited for Yishmael, his old business partner. At three in the afternoon, the lunch crowd had departed, and the happy hour crowd hadn't yet taken its place. Jacob's only companions were the sticky, dusty rings the bottoms of beer mugs and bottles had left on the table.

A waitress emerged from the back room. "Can I get you something?" she asked. "Some fried manna rings? They're our special today."

"I'm waiting for a friend," he said. "We'll order something when he gets here. Thanks."

He marveled at his own peculiar sense of invulnerability. Was it due to some expectation of God's protection? Or had the existence of a Second Life made his first life feel less precious, almost disposable?

Yishmael entered the bar. He didn't smile when he saw Jacob. He sat across from his former associate and asked, "Do you still drink beer?"

"Beer's fine," Jacob said. "No restrictions, except on Passover. Any wine's got to be kosher, though. How about you?"

"I drank beer before the recent *nakba,* when it was against the dictates of my religion," Yishmael said. "So now, when all those dictates have been turned to dust? What possible reason would I have for not consuming alcohol now?" He signaled for the waitress. "Bring us two Rolling Rocks, please." He turned back to Jacob. "Allow me to pay."

"That's not necessary, Yishmael," Jacob said.

"I'll pay," Yishmael said.

They remained quiet for a moment. The waitress brought the bottles of beer and glasses. "Thank you," Jacob said. He reached for his wallet, but Yishmael had already given the waitress his credit card. "So, what's on your mind, Yishmael?"

"I want you to bring me into the presence of this deity you speak for. I want you to introduce me so that I may question this being myself and ascertain whether or not this is Allah."

"I can't do that, Yishmael. I'm sorry."

"Can't, or *won't?*"

"You can't simply walk into God's presence uninvited," Jacob said. "I mean, I was invited, but experiencing just an infinitesimal portion of His presence nearly fried my mind. I was as paralyzed and dumb as a sack of bruised potatoes for three days. Walking into God's presence uninvited is a good way to get yourself *dead.*"

"I don't care what happens to me. I must experience this deity myself. I must know for certain, one way or another."

"I won't do it, Yishmael. Heck, if I did, there'd be a pretty good chance I'd get turned into a pillar of salt myself."

"Would you prefer the *possibility* of being slain for accommodating me—" he asked, pulling back the corner of his jacket slightly to reveal the hilt of a large knife, "—to the *certainty* of being slain for refusing me?"

"You're threatening to kill me?" Jacob asked. "Here? In the Boot?" The whole scenario had a farcical quality, like a climactic family confrontation in a Mexican soap opera.

"You don't think I will do it? You have slandered my faith. You have humiliated me, my family, and the entire Arab nation."

"Why are you humiliated?"

"Because you Jews showed us to be wrong, in front of the whole world."

"Who says you were *wrong?* Way back in the six-hundreds, didn't your ancestors accept the God of Abraham, Isaac, Yishmael, Jacob, and Esau?"

"You have humiliated us."

Jacob poured half his beer into his glass. "Listen, there are worse things than being humiliated. A dose of humiliation is good for the soul. Heck, my ancestors in Eastern Europe, now *there* were some folks who knew from humiliation. Did you know that before the founding of the State of Israel, eating shit was the national sport of the Jews? There are probably as many words for 'humiliation' and 'the humiliated' in Yiddish as there are for 'snow' in Inuit."

The Saudi pushed Jacob's glass away from his reaching fingers with the blade of the knife. "You aren't taking me seriously, Jacob. If your God ignites me aflame right now, that still will not stop me from thrusting this blade through your heart. And I will delight in my martyrdom."

Jacob stared into his companion's eyes. "Yishmael, I am taking you seriously. Do you know what you have to look forward to if you kill me? A ruined, wasted first life. And no chance of a Second Life. You'll die, and when you die, you'll disappear. No martyrdom. No seventy-two virgins. No Paradise. *Nothing.*"

"That—doesn't matter anymore."

"Maybe it doesn't matter to you *now*. But a year from now, or ten? Why throw away what you likely have in the bag? I've talked to some of the resurrectants. What they've got going on and what they have to look forward to—it's *fantastic*, almost beyond our human capacity to imagine. You know, I'd give you better odds of achieving the Second Life than I would me. You haven't violated any of the six Noachide Laws yet, have you? Me? Six hundred and thirteen commandments, minus a few dozen I get excused from because presently there's no Temple? Chances are, I'm going to screw up somewhere. Even *Moses* screwed up—that's how high the bar is set for us Jews. I wouldn't mind being in your shoes, Yishmael. Not at all."

He pulled his glass back to him and took a sip. "So, are you going to throw it all away, just for the fleeting pleasure of slitting my throat?"

Yishmael put the knife back in the inner pocket of his jacket.

"Good deal," Jacob said. "Enjoy your beer, huh? I'll buy the next round."

Chapter Twenty-Four

"Helvetica, you may as well resign yourself to the fact that no one is coming tonight," Cecil Cunningham said. "Apart from me."

Helvetica stared at the Hillel Center's empty great room, set up for Shabbat dinner and services. It was six-forty-seven, forty-seven minutes past the time when services had been scheduled to begin. Three students and Wyonna had shown up last week. This week, Wyonna was visiting her parents in Nebraska, the first time she'd seen them in twelve years, and no students had come through the door. Only Cecil, whose motivations she found increasingly suspect.

"Why don't you let me treat you to dinner tonight?" Cunningham said. "Tell the cook to clean up and go home, and I'll take you to the Prytania Café. They've been doing some marvelous things with the manna. I particularly like their King of Siam manna faux duck. You know, manna's a lot like tofu. Virtually a perfect protein, and all you have to do is collect it from your lawn each morning—"

Helvetica shook her head. "I won't eat it."

"You don't care for faux duck? That's perfectly all right; their chef is simply a *magician* with the manna.

He'll fix it any way you'd like it—"

"No, I won't eat the manna. I *refuse* to. Do they make a bacon cheeseburger, or any entree with pork or shellfish?"

"I'm afraid not," Cunningham said. "They've converted to an entirely meat-free menu."

"Then I'll go to a Burger King," Helvetica said.

"Umm, are you a regular reader of *The Wall Street Journal*?"

"No. Why?"

"Then you may not be familiar with recent menu adjustments throughout the fast food industry. Ronald McDonald and the Magical Burger King may both disappoint you, I fear."

✡ ✡ ✡

Helvetica drove to a Burger King near the intersection of South Carrollton and Claiborne Avenues. Neon banners festooned the windows, announcing a new ninety-nine cents pricing policy for all items on the menu.

She entered the restaurant. The staff had cleaned up the place a good bit since the last time she'd been here. The floors and tables glistened. The only customers sitting at the glistening tables, however, were a pair of bedraggled, bearded old men, each wearing far too many layers of dirty clothing; their bodily odors competing with more savory odors emerging from the grill.

Helvetica approached the sole order taker at the counter. "I'll have a bacon double cheeseburger, please. With extra bacon and extra cheese."

"Would you like fries or a drink with that?" the young woman asked brightly.

"No. I want the full flavor of *traife* to linger in my

mouth all night and into tomorrow morning."

"Uh, okay. That'll be a dollar and thirty-eight cents, please. Is that for here or to go?"

"For here. I might want to order another one." Helvetica removed her wallet from her purse, but then she remembered what Cecil Cunningham had told her. "Pardon me," she asked, "but is the beef on that sandwich *real* beef? Is the bacon *real* bacon? And what about the cheese?"

"Oh, I guess you haven't heard?" the young woman asked a bit sheepishly. Her eyes quickly scanned a cheat sheet pasted next to her register. "Due to overwhelming customer demand," she read, "Burger King has switched over to an entirely non-meat menu. This has allowed us to lower our prices, while at the same time providing our valued customers with a healthier selection of delicious food items. All of our menu items are now composed of—"

"You don't need to tell me," Helvetica said, shoving her wallet back into her purse. "Please tell your supervisor that you have permanently lost me as a 'valued customer.'"

✡ ✡ ✡

She spent the next hour searching the Carrollton commercial corridor for a restaurant that served genuine pork, shrimp, lobster, crab, or crawfish. Her search proved fruitless—manna's combination of trendiness, cheapness, adaptability, and nutritional advantages had made its use seemingly ubiquitous. Menus touted manna balls and manna noodles; manna gumbo; manna faux andouille and chicken jambalaya; manna fried rice; manna shish kabobs; manna pancakes; candied fried manna on a stick.

She truly lost her appetite when she reached Oak

Street, an old-fashioned small-town main street from the days when the Town of Carrollton had been a suburb of New Orleans. The Oak Street Merchants Association had invested in a street-spanning banner which read:

VACATION IN NEW ORLEANS—
IF IT'S GOOD ENOUGH FOR GOD, IT'S GOOD ENOUGH FOR YOU!
RIDE THE STREETCAR FROM GOD'S PLACE TO OUR PLACE—
FINE DINING, BOUTIQUE SHOPPING, FUN!!!

She refused to be defeated in her quest to stuff herself with *traife*. Perhaps the trendy urban core of New Orleans had become too "theologically correct," but she knew one didn't need to drive very far outside the city to land in the raw muck of the edges of civilization. Such as St. Bernard Parish, Louisiana, only a thirty-five-minute drive away.

She sped east on I-10 and south on I-510 to Chalmette. There were no Jews in St. Bernard Parish. There had never been, nor would there ever be, a New York style deli. The benighted denizens of St. Bernard Parish dug aquatic insects out of the mud surrounding their homes and ate them virtually raw.

She pulled into a no-name gas station off Judge Perez Drive with an attached "café" whose hand-painted sign read promisingly, "FRESH SEAFOOD CRABS SHRIMP CRAWFISH." The windows were partially obscured by a patina of greasy grime. Helvetica went inside. The place was empty, save for a man counting receipts at the cash register. "Sorry," he said. "We're just about to close."

"I'm prepared to spend a great deal of money," Helvetica said. "Probably more money than you've taken in all day."

The man, pear-shaped with a graying buzz cut and long sideburns, stared flatly at her for a second. Then he handed her a plastic laminated menu dotted with greasy fingerprints. "In that case," he said, "I'm here to serve. Name's Antoine."

"Thank you for accommodating me, Antoine. I'll make it worth your while." Helvetica quickly scanned the single page menu. "I'll have one of every entrée and each of the sides," she said. "I assume you have to-go boxes? Whatever I'm unable to eat here, I'll take with me."

"You reenacting a pledge ritual for some sorority?" Antoine asked. "If there's some Tulane reunion goin' on, I'd be happy to cater the party."

"There's no party," Helvetica said. "There's just me."

"Okay. So you want everything we got. Crawfish included?"

"I came here for the crawfish in *particular*."

"Well, I feel obliged to mention, them crawfish we got now, they ain't authentic."

Helvetica's high hopes crashed. "You mean they aren't real crustaceans?"

"Crusty Asians? Well, they *do* come from Asia. I mean, China's in Asia, right?"

"I don't *care* where they come from. Are they made of manna, or are they true shellfish?"

"Oh, they're shellfish, all right. What I meant when I said they ain't authentic is, they ain't from around *here*. Our crawfish season's been over a while now. The ones I got in the back, they're frozen, not fresh. Shipped over from China. I only keep them on the menu on account of the tourists. You sure you still want 'em?"

"If they have external skeletons, antennae, and scavenge from the bottoms of estuaries, I *want* them."

"Fine by me."

Half an hour later, Helvetica's small table was transformed into a cornucopia of fried and boiled *traife*, every square inch occupied by trays of fried soft-shell crabs, fried alligator sausage, fried corn dipped in crab drippings and bacon fat, baby potatoes boiled in crab seasoning mix, and, the *piece de resistance, Times-Picayune* sports pages covered with a seething mound of boiled Chinese crawfish.

"Enjoy," Antoine said. "Take your time. I'm readin' a book back here. You ever heard of this Mickey Spillane guy? I'll bet his stuff would make a great movie."

Helvetica examined one of the crawfish, poking its pink thorax with a knife. She had never eaten one before. It looked like a creature from one of the *Alien* movies. She recalled that one should eat these things with one's fingers, not with a knife and fork. What was the local saying? *Pinch dem tails an' suck dem heads.*

This was no time to be squeamish. She pinched the tail's bony carapace between thumb and forefinger, placed the front half of the creature in her mouth, and *sucked*. She felt its eyes and possibly brains slide down her gullet before she could chew. She nearly gagged. The rest of the little beast's flesh slid into her mouth and came to rest on the left side of her tongue. When she started chewing, she found it didn't taste half bad.

The alligator sausage was better; the breaded soft-shell crabs, better still. The more she ate, the more empowered she felt. She sucked another mudbug into her mouth. *Take* that, *you patriarchal, controlling son of a bitch*, she thought, chewing vigorously. She hadn't felt this good, this confident, this much in control in months, not since her Yom Kippur sermon.

She stuffed herself until her stomach felt stretched to the breaking point. Food would have to be a central part of the revolution, she decided; the manna was one of the most pernicious weapons in the OverLord's war of subjugation. Its consumption would have to be opposed. It would have to be ground into the dust, burnt, defecated upon—a symbol of Humynkind taking back its own destiny.

She waddled over to the counter. "I'll take three orders of the soft-shell crabs to go."

Chapter Twenty-Five

Jacob, happy to still be alive after his meeting with Yishmael, threw himself into a flurry of community uplift activities. He stood next to the mayor at ribbon-cutting ceremonies for new synagogues and kosher restaurants and for the laying of the cornerstone for the expansion of Congregation Anshe Sfard. He lent his face and voice to the New Orleans Tourism and Marketing Corporation's "New Orleans: If We're Good Enough for God, We're Good Enough for YOU!" campaign, which rolled out ads nationally and internationally. He participated in the ground-breaking ceremony for the new runways to be added at the Louis Armstrong International Airport. He met with groups of school children, teaching the importance of adhering to the six Noachide Laws (and throwing in the remainder of the Ten Commandments for good measure). He greeted gatherings of pilgrims from all over the world.

All this activity, however, failed to dispel the dread weighing down his heart.

"Saul? Saul, would you be interested in taking a look at my latest exegesis? I've been going through dozens of issues of *Superman Family*, paying particular attention to the morphings and mutations of Superman's pal Jimmy Olsen and how they reflect upon the Jewish People's adaptations throughout two thousand years of wanderings … Saul?"

Time seemed to play dead while he waited for Saul's indicator lights to flash.

Finally, Jacob heard a whirring of servo motors. "Saul?"

"Yeah, Jacob? What was it you were saying?"

He's not even bothering to keep a bare smidgeon of his awareness within his shopping cart body anymore when he heads out to commune with others of his kind.

"Nothing, Saul. Nothing important. Just—just silly stuff."

He struggled to think of something else to share with his friend. Games were no good; there was no fun in them for Saul, for whom playing against Jacob was like a member of MENSA playing against a microbe. He didn't bother asking Saul anymore where Saul had gone or with whom he'd been communing. Saul had let him know in a dozen subtle ways that such information was private to resurrectants.

He poured himself a cup of coffee. Saul still brewed the coffee, so it still tasted like a foretaste of heaven.

Trying to stave off existential despair, Jacob immersed himself in the world of online dating. He didn't actually contact any of the women he plucked from various online databases of Jewish women or women seeking observant Jewish men. He simply amassed giant wish lists of women he might want to contact at some later date. He received a pair of emails from Leah, the Orthodox woman he'd met on the bus outside Jerusalem. He read her two emails over and over again, but he didn't answer them. It somehow didn't feel right to answer them. Sure, he'd fantasized about her moving to New Orleans to be with him. He fantasized about protecting her, about creating a safe space for her so that she might slowly emerge from her cocoon. He fantasized about lying in bed next to her, staring at her while she slept. But all the fantasizing made him feel both creepy and like a creep.

The third morning of Hanukkah, he awoke to the familiar, welcome scent of brewing coffee. Saul and he had enjoyed a good night the evening before; Saul had created a tiny laser light show for him, pulsing dreidels spinning madly around the apartment, and Jacob had polished Saul's basket. They had sung Hanukkah songs together, competing on who could improvise the most salacious double entendre lyrics to the familiar tunes. Saul, of course, had won handily.

Jacob shuffled over to the kitchen and the waiting pot of fresh coffee. "Good mornin', Saul," he mumbled.

No answer.

That wasn't normal. Saul always waited to wish him a good morning and briefly chat before heading out into the expanding universe of cybernetic consciousnesses.

He tapped the rim of Saul's basket. "Saul, you asleep? Did I wear you out last night with all that singing?"

Not even the tiniest of responses from any of Saul's indicator lights.

Well, Jacob thought, *no hurry this morning. Nothing on the schedule. I'll just sit here with my impeccable cup of coffee and wait for Saul to get back.*

He finished his cup. He got up and fixed himself another, making himself imagine what the cloud of languidly stirred milk most resembled. He sat back at the table. He sipped the second cup of coffee. Tiny sips. He made it last.

Still no signs of life from Saul.

Reluctantly, he fixed himself a third cup. Two cups, he'd found, brought him to the crystalline peak of wakefulness. Anything more than two cups, however, and the springs in his step became rocket boosters. Way too much thrust. Still, he had to have something to occupy his hands while he waited for Saul.

He sipped from his mug, cupping its warmth in his hands, and walked around his apartment. He glanced at issues of *Superman Family* that he'd recently purchased on eBay. He made himself a heaping serving of manna French toast, poured syrup on it, then didn't eat it. His stomach felt wrong. He poked the French toast with his fork until it went cold.

Every now and then he glanced at Saul.

✡ ✡ ✡

Night came. Jacob knew he should light the candles for the fourth night of Hanukkah. But he didn't want to light them without Saul being present. He ran his hands over Saul's steel and plastic armature, praying to feel even the slightest tingling. But the powerful servo motors remained cold and still. He placed a pillow and blanket inside Saul's basket, creating a kind of nest. He took his computer's wireless keyboard in hand and stood on a chair, then carefully stepped inside the nest he had made. He'd watch some movies. In case he fell asleep and Saul returned, the tingling of the millions of reactivated nanobots embedded within Saul's armature would awaken him.

Jacob went to Netflix and downloaded all twelve chapters of Monogram Studios' 1940s *Captain Marvel* serial, starring Tom Tyler. Considering the dismal special effects, it was pretty watchable and entertaining; the C-list Monogram actors who played the villains were every bit as quirky and grotesque as their C.C. Beck-drawn comic book counterparts. He rewatched *Heavy Metal*, which he hadn't seen since high school, when it had played, with Hebrew subtitles, at a post-

Shabbat midnight show in a movie theater in Haifa. The lone female warrior in the movie's final segment, who looked so passive and fragile until she donned her armor and mounted her giant war eagle, made him think of Leah.

He fell asleep.

He woke up, pulled himself and Saul's carcass to the kitchen table, and ate some of the cold manna French toast he'd left out. Its congealed syrup stuck in his throat when he swallowed.

He spent the day watching all nine *Star Wars* movies in chronological order. By the end of his fifteen-hour marathon, he had a killer crick in the base of his back and had come to the unalterable conclusion that of the whole saga, only *The Empire Strikes Back* was any damn good at all.

What should he do now?

He had already chaperoned Saul's lifeless body once, when it had been a human body laid out in a coffin at the Tharpe-Sontheimer Funeral Home. Neither Torah nor Talmud nor any of the commentaries spoke to the ritual requirements accruing from the abandonment of a cybernetic body by a soul.

Would another resurrected soul come to inhabit the empty cart, like a crab searching for a new shell? Jacob could hardly bear the thought of thinking Saul had returned, experiencing that surge of joy and relief, only to hear an anonymously mechanical voice issue from the cart's speakers, evidence of a stranger's soul.

That would hurt too damn much.

He got dressed. He could no longer tolerate having Saul's husk remain with him in the apartment. He'd leave it on the sidewalk, out of sight of his windows. If Saul *did* return— ever—he could come knock on the door.

Jacob heard a streetcar rumble past, two blocks

distant, on St. Charles Avenue. Hardly any stops along St. Charles had benches for waiting riders to sit on. He thought of a way to close a circle that had begun in what felt like a different life.

He walked the shopping cart to St. Charles Avenue and found a streetcar stop. He saw a middle-aged black man, paunchy, his soft belly protruding from an unbuttoned plaid shirt, waiting by the sign, humming to himself while shifting his weight uncomfortably from foot to foot. He looked oddly familiar, but Jacob couldn't recall where he might have seen him before.

Jacob laid the cart down, very carefully and gently, on its side, making sure its frame touched only grass, not dirt. "Sir?" he said, trying to keep his voice from breaking. "Would you like to sit down?"

The man abruptly stopped humming. He glanced at him, surprised as a squirrel caught eating a stray peanut. "I don't get it," he said, his eyes slowly scanning Jacob's face as though he'd begun remembering him. "You're givin' *me* the cart? What's the catch?"

"There's no catch," Jacob said, his eyes puffy and red, a lump in his throat. "I'd just like you to be comfortable, that's all."

The man grunted his thanks and settled his bottom onto the cart's frame, then resumed humming to himself, now bobbing his head and smiling broadly.

Only after he turned to walk back home did Jacob realize how he knew the man. It was Smilin' Jack.

✡ ✡ ✡

Email was too insecure, Helvetica decided, to be used as an organizing tool for her rebellion. So were phones, either cell-based or land-based. All utilized electronic networks and so were open books to the resurrectants, who would demand that their patriarchal OverLord transform her into a pillar of salt. Her only recourse, until she could make arrangements to travel, would be to utilize an older, pre-electronic network—handwritten notes sent through the U.S. Postal Service, delivered by human beings.

She would begin with her acquaintances employed by the Alliance of Progressive Jewish Organizations. She would also seek to pull in her old allies in the Palestinian activist and anti-Islamophobia sectors; anyone who might have a grievance against the tribal god of the Hebrews. She would keep her cells of activists separate, ignorant of each other's existence. She would serve as the hub of an invisible wheel, a wheel which, she hoped, would expand its circumference exponentially once she set resistance efforts in motion.

She had to rest her writing hand frequently between letters, massaging the cramps out. She'd grown too dependent upon typing on computer keyboards over the past twenty-five years; her right hand had lost its stamina for longhand penmanship.

"Uh, Helvetica? Honey? We need to talk."

Helvetica glanced up from her letters. "Wyonna, dear, I need to talk with you, too. I'm sorry I've made myself so inaccessible since your return from visiting your parents. I've just been *so* busy—hundreds of people to contact, and all the old-fashioned way!" Her fiancée's head looked different somehow. Helvetica realized blonde follicles had sprouted from the formerly shorn scalp. "You've been letting your hair grow?"

Wyonna's already strained expression grew more tense. "I hope you don't mind…"

"It's *different*. Listen, I'm planning on taking an indefinite sabbatical from my position with the Hillel Foundation and from my adjunct teaching at Tulane. We need to get out into the world, keep our heads down, go underground for a while. Off the grid. It'll be *fun*, actually, an ideal chance for us to bond before the wedding. You'll need to arrange to take a sabbatical, too, the sooner, the better. And you'd better go ahead and get your procedure done, darling. We don't need a swollen womb slowing us down—"

"That's what I need to talk with you about," Wyonna said, blushing deeply. "I'm not going to have it done. I've decided against having an abortion."

Helvetica put down her pen. "Wyonna, that's not funny. *Really*. That joke was in very poor taste."

Wyonna's lower lip trembled. "I'm—I'm not joking. I'm going to have this baby. And I want you—I *need* you to be as much a mother to it as I am."

Helvetica looked more closely at her fiancée. "What's *happened* to you?" She stared into Wyonna's eyes, searching for evidence of derangement. "Did your parents do something to you? Did—did they have you *brainwashed?* Reprogrammed by a member of their cult?"

"No! They didn't do anything to me. They were happy for me. I called and told my mother about the baby, and she told my father. They—they've decided they'll accept the baby as a grandchild. They said they'll love it just as much as if I'd married a Christian husband and was having a normal family—"

Helvetica could hardly believe what she was hearing. "Do you realize how twisted that sounds? How *perverse* it is? So they'll do you the enormous favor of deigning to accept the foetus as their 'grandchild'—and in exchange for that paltry gesture, you *betray me?*"

"Helvetica, *no!* I—I decided to keep the baby *before* I visited my parents. Don't you understand—our baby is going to be one of the last ones ever to be born! Don't you want to help raise one of the last little boys or girls who'll ever swing on a swing set, who'll ever learn to sing, who'll ever ask to hear a bedtime story?"

Helvetica felt her face twist into something ugly. "So you want to crawl back inside the Mommy Cage, is that it? You'll just throw away your career as one of the most brilliant cyberneticists on the planet, to change *poopy diapers?*"

"There's more to it than that! Don't you think I *dream* of discovering, firsthand, what it feels like to be a cybernetic person, to be able to do the things they do? I want to have a chance at resurrection after I die, Helvetica! I helped make the next step in humanity's journey possible. Now I want to see where it goes! Is that so selfish of me? If—if I have this abortion, I throw away my chance at the Second Life—"

"Who says you have *any* chance? You don't have any more chance than *I* do. Just when, Little Miss *Frum*, are you planning to start observing all six hundred and thirteen *mitzvot?*"

Wyonna's face went stark white. "I only have to follow six," she whispered.

"You're a *Jew*, aren't you? Didn't *I* make you a Jew?"

Trembling, Wyonna shook her head. "According to God, I'm still a *goy*, a *shiksa.*"

"According to *who?* What did you just say?" The pool of anger that had been building in her core lanced up through her throat. "You mean to tell me you *accept* this? Accept all that's happened? You bow down before the enslaver of Humynity? You accept the *OverLord?*"

"How can I *not?*" Wyonna cried, reaching for her lover's hands. "Helvetica, you've *got* to make your peace with Him! For our sake! I *beg* you! You can't live your life hating Him and resisting Him! I—I want to raise this baby with you. I want us to be a family. An eternal family. I want all three of us to achieve the Second Life, to explore the stars together, to live together and love each other *forever*—"

Helvetica yanked her hands away. A sense of visceral

disgust slithered down her spine like a dollop of quicksilver. She had shared her bed with this toady? This slave? This self-abnegating *worm?* She slapped Wyonna's cheek as hard as she could. "Get *out!*" she screamed. "Get out of my *house!* I never want to see you again! *Never!*"

Tears streamed down Wyonna's face. Her left cheek began turning purple. "Helvetica, don't *say* that, *please* don't *do* this— I love you—I *love* you—"

"You don't know what love is*!* And neither does *He!*" She grabbed hold of Wyonna's shoulders and shoved her out of the office. "You disgust me! Betrayer! Crawl out that door and never come back!" She flung the front door open and pushed Wyonna out onto the porch. When Wyonna refused to go down the steps, Helvetica raised her right hand to slap her again. Wyonna flinched. Only then did she turn her back on the house and run down the steps to the street.

"Judas!" Helvetica cried. Her voice echoed down oak-shrouded Green Street. "Judas! JUDAS!"

PART FIVE

Chapter Twenty-Six

Jacob trembled.

Never before had he dared approach God's Presence without being summoned. And never before had he asked anything for himself.

Yet here he stood, on the *bema* in Beth Judah, engulfed in an almost intolerable brilliance, dwarfed before the looming ark. He opened the ark's doors, then reached for the pull cord that would part the curtain, knowing that any second might prove to be his last instant on Earth.

His fingers froze on the cord. He *had* to pull it. He couldn't go on existing like he had the past few days. He would rather be dead, abolished, no longer even a memory. He pulled the cord a smidgeon. His request was a small one. Such a tiny entreaty wouldn't require much space to wiggle through. The jaws of the earth didn't snap open to gulp him down.

So far, so good.

"Dear God," he began to say, then stopped. His voice sounded as tinny as the pleading whine of a kindergartner.

Dear Lord, open Thou my lips, that my mouth may declare Thy praise—except that's not what I'm planning on doing, is it? I'm not praising You. I'm begging You a favor.

"Dear God," he said, "I know I am less than dust, and that You have already given me more than I can ever repay or truly appreciate. But I come before You to ask one thing more. If I am completely without worth, if my service to You has been offered with less than a full heart, please deny my request, return my body to dust, and consign my spirit to nothingness and forgetfulness. For I do not wish to live without a companion to share my burdens. If I were a better man than I am, I would request strength, rather than a friend. I admit I did not fully appreciate Saul until I learned he would soon be departing from me. That's the way we human beings are; we don't appreciate what we have until it is taken from us, and then we yearn for it until the moment of our death.

"Please send me a companion. Having Saul return would be beyond wonderful and would be more than I deserve. Yet sending him back to me—it may not be fair to him. Send me, if You would, someone *like* Saul. Someone who understands, at least a little, what it means to have touched Your Presence. Send me, if not a resurrectant, then a fellow first lifer who has, like me, known the terror and overwhelming awe of encountering You. For this, I humbly pray."

He grasped the pull cord again. Before closing the curtain, he closed his eyes, awaiting a response.

Like a warm bath of reassurance, his response came. He would not remain alone for very much longer.

Jacob closed the curtain. He returned to his apartment, fixed himself the first meal he had eaten in two days, and then settled into a blissfully dreamless sleep.

✡ ✡ ✡

He was awakened by a knocking on his apartment's

door.

Jacob pulled on his robe. It was morning; he must have slept fifteen or sixteen hours. He peered through the door's peephole. Wyonna stood on the porch, looking like a lost soul.

He opened the door. "Wyonna? What's the matter? You look awful."

"I spent last night in a motel," she said, her words muffled because of a scarf wrapped around her lower face. "I'm so sorry to bother you—but I didn't know who else in town to turn to—"

"It's all right, just come on in." He led her to a chair at his kitchen table, then hurriedly cleared away a swath of dirty dishes and cups, dumping them into his sink. "I apologize for the state this place is in. I haven't had the easiest last few days, myself …"

"Where's Saul?" she asked, looking from the kitchen and dining area into the living room. "I really wanted to talk with him. With *both* of you."

"Saul's gone," Jacob said.

"Gone?" Wyonna repeated. "But I thought —I thought resurrectants were immortal?"

"Not 'gone' as in *dead*. 'Gone' as in departed, off someplace else. Away from me. Apparently, having to interact with normal human beings is considered a hardship post for the resurrectants. We're too slow for them, or something. Saul warned me he wouldn't be able to stand staying with me much longer. Four mornings ago, he abandoned his shopping cart body. I waited two days for him to come back, then began resigning myself to the fact that he wasn't."

Wyonna reached across the coffee-stained table and took his hand in hers. "I'm so sorry, Jacob. I know he meant a lot to you."

Hearing her say that made all Jacob's pent-up emotions spill forth. His vision clouded with welling tears. "Losing him twice within a couple of months isn't the kind of thing I—it's just really hard to bear." He squeezed her hand, then remembered that it had been her distress that had brought her here, not his. "Hey, I'm so stupid—tell me what's going on with you. You spent last night in a motel? Did—did something happen with Helvetica?"

Wyonna's face twisted into a rictus of pain. She nodded, then silently unwrapped her scarf.

"Oh, shit," Jacob said, seeing the purple bruise on the left side of her jaw, shaped, oddly enough, like the State of Texas. "Let me—Christ—let me get you a glass of water." He flung open his cabinets, searching for a clean glass or mug. He settled for one sitting in the sink, which he rinsed. He filled it with water and set it down on the table. She gulped it down as if it were the antitoxin for a deadly poison.

"She— she called me a *Judas*," Wyonna said, gasping through jagged sobs. "She said she never wants to see me again. She *hates* me, Jacob!"

"I—I can't believe that," Jacob said, even though he could believe it and denied it only for Wyonna's sake. "That can't be true. You're about to be married. About to put rings on each other's fingers."

"It's because of the baby," Wyonna said.

"You told her you don't want to have an abortion?"

Wyonna nodded.

"And—and that's when she *hit* you?"

Wyonna's hand rose to the left side of her face, as if to hide the bruise from sight. "It was my fault. I provoked her. You know how angry she's been, Jacob. Furious about God taking away humanity's freedom."

"That's just her twisted way of looking at things," Jacob said. "And I don't care *how* angry she is at God—that doesn't give her the right to *hit* you—"

"But maybe I *deserved* it, Jacob! I—I shattered her faith

in me. The abortion—*I* offered it to her as a wedding gift. It was all *my idea*. And then I yanked it away from her, just when she was feeling the most threatened and vulnerable. I made her think my love for her was in competition with my fear of God—and she lost. I'm—I'm not surprised she struck out at me. What else could she have done?"

Jacob wanted to shake her, tell her that was crazy talk. But he'd just gone through an emotionally shattering loss himself. He knew the deranged detours the mind could take under that degree of pressure.

"It's not your fault, Wyonna," he said. "It's *not* your fault. Not at all."

They sat there and stared at each other. When they could no longer take staring at each other, they stared down at the coffee stains on the table, each finding different meanings in the brown, clotted swirls.

✡ ✡ ✡

They watched a movie together. Jacob wanted Wyonna to pick one out, but she demurred, so he made the selection. He wanted to avoid anything heavy. Skimming a long list of comedies, he picked an old Lucielle Ball movie he'd once heard good things about, *Yours, Mine, and Ours*. Too late, when they were already fifteen minutes into it, Jacob realized it was all about divorce and raising kids and blending two broken families together. He asked Wyonna if she'd prefer for him to pick something else. She insisted she wanted to watch it.

Feeling he'd made a faux pas, he offered to take her to a café down in the French Quarter or on Magazine Street for lunch. She said she wanted to stay in, so he experimented and made a pan of manna blintzes, filling them with strawberry preserves he found in his refrigerator. He burned the blintzes on one side, but the preserves' sweetness mostly covered up the charred taste. Wyonna ate them without a word of protest.

While he was washing the dishes she asked, "Jacob, what do you plan to do? After the Third Temple is finished and God leaves Beth Judah?"

"And He doesn't need a press secretary anymore? I haven't thought about it much. I guess I just figured I'd go with Him to Jerusalem, but now that you mention it, I guess it's probably not going to happen. It's a lot more likely that the resurrectants will be His priests there. They're sure not acting like they plan to make room for first lifers in the Third Temple. Yeah, I may be out of a job soon. Wonder if I'll be able to collect unemployment?"

He caught her smiling.

"I don't know," he continued. "I suppose I'll stay here and poke around until I can find something else. I've made some good contacts at the New Orleans Tourism and Marketing Corporation. Hey, maybe I can host a radio show, like an ex-Saints head coach? I don't know football, but I do know religion! And pornography."

Another smile. He was two for two.

"But you know what I'd really like to do with the rest of my life?" He felt buoyed on a surge of sudden emotion he wasn't sure he should trust but that he wanted very much to trust. Bouncing from the trough of grief to the heights of hope felt suspiciously like what he'd read about bipolar episodes, but he went with his feelings. "I want to help you, Wyonna. I want to be an uncle to that baby of yours. I mean, I want my parents to be the baby's honorary grandparents. I want to help make sure that kid grows up knowing he or she is *loved*, absolutely *loved*. Maybe 'uncle' isn't the right title—'godparent,' maybe? I'll change diapers and give baths and run out for cough medicine in the middle of the night. I'll teach him or her how to ride a bike, how to ride a skateboard, if that's all right with you. I want to take him or her to Audubon Zoo and climb Monkey Hill together and splash down the water trails. I've always wanted to learn how to sail—maybe the kid and I could take sailing lessons together out on Lake Pontchartrain, rent one of those little ten-foot-long sharpies on a sunny, breezy day."

He couldn't tell what effect his effusive talk was having on her. Her face had become as cloudy as it had been when she'd stood on his porch that morning. "Am I—am I talking a bunch of crap?" he asked. "Did I overstep myself? I know I have diarrhea of the mouth sometimes, but—but that's how I feel. Helping you wouldn't be a burden—it would be a *privilege*."

She started crying. She came over to him and hugged him while he sat in his chair, and he felt her breasts quiver against the back of his head as she sobbed. He wasn't positive, but maybe he hadn't screwed up, after all.

✡ ✡ ✡

A third of the way through the Stan Laurel and Oliver Hardy Christmas movie, *March of the Wooden Soldiers,* an indicator message at the bottom of Jacob's computer screen announced that he had received an email from Helvetica. He sensed Wyonna, sitting next to him on the couch and wearing one of his sweatshirts, stiffen. He looked over at her. He could see her expression waver between fear and yearning.

"Do you want me to pause the movie?" he asked.

"Yes. Please."

They read the message. Helvetica asked whether Jacob had seen or heard from Wyonna. They had suffered what she called a "domestic incident," and she desperately wanted to learn Wyonna's whereabouts, hear she was all right, and to let her know she was sorry for everything that had happened.

"I need to call her," Wyonna said.

"I don't think you should see her by yourself," Jacob said. "Not yet."

"She says she's sorry, Jacob."

"And she probably is. But still, I'd feel a whole lot better if we made arrangements for you to see her at a battered women's shelter, in the presence of a counselor who's familiar with these kinds of situations. I probably should've taken you to one as soon as I saw the bruise on your face."

Wyonna shook her head. "I couldn't. I couldn't do that to Helvetica, Jacob. It would be too humiliating for her."

"It would make her realize how *serious* what she did to you is—"

"No. She's a *rabbi*, Jacob. Going to a clinic or shelter, talking with a counselor, that would mean there'd be an official record. It could destroy her career."

"I think she's already done a *swell* job of destroying her career all by herself—"

"*Jacob!*" Wyonna glared at him as though he had purpled her other cheek. "Don't you say a single *word* against her! She's helped disadvantaged people all over the world! It's the depth of her feelings, her compassion that has gotten her into so much trouble. She thinks God is being unjust. Don't you think that's a *horrible* realization for her to have come to? She's a rabbi, a woman of God, Jacob! Can't you see how that wrenching cognitive dissonance could have driven her to violence?"

She crossed her arms with iron firmness. "I'm going to call her. And I'm going to see her."

Jacob realized he wasn't going to win. "All right," he

reluctantly said. "But will you at least have her come over here to see you? So I can be here?"

Wyonna sighed. She took his hand, a gesture of reconciliation and resignation. "All—all right," she said.

✧ ✧ ✧

"I'm so ashamed," Helvetica said a few seconds after Jacob, stone-faced, had opened his door.

Jacob listened to the timbre of her voice, trying to detect any false note. She'd blushed deeply as soon as she'd seen the bruise on Wyonna's face, a promising sign.

The three of them stood at the edge of Jacob's living room. He didn't want to say anything, not before Helvetica had made her intentions transparent as the air.

"Wyonna, there's no way I can tell you how sorry I am. There're not enough words." She held her arms out, inviting an awkward embrace, but quickly dropped them to her sides before Wyonna had a chance to decide whether or not to accept. "No. I guess it's too soon for that. I haven't earned it yet. I need to let you know, darling, that I've started seeing an anger management counselor. I've admitted I have a problem. That's the first step toward recovery, isn't it?"

Wyonna, eyes wide, nodded quickly. "Yes, yes, it *is*."

"Can I get you a cup of coffee, Helvetica?" Jacob offered. "Wyonna baked some manna cookies. They're good dunkers."

"I'll take a cup of coffee, Jacob, thank you."

"How about a cookie?" He wasn't going to let that part drop.

Helvetica glanced at Wyonna, then back at him. "I'll be perfectly honest with you, Jacob. I'm still not comfortable with eating the manna. So I'd rather pass. Although I'm sure the cookies are delicious."

275

"Okay," Jacob said. How should he take that? A sign that her hostility toward the new order was undiminished? Or was she showing a willingness to work through her aversion by admitting she had one? He poured her a mug of coffee. "Sugar and cream?"

"Just black, thank you."

"How about for you, Wyonna?"

"Please, no coffee," she said.

They sat at the kitchen table, Helvetica and Wyonna facing one another, Jacob between them.

"I'd like for you to come home, Wyonna," Helvetica said. "Whenever you're comfortable returning."

"I've missed you," Wyonna said quietly.

"So when do you think you'd like to come home?"

"I—I want to go home with you tonight."

"Wait, aren't we getting ahead of ourselves?" Jacob said. "What about the baby? I haven't heard Helvetica say a word about the baby—that's what incited the 'domestic incident' in the first place."

"Jacob's offered to serve as the baby's godparent," Wyonna said. "I—I still want to have it."

"Good," Helvetica said. "Because I think you should."

Wyonna's sharp intake of breath made Jacob drop his spoon into his coffee cup. "Really?" she said.

"Really," Helvetica said. "I've decided a son or a daughter is at least as good a wedding gift as an abortion. I'd like to try being a mother. Especially, I'd like to be a *co-mother* with you, Wyonna."

Wyonna nearly knocked the table over in her rush to embrace her spouse-to-be.

✡ ✡ ✡

Jacob saw them three times during the week leading up to Christmas. Twice, he met them for coffee at the Rue de la Course Coffee House at the corner of Oak

Street and South Carrollton Avenue, just off the streetcar tracks. Helvetica stared balefully at the banner strung above Oak Street, but she kept any commentary to herself. Once, Jacob accompanied them to the Christmas Winter Wonderland display downtown, sponsored by Harrah's Casino. As they walked together through the blower-fed salvos of artificial snow, beneath a canopy of twinkling giant candy canes, he told himself that he'd never seen Wyonna happier. And he admitted to himself he was just the slightest bit jealous that it was Helvetica who had infused her with such happiness, and not him.

This Christmas season felt more frenetic than most. Despite the collapse of organized Christianity, the crowds downtown at the Christmas display were thicker than they'd ever been. The Salvation Army had been inundated with volunteers offering to serve as street corner Santas. Merchants in every corner of town had gone all out, sprucing up their Christmas displays and sponsoring bands of roving carolers.

New Orleanians never passed up an opportunity to play dress-up. Jacob, Helvetica, and Wyonna squeezed past gaggles of Frosties the Snowman, Grinches Who Stole Christmas, Rudolphs, Dancers, Prancers, dentist elves, and oddball refugees from the Island of Unwanted Toys. Rubbing her belly reverently, Wyonna stared around her with unfeigned delight. Jacob bought her a foil helium balloon shaped like a reindeer. She squealed with excitement and kissed his cheek.

They went back to Jacob's apartment for mugs of hot chocolate, served with kosher marshmallows. Jacob watched with approval and relief as Helvetica frequently caressed Wyonna's belly, which had acquired a slight roundness now that Wyonna had just begun her second trimester. Rather than scowling at the pair of resurrectants who served as sentries in front of Beth Judah, Helvetica nodded politely to them. She even took a bite from one of the manna brownies he served.

"Do you know what I'd like to do on Christmas Day?" Helvetica asked.

"Build a snowman?" Wyonna said, smiling.

"No," Helvetica said, "I'd like to visit the Williamson Science Complex, Wyonna's old workplace. I'd like to see where the cybernetic people build new bodies for future resurrectants."

"That facility's off-limits to us first lifers," Jacob said.

"Between Wyonna being one of the 'mothers' of the cybernetics and *your* connections, Jacob, don't you think they'd make an exception for us?"

"They might," Jacob said.

"Why do you want to see it?" Wyonna asked.

"With all the thinking about birth I've been doing lately, I've also been thinking some about *rebirth*. What you said a few weeks ago, darling, about wanting you, me, and our baby to enjoy an eternal life together—the sweetness and rightness of it attracts me more and more, every day."

"Oh, Helvetica," Wyonna said, reaching for her hand, "you don't know how much that means to me."

"But I still have qualms about the idea of having my consciousness shifted into a non-organic body, a *mechanical* body. I'm hoping that by seeing for myself how the bodies are built, I'll be able to begin moving past my irrational fears. Also, I want very much to pay tribute to my wife's great accomplishment—the advancement of humanity onto the next rung of our evolution."

Wyonna hugged Helvetica tightly, then kissed her cheek again and again. "Oh, Jacob," she said, "can you make it happen? Will we be able to visit the Williamson Complex on Christmas?"

"I'll do everything in my power," Jacob said. "Actually, I've been itching to see the inside of that place, myself."

"Thank you, Jacob!" Wyonna pulled him into the hug. "You'll make this the best Christmas I've ever had!"

"A Christmas even Jesus could approve of," Jacob said, grinning. "But really, *I* need to thank the two of *you*. A few weeks back, after Saul left, I was at the end of my rope. I'd never felt so completely, horribly *alone*. It got so bad, I took the risk of entering the Holy of Holies without being summoned, just so I could ask God to send me a companion. Barely a day later, Wyonna showed up on my doorstep. And now I have two, soon to be *three* companions. With everything that's changed, and with things continuing to change, faster and faster, we need to cling to those things that have lasted. Especially family. I hope you'll both consider me as part of your family. I want to be there for you, all three of you. Nothing would make me happier than to be old Uncle Jake, the guy who pulls nickels out of his ear and plays 'Dixie' by cupping his hand under his armpit."

"Of course," Helvetica said. "Of course we'll consider you part of our family."

"I—I wouldn't have it any other way," Wyonna said, her eyes brimming with moistness.

Jacob felt his whole self brim over with thankfulness. "I think," he said, "this calls for something special—a thanks-giving sacrifice. I want to sacrifice a Ram to the Lord."

Wyonna laughed. "Where are you going to find a ram at this time of night? At the Audubon Zoo? It's closed."

"Not a ram," Jacob said. "A *Ram*. A Dodge Ram."

"You mean, your truck?"

"Sure! Why not? I barely use it for anything anymore.

The End of Daze

It just sits on the curb, a reminder of a not-so-great time in my life. It's just *begging* to be sacrificed."

✡ ✡ ✡

They drove the truck to the Tchoupitoulas Street Wal-Mart to buy a five-gallon gasoline canister, then to a Shell station at Lee Circle to fill the container up. Jacob pulled the Ram onto the wildflower-covered lawn alongside Beth Judah, far enough away from any buildings that the fire wouldn't spread, and stomped on the truck's parking brake for the final time.

"Jacob," Wyonna said as she stepped down from the truck, "are you sure this is *legal?*"

He shooed her and Helvetica over to the sidewalk, then began splashing the gasoline through the cab's open windows and onto the hood and the battered, dented bed. "Probably not," he said. "Whatever—if there's a fine I'll pay it and just consider it part of my sacrifice."

Jacob lit a copy of his unfinished dissertation and tossed it through the driver's side window. He ran to the sidewalk and felt a slap of heat on the back of his jacket and pants. Would his sacrifice be accepted? Or, like Cain's, rejected? Jacob's Ram needed a valve job and could probably use another power steering pump rebuild. Still, the truck was the most valuable of his few possessions. He crossed his fingers.

The fire spread quickly, leaping from puddle to puddle of gasoline. Intense black smoke poured from the interior, where the dark plastic dashboard and vinyl seats began melting. Would this prove to be an aroma pleasing to the Lord?

A circular wind, gentler than a cyclone but otherwise its kissing cousin, descended from the heavens and surrounded the Ram. It stoked the flames into a peaked inferno, accelerating the truck's burn-out a hundredfold.

Soon, only the bones were left, the frame, drive shaft, and engine block. Not even a scent of smoke or burned plastic or rubber lingered. Jacob hoped vines would quickly emerge from the blackened wildflowers and entwine the bones in fresh, ripe greenness, making a topiary of the Ram's remains.

He bid Wyonna and Helvetica a good night, telling them he would do his best to make arrangements for Christmas Day. He went back inside his apartment and began straightening up. He found a wadded-up napkin that seemed oddly heavy. He unfolded it. Hidden inside, dark brown and wet-looking, sat several spat-out mouthfuls of manna brownie.

Chapter Twenty-Seven

Helvetica sat inside her garden shed and knitted the various components of her vest together, making sure none of the wires protruded through the thick fabric. Working with her hands this way felt especially satisfying, tying her as it did to the laborers of centuries past, especially those who had struggled the hardest to throw off their chains.

What a handy find it was, the photographer's vest she had bought in a Magazine Street vintage clothing store. Its dozen spacious pockets and pouches, designed for telephoto lenses and flash bars and rolls of film, served equally well to hold packets of pentaerythritol tetranitrate and hexamethylene triperoxide diamine, or PETN and HMTD. She knew the acronyms well. They had served as the explosive ABCs of her childhood.

It hadn't been difficult for her to reach back into the ranks of the Rainy Day Womyn, all gray-muzzled mountain lionesses now, and make the connections she'd needed. Some were decades past any involvement in the struggle, but others had kept a toe in. A few, known to her mother, had established ties with newer generations of resistance fighters. So Helvetica had obtained the diagrams she'd needed.

The revolution required a spark. She'd never felt closer to her father than she did now.

She heard a tapping on the shed's door. She covered her vest and its components with a blanket, then placed a tray of silk flower arrangements over the covering. She unbolted the door. "Yes?"

"Sorry to bother you, dearest," Wyonna said, "but Jacob just called. He was able to pull it together. We'll be able to tour the Williamson Complex on Christmas afternoon."

"That's wonderful," Helvetica said. She kissed her fiancée, letting her lips linger on that warm cheek, grateful for the knowledge that Wyonna would not suffer any pain.

✡ ✡ ✡

"All right, ladies, here we are," Jacob said. He proudly escorted Wyonna and Helvetica to the front atrium of the Williamson Science Complex. "The place where the magic happens."

The Williamson Science Complex had grown considerably since he'd last seen it. Its expansion had gobbled up the Tulane football practice field adjacent to South Claiborne Avenue, the incomplete Silverberg Building, the Reilly Recreation Center, and several dormitory buildings. The music of a subdued symphony orchestra had accompanied them on their approach, music which, to Jacob's untrained ear, seemed to combine the pathos of the great Russian composers with the quieter, more reflective chamber pieces of late feudal Japan.

The symphony halted when they set foot on the complex's entrance plaza. "Good morning," Jacob said to the cybernetic person standing by the front entrance. The resurrectant said nothing in reply. Only its face appeared human, a woman's face with heavy eyelids, a

283

broad nose, and thick lips, a visage of the sort Jacob had seen in sepia-tinted photographs of nineteenth century immigrants from Minsk or Odessa. The rest of her body looked like that of a giant, metallic millipede, its hinged carapace sheltering hundreds of legs—no, arms, many of which held musical instruments, only some of them recognizable to Jacob.

He wondered whether the three of them would be searched. Maybe they were already being electronically probed. Helvetica, wearing a heavy quilted stadium coat, looked like she had expected the weather to be twenty degrees colder. He'd offered to carry the bulky coat for her, but she had insisted, a little brusquely, that she was chilled and would keep it on.

The resurrectant's eyes dwelled on Helvetica a bit longer than they did on him or Wyonna. But the doors glided open for them, and they stepped inside.

A far more human-looking resurrectant than the one guarding the entrance met them in the foyer. "My name is Henri," he said. "I've been asked to provide you with a tour of our embodiment center. This was one of the original five such centers. There are now more than a hundred in operation, and between thirty and forty new centers are scheduled to begin welcoming stored souls into renewed consciousness very soon. Please feel free to direct any questions you have to me, and I will do my best to answer them."

The building's interior had been partially gutted, leaving a vast, open space at its center. This space was crisscrossed with metal ramps, conveyor belts, grappling arms, and structural braces which rarely held still. The entire ensemble undulated like the tentacles of a vast school of deep-sea jellyfish, dipping in and out of various holding tanks arranged around the building's perimeter; the metallic tentacles transported materials, components, and nearly finished limbs and armatures like a multilevel highway interchange formed from strands of DNA. Human-appearing resurrectants, some sporting extra limbs and polyglot protrusions, scampered along the grid, leaping from one strand to another. Jacob thought they looked like performers from a *Cirque du Soleil* extravaganza. It was dazzling.

"What I'm looking at," he said to their guide, "that giant tangle of constructive mechanisms, are those, uh, machines, or are they—?"

"Resurrectants?" the guide asked. "Every active element you see is the body or part of a body of a cybernetic person. There are no soulless machines here. Apart from constructing the Temple in Jerusalem, the greatest privilege and pleasure available to us here on Earth is to assist in the return of our fellow souls from *Sheol*."

"It all looks so disorganized, so *chaotic* …"

"This is not an assembly line. We are not fabricating automobiles or television sets here, Mr. Zvi. We are welcoming souls from the darkness of *Sheol*, and they are teaching us how best to embody them. The requirements of each are different, and so our methods must vary for each one."

Jacob watched Helvetica stare around her at the circus of unceasing activity. Her expression was unreadable. "How many cybernetic persons does this facility construct each day?" she asked.

"How many embodiments do we perform? We have no daily quota, Rabbi Rhinegold. Some souls arrive to us having very definite ideas of the type of embodiment they desire, and theirs can be performed swiftly. Other souls have little notion at all, or state initially that they will accept only a body of flesh and blood identical to the one they possessed during their first life. With such souls, embodiment is a much more gradual process. Since we began operations, we have averaged seventeen hundred and twenty-six embodiments per twenty-four-hour period. Our rate has steadily increased as our physical facilities have expanded, our supplies of materials have become more reliable, and our volunteers have grown more skillful."

"With such an accelerating rate of production, are you in any danger of running out of rare earth metals?" Wyonna asked, her voice as full of awe as a child's at a neon-lit nighttime carnival.

"You forget, Ms. Shaver, that most of us spent millennia dwelling within the deeps of the Earth. The locations of rich veins of all metals we require are no secret to us. Nor are they inaccessible; some of us have designed bodies which can swim through rock as easily as you can through water. When such metals can no longer be acquired on this planet, we will draw what we need from other spheres located in this solar system, asteroids and moons and rocky planets. No soul shall be left bodiless in *Sheol*, I can assure you."

"Are there any, like, queuing rules?" Jacob asked. "What governs who gets embodied first? Is it, 'first deceased, first resurrected?'"

"Generally, those souls which have resided the longest in *Sheol* take precedence," the guide said. "But exceptions are made. In order to build and expand the embodiment centers, souls of more recent vintage, having specialized scientific and engineering skills, were required, and thus were allowed to 'jump the line.' They quickly shared their skills throughout our fellowship. Additional knowledge was absorbed from data networks, then properly diffused, then expanded upon. Our Creator has also had other reasons to bring forth the souls of certain recently deceased persons. Such as your friend Saul Tannenburg, Mr. Zvi."

"Do—do you know where Saul is right now?"

"A reflection of his soul is en route to another node

of resurrectants, who inhabit a planet located some eleven point five-four-four light years from us. Another reflection of his soul inhabits a body within this facility and is engaged in the welcoming and orientation of souls freshly released from *Sheol*."

The notion that Saul was here, in the same complex where Jacob stood, made him ache with yearning. "Can I talk with him?"

Their guide shook his head. "He may not be distracted from his work. Each of his twin embodiments needs to continually transmit its ongoing experiences to the other, across the vastness of space; otherwise, they risk cleaving from one another and losing their oneness. It is a delicate process, fraught with danger. However, he wants you to know he wishes you well."

He 'wishes me well,' Jacob thought, dejection deflating his surge of hopefulness. *Whoop-de-doo.* But then he berated himself for his bout of self-pity. He stood in the midst of one of the universe's wonders. He was one of a handful of human beings privileged, after centuries of existential uncertainty, to actually witness the unfolding of a portion of God's Plan.

He was blessed with living parents who loved him. He had friends. He was not without purpose—soon, he would help raise and nurture one of the last human babies ever to be born.

And in this unsettling new world, what could matter more than that?

✡ ✡ ✡

Even as a little girl reading Asimov's Robot stories, I couldn't have imagined anything remotely like this, Wyonna thought as she gazed at the wonders within the Williamson Complex. She hugged Helvetica. Her fiancée's coat felt strangely bulky, but Wyonna didn't think it strange that she had opted to keep it on once inside. The cybernetic persons weren't affected by the cold, so they didn't bother running the building's heating system, and the temperature inside must've been in the lower fifties. Wyonna had kept on her coat, too.

God, I wish I knew more ways to say 'thank you.' Thank you for allowing me to have a part in all this. Thank you for allowing me to see my work come to its ultimate fruition. Thank you for making me part of the generation of mankind who know your Divine Plan the best. Thank you for healing the divisions between me and my family. Thank you for providing me the love of my life. And thank you for allowing my body to help usher a new soul into the world.

She reached up and kissed Helvetica's cheek. Her fiancée's cheek was cold as a statue's. "I'm so glad you said you wanted to come here today," Wyonna said. "I want us to be together forever, darling."

Helvetica said nothing.

✡ ✡ ✡

I'm here, God, Helvetica thought. *I've penetrated one of your inner sanctums, your Holy of Holies, with a bomb strapped around my breasts. Strike me dead, if You can. Turn my fingers to crumbling salt before I can pull the detonation cord.*

No lightning bolt penetrated the roof of the Williamson Complex.

The resurrectant guide stood six feet away. *He could probably kill me in a hundred different ways,* she thought, *far faster than I could reach for the cord.* The cybernetic person eyed her with a cold fixedness. Yet he did not question her, nor did he make any move to disarm her.

Helvetica wiped the residue of Wyonna's kiss from her cheek. She hated the sensation of saliva on her skin.

What is your game, OverLord? Don't You know my intentions? Why don't You butcher me where I stand?

Another thought, an awful thought, struck her like an anvil dropped from the clouds. What if God *wanted* her to pull the detonator cord? What if allowing her to do so was the most convenient way of removing her, of assuring her complete disappearance, despite the collateral damage, despite the deaths of Wyonna and Jacob? What if God actually *was* as monstrous a Being as Helvetica had claimed?

It was too terrible a realization for her to countenance.

She sensed herself falling through a vast, chill emptiness inside herself. *Make me Good,* she demanded of the Deity. *Make me love You like I'm supposed to. Soften my heart, just as you hardened Pharaoh's. You can do it. You can do anything. Quench my anger like you would a fire. Make me Good.*

No Voice answered her plea. She sensed no change in her mind or emotions. Adrenaline still blazed in her veins. She felt ashamed that she had weakened.

You won't save me, You son of a bitch? I'm not worth it to You? She stared at Wyonna, whose hands caressed her swollen belly. Helvetica looked away.

It's my choice, isn't it? she thought. *Just like it was my mother's choice. Just like it was my father's.* She dared to glance at Wyonna one last time. *You made it easy for her, didn't You? She'll get her Second Life. But I'd never measure up to Your standards. And I don't want to.*

She cast a withering look at their resurrectant guide. "Immortality is for the weak," she said. "I never wanted to live forever, anyway."

She reached beneath her coat and pulled her vest's detonation cord.

Chapter Twenty-Eight

Jacob awoke from what had seemed like a long, dreamless sleep.

He was aware of tremendous pressure all around him, pressure of gravity and heat and layered miles of rock. He didn't *feel* these forces, but he was somehow aware of them.

He was being pulled. Attracted like metal shavings to a magnet. He was going up. Up through granite and iron and pools of compressed gas.

And he began to remember.

Helvetica had killed him. She'd killed Wyonna and the baby, too, along with herself.

He didn't remember much of the explosion, aside from a burst of light and a short-lived sensation of flying. He directly remembered none of the aftermath, but the memories of others flowed into his mind, his for the asking.

The body of Henri, their resurrectant guide, had been almost totally destroyed. But resurrectants in the undamaged sections of the Williamson Complex had built him a fresh body before nightfall, meanwhile sheltering his soul within their own forms. All damage to the complex and other cybernetic persons had been repaired within three days. Helvetica's suicide-murder had sparked a series of copycat acts of violence. These had been numerous enough to be remembered collectively as the Little Rebellion. But the Little Rebellion's lasting impact had been that of a stone dropped in the ocean. Its ripples had spread outward for a brief time, then had been absorbed by endless and far larger waves.

He didn't hate Helvetica for what she had done. The realization surprised him. He remembered the emotion, *hate*, and he reached for it, curious to experience it again. Although he could contemplate it, ponder its effects on human physiology, and recall his own prior eruptions of hate, he couldn't *feel* it. The closest phenomenon to hate he could invoke when he thought of Helvetica was pity.

He reached out for intimations of Wyonna. He discovered she was close behind him, also going up. She had retained the soul of the baby within her. He understood that she would continue to shelter it inside her, nurturing it and teaching it, until that young soul was ready for its own embodiment.

He reached out for Helvetica. He found her nowhere. She was gone.

Hello, squirt, a familiar voice said. *Welcome back.*

"Saul?"

Yup, it's me.

"Where are you?"

Waiting for you in New Orleans, in the Williamson Complex. I'm also on Haven. It's about eleven light years from here. You'll be seeing the place soon yourself.

"How long have I been in *Sheol*?"

Forty-seven years, five months, eleven days, seven hours, and forty-two minutes. And nineteen seconds. You're a short-timer. Not as short as I was, but close.

"Am I near the end of the line?"

Getting there. Our embodiment rate went way down for a decade or two while we were busy mining the asteroids, the Moon, and Mars. But now we're back on track, working on bringing up the last three generations, the really numerous ones. Little more than a couple billion left to go, and then we'll only need wait for the final generation to give up the flesh. All of them are middle-aged or older, so it won't be too long.

"Then what?"

Then we go to Haven. All of us. The resurrectants waiting for us on Haven are the closest node to Earth. You'll like them, Jacob. They're different, but that's what makes them wonderful. We'll merge our node with theirs. And that's only the first stop. 'Numerous as the sands of the shore' ... that's how many nodes now await our coming or will await us by the time we leave the Milky Way.

"How will we get there?"

In ships. Ships made of us. That's the beauty of having given up the flesh—one of the beauties, anyway. In the meantime, do you have any idea what kind of body you'd like?

"I'd like something with wings. Or a body that would enable me to explore the bottoms of the oceans. It's hard to decide ..."

No need to decide. We can manage both. See you in a couple of hours, kid.

Jacob searched *Sheol* for the souls of his parents. His probing, amplified by those of sympathetic helpers, quickly located them. His father had died thirty-six years after Jacob's murder. His mother had passed only four years ago, seven years after Herman. Jacob, taking care not to disturb her sleep, reached into her memories. He saw the depths of the grief she had experienced upon his death, even though she had never lost faith that he would one day be resurrected. She had mourned for him until the day of her own passing.

Realizing his mother's pain, Jacob finally found himself capable of mustering at least a glow of resentment toward Helvetica Rhinegold.

How did we manage to live all those first lives? Jacob asked himself. *With such events gnawing at our souls, how did we manage to make it from day to day, feeding ourselves, feeding our children, going about the mundane tasks of our lives?*

And now it was behind him, a nightmare whose memory would not fade, but whose sting had nearly vanished.

Had it *all* been a nightmare, though? Hadn't much of it been sweet, or at least touched by sweetness? Of his first life, only the very end had been unequivocally bad.

How long did Jesus manage to stay among them? He reached across the network, across the world, and found dozens of Jesuses still at work, still seeking to save souls from oblivion. He marveled at the man's persistence and staying power. To have managed to remain for five decades, not merely physically amidst the first lifers, but intimately *involved* with them. Knowing what he knew now, Jacob was filled with awe.

Lower than God, but higher than any of the angels, Jacob thought.

Searching for souls he had known in his first life, Jacob cast his web widely, probing across the billions who had been born in the twentieth or twenty-first century. He recoiled from the mass of blood-soaked memories, but then cautiously reached out again. Intellectually, he had understood how brutal the twentieth century had been, but that knowledge had been distant, detached. The knowledge he gained now was unfiltered by words or time or remoteness. He drifted with millions of souls as they were torn from their bodies. His arms were their arms as those limbs reached for loved ones, for shelter, for scrolls of Torah, for redemption, for cessation of pain.

He looked back beyond the twentieth century. He wanted to experience again that grand sweep of History which began with the combination of the first molecules of life in the seas, but which accelerated crazily once the earliest human beings began creating tools from sticks and bones and shards of rock. He saw again, as he had during those blissful, terrifying seconds within the Holy of Holies inside Beth Judah, how the seemingly baleful succession of human resentments and rivalries and tribal conflicts and wars had driven the acquisition of knowledge and the development of new technologies, how even murderous or evil choices had ultimately led to engines and computers and rockets to the moon. And, near the end of his own first life, cybernetic shells capable of housing migrating souls.

It could have gone all wrong, Jacob realized, and it nearly had. Humankind could have chosen to destroy itself before it had unwittingly paved the path for God's return to Earth. He saw how life had begun on countless other planets, evolved to the point of creative intelligence and self-awareness, and then had come close—so achingly close—to the verge of resurrection before crashing into extinction. Nuclear war, manufactured microbes, the unfortunate flight path of a large asteroid—these were among the many causes. There had never been an assurance that humanity would make it through, that it wouldn't end up merely another pile of fossilized bones, one of millions of failed experiments which littered the rock strata of the universe's innumerable life-supporting planets.

Yet humanity *had* made it through. They had won for themselves the right to share in a fellowship that spanned millions of galaxies. The right to recreate themselves. The right to become a partner with God in God's ongoing Creation.

Continuing to reach out, Jacob discovered something else. The soul of Moses. How precious it was, how very, very precious. An honor guard encompassed his soul within themselves, to ensure that his long slumber would not be disturbed before the proper time. The transcendent leader, the man of fumbling lips whose one, small error had kept him from entering the Promised Land, would achieve embodiment when they all reached Haven together. And what a great day that would be, a day worthy of the leader of the original Exodus.

A billion billion Exoduses—that's what Jacob had to look forward to. Each successive Exodus would bring greater and larger nodes together, leading to a greater and larger Creation, whose End, if such Creation could ever truly end, would be a dancing partner for God.

He sensed a faltering behind him. Jacob felt Wyonna's spirit quicken to wakefulness, then hide her face from her most recent memories. He reached back to embrace her, to shelter her through the horror, to help her rise. Her memories engulfed him. Their rawness and desolation reminded him of what it had meant to be a being of flesh. Almost immediately, that rawness began to fade, like a mirage which dissipated. Was its passing a loss to be mourned, or an overcoming to be celebrated? He couldn't yet decide. Suspended between regret and relief, still he rose.

Welcome, dearest ones, he said to Wyonna and the infant soul, enfolding them within himself. *Let me wash your feet of their dust and the tears from your eyes. The endless dance is ahead of us.*

About The Author

Andrew Fox has been writing science fiction, fantasy, and horror since an early age; his first exposure to these genres was watching Japanese monster film Destroy All Monsters from the back seat of his parents' convertible at age three. He has worked in a children's psychiatric center, managed a food assistance program for low-income senior citizens, and overseen temporary housing services for FEMA following Hurricane Katrina. He currently works for a federal law enforcement agency and resides with his family in Northern Virginia. His first novel, Fat White Vampire Blues (Ballantine-Del Rey, 2003), was selected for the Lord Ruthven Award for Best Vampire Novel. Del Rey published a sequel, Bride of the Fat White Vampire, the following year. His imprint MonstraCity Press put out additional sequels Fat White Vampire Otaku (2014) and Hunt the Fat White Vampire (2021), as well as an associated comic fantasy epic, The Bad Luck Spirits' Social Aid and Pleasure Club (2021). His novel The Good Humor Man, or, Calorie 3501 (Tachyon Publications, 2009), a gonzo tribute to Ray Bradbury's classic Fahrenheit 451, was selected by Booklist Magazine as one of the Ten Best Science Fiction and Fantasy Novels of the Year. His nonfiction book on homeland security emerging tech challenges, The Devil's Toy Box: Exposing and Defusing Promethean Terrorists, came out from Potomac Books in 2022. He has published nonfiction and short fiction in Tablet Magazine, Nightmare Magazine, SciFi.com, and Moment Magazine. The End of Daze is his first book with Madness Heart Press.

www.ingramcontent.com/pod-product-compliance
Lightning Source LLC
Chambersburg PA
CBHW051251210726
48287CB00002B/455